3/01
5.99

EVEN PARANOIDS HAVE ENEMIES . . .

use

Dal

pla

at

viru

car

in

we

o

b

n

d

s

ROBERT DOHERTY

PSYCHIC WARRIOR:

PROJECT AURA

A DELL BOOK

Published by
Dell Publishing
a division of
Random House, Inc.
1540 Broadway
New York, New York 10036

ISBN: 0-440-23626-6

Printed in the United States of America

Published simultaneously in Canada

August 2001

10 9 8 7 6 5 4 3 2 1

OPM

The Past

Prologue

The Himalayas
1220 A.D.

Jagged white-topped peaks crowned the horizon in all directions, cut only by the narrow river valley. Like an invasion of locusts, the great Genghis Khan's army marched up the chasm, driving hostages they swept up before them. Finally, deep in the high country, the valley broadened, opening to a lake, next to which was a small town of whitewashed stone buildings. A thick layer of ice covered the water, even though it was the height of summer.

Horses' and men's lungs labored for oxygen as the Khan deployed the bulk of his warriors in a semicircle around the captives at the near side of the village. More than a thousand hostages, every person who lived in the lower valley, milled about in fear in front of the Mongol soldiers.

At over ten thousand feet in altitude, the valley was a desolate place holding little of obvious value. The twenty-thousand-foot-high peak of Kharta Changri loomed to the west, overlooking massive glacier fields that fed the lake and river, known as Kharta Chu to the locals, that came out of it. Ten miles to the south, Chomolungma, which was not to be called Mount Everest for another six centuries, filled the horizon.

Khan rode forward, one hundred of his elite guard behind him. He was flush from recently having destroyed the great city of Samarkand several hundred miles to the northwest, in a more temperate and lower land. Astride the Silk Road, Samarkand had boasted a population of over two hundred thousand souls. Khan had ordered his troops to slay everyone except the most skilled artisans, whom he sent back to Mongolia in chains. Men, women, children, even cats and dogs, were put to the sword. The walls of the city were razed and broken into dust. A nearby river was diverted to wash over where the city had been so that no trace of it would survive—such was the fate of those who were in the Khan's path. The world had never known such a conqueror—not even Alexander or Caesar had come close to inflicting the level of destruction that had been dealt by the Golden Horde led by Genghis Khan. It would take weapons of mass destruction in the twentieth century to approach the scale of the millions his forces killed, the cities he destroyed, the land he left barren behind him.

None had stopped Khan so far, so he rode forward without fear, his warriors guarding him with arrows notched to the sinew strings of their bows. He paused as he approached the town. A lone figure barred his path: a slight old woman, seated in a chair made of reeds, set in the center of the small track that led into the town. Some of the hostages were crying out to the old woman in a strange tongue, no doubt pleading for her help. The town behind her, though, appeared deserted, as if it had not been occupied for a very long time. The cold air had preserved the buildings, but there was no other sign of life, and certainly little of wealth.

The woman had light skin, unlike the darker tone of the hostages. Her hair was long and white, flowing over her shoulders like a waterfall. Lines etched her face, surrounding eyes the likes of which the Khan had never seen—they were icy blue and their gaze pierced into him.

She wore a long robe of white that stretched to the ground.

Less than ten feet in front of the old woman, Genghis Khan raised his left hand, halting his troops. Khan saw no fear in the woman's face, something that gained his immediate respect after dealing with so many cowering noblemen from towns he had encountered on his march. Among the Mongols, women were held in esteem and their wisdom listened to, so Khan held back from immediately slaying her. Also, this strange situation interested him. It was not what he had been told to expect.

"I speak your language," the old woman said in Mongol, which surprised the Khan.

This land was far from his home, and he had only come here because he had been told stories of a wonderful valley full of riches, hidden high in the mountains. The ones who told him of this place, wanderers without a home, were a group of outcasts. These people had assured him that he would find treasure beyond belief high in the rooftop of the world, as they called it. This place did not look rich, but it had been an arduous trip here and Khan did not want to go back empty-handed.

"I am the Great Khan, ruler of all you see behind me, and soon to be ruler of all I see before me."

"I know of you, Great Khan of the northern plains," the old woman said.

Khan was not surprised the woman had heard of him. All the world trembled at the approach of the Khan and his army.

"You are far from your path," the woman continued.

"My path is whatever I choose it to be."

"So it seems."

"What do you know of me?" Khan demanded.

The old woman's voice became surprisingly loud. "Your greatest pleasure is to vanquish your enemies and chase them before you. To rob them of their wealth and see those dear to them bathed in tears, to ride their horses and clasp to your bosom their wives and daughters. Is that not what you believe?"

Khan slammed a fist into the armor on his chest. "It is what I live for."

"Your goal is to conquer all the world."

"As far as I can ride will be mine," Khan said. "None can stop me."

"There are forces in the world that you do not know about," the old woman said.

Khan spit. "The sword and bow are great equalizers. None have stopped us so far."

She waved a frail hand. "We are not your enemy."

"I decide who my enemies are."

"You do not want my people as your enemy. It would gain you nothing."

Khan stiffened. He lifted his left hand and slashed it down. A troop of his warriors fired their short bows into the hostages. A hundred fell, most dead, the wounded screaming in agony. Warriors waded among them and slit the throats of those that cried out.

"We are enemies now, aren't we?"

"Those are not my people," the woman said. "They till the land in the valley far below. Why kill them? They are not your enemy either."

Khan looked about. "I don't see your people."

She waved her hand once more. "They are all around you. They watched you come up the valley."

"We saw no one other than these."

She rested a hand on her chest. "Of course not. You see of us only what we allow you to see."

"You know me, old lady. Who are *you*?"

"You may call me Kirati."

Khan got off his horse, his squat, bowlegged form wiry

and used to the harsh life in the field. "What are your people called?"

"We are the spirits who ride the wind."

Khan could sense the uneasy rustling among his men close enough to hear. He gestured with his left hand, indicating for his guards to move back out of earshot. His mother had told him tales of the wind spirits, the souls of those who had died, who flew over the steppes. But the old woman looked very much alive to him.

"You are the dead?"

The old woman smiled. "No. We came here to the high country long before your ancestors first rode the great grasslands that you call home, and we will be here long after your name is legend. We came here to be left alone. To be away from men's wars."

Khan squatted, running the strands of a leather lariat through his callused hands. "Where there are men, there are wars. It cannot be avoided. It is our nature."

"We know," Kirati said. "That is why there are few men with us. We came to this place, far away from all others, to dwell. We lived in this village for many years beyond counting. Then we fought among ourselves. Some left and became the wanderers who told you of this place. Others, most of the men, they went far to the west. And we went higher into the mountains where no one can dwell."

Khan ran a hand through his dark beard. No men to fight, no wealth to steal, no city to destroy. Just an old woman in a chair.

"If no one can dwell in the high mountains, then how can you?"

"I told you, we are the spirits who ride the wind. We have no desire to leave the mountains," Kirati continued, "so we are not a threat to you and there is nothing here that you would want. There is no way through the mountains to the land of the Sultan of Delphi far to the south." She pointed at the highest mountain. "The great Chomolunga guards the way. You must go around the mountains with your army if you wish to conquer there."

"I will conquer that land and many others. But as far as riches hidden in these mountains, your words are not what I have been told," Khan said. "I have heard there is great wealth hidden here."

"You hear this from those who wander." It was not a question, nor did Kirati wait for a reply. "As I said, they who told you this were once our people and lived here also. They choose a different path and now must wander the world. They will never have a home. I am afraid, Great Khan, that they lied to you in order to have you wreak their vengeance on us for past angers and to keep you from destroying them."

"Maybe you are the one who lies."

Kirati sighed and seemed to grow older. "There is great wealth. But not in the manner you think of wealth." She tapped the side of her head. "Our wealth is here. You cannot use it."

"If I cannot use it, then I will destroy it." Khan stood and turned for his horse.

"Great Khan!" Kirati's voice had changed timbre, a vibration of power in it. "Listen to me."

Khan turned. The old woman got off her chair and walked to the Mongol leader, hands out from her side. When she was close enough to touch him, she spoke in a low, powerful voice. "I will tell you who has more wealth— in the way you view such a thing—than you could imagine.

"We do have enemies and they are very rich and very powerful; worthy adversaries even for you. Far to the west. Past the kingdom of the Persians and the Greeks. South of the Russians, across the Volga River. They hide in secret places among the peoples there, but if threatened they will come out of their holes. They rule in the shadows, pulling strings that make others jump. They are like you—they enjoy war, and they enjoy wealth—but unlike you, they get others to do it for them."

"Whom do you speak of?"

"Search for those called the Priory."

"The pope in Rome? I have heard of him."

"Not the pope. He too is just a lackey for the Priory."

"How will I find these people who hide in the shadows?"

"They will find you if you threaten the world they have built to protect them."

The old woman reached forward, and to the shock of the Mongol warriors watching, her hand went into Khan's chest as if it were made of nothing but air. Her other hand reached up to his head, the tips of the fingers passing through his helmet, into his head. Several warriors cried out in alarm, but Khan signaled for them to be still with a slow gesture of his right hand, his entire being focused on the old woman before him.

Kirati smiled. Her eyes pierced into Khan's as she spoke in a low voice, the power in it growing stronger, echoing inside Khan's head, beating in rhythm with his heart. "Our spirits are joined now. You will leave here and go no further into the mountains. It is dangerous and there is nothing here that you want. What you want is the Priory. They are your enemy. Your people's enemy. The enemy of all. Destroy them. If not you, then your son. And your son's son. As long as the Mongols ride. The Priory are the enemy of your people."

Khan slowly nodded. "The Priory. I will leave here. I will ride west with my army."

Kirati stepped back, her hands coming out of Khan's body. She seemed to diminish in size as she sat back down. Khan staggered, almost fell, then regained his balance. He shook his head, a quizzical expression on his face for a moment. His thick eyebrows knit together as he stared at Kirati.

"Go back to your people, old woman. Tell them I will spare them. But they must stay here, in the high country, and never come down to the plains."

The old woman inclined her head. "We will do as you say, Great Khan."

Khan turned away from Kirati. He ordered his warriors to kill the rest of the hostages, and the ground flowed with their blood, which then seeped into the ice that covered the lake. The woman's expression did not change during the butchery.

Then, without another look at her, Khan led his troops back the way they'd come. As the last warrior disappeared down the trail, Kirati raised her arms to the sky and her figure slowly faded from view until only the dead and the abandoned village were left.

The Banks of the Volga River
1241 A.D.

Rows of bloody and dented armor and weapons lined the road that led to the magnificent silken tent. The golden cloth marked the headquarters of Bhatu Khan, grandson of the Great Genghis Khan. The booty had been gathered from the dead who littered the field after the battle at Legnica two days ago, where the Golden Horde had overwhelmed a combined force of Silesians, Poles, and Teutonic knights in a devastating victory. In one dark day, the cream of Eastern European military might had been smashed. It was the latest in a string of victories moving the Mongol forces further west, out of Asia and into Europe, a bloody tide that sent shivers of fear ahead of it to lands that knew of Asia only through rumors. Marco

Polo, the first European to visit the Mongol court, would not even be born for another thirteen years, and the vastness of Asia was a great mystery.

Five years earlier, in 1236, Bhatu Khan had begun to lead the massive force given him by his grandfather westward, killing millions in the process and leaving a massive swath of destruction across Russia into Europe. Bhatu had crushed the northern Russian armies in the winter of 1237–1238; history would record this action as the only successful winter military campaign against Russia ever, something Napoleon and Hitler would fail to do. In 1240, his army had razed Kiev, massacring every inhabitant. That had scared the other Eastern European empires that lay in the Golden Horde's path, and a massive army had been raised, old hatreds put aside, all in an effort to stop the Mongols. That army now lay dead on the fields of Legnica or prisoner in the Khan's camp.

The way into Europe lay open to the forces of Bhatu Khan and the Golden Horde. It had been his father's dying command for him to attack to the west, something internal rebellions and other enemies closer to the first Khan had delayed Genghis from doing before his untimely death. What else the Great Khan on his deathbed had passed on to Bhatu remained locked inside the mind of the leader of the Golden Horde. Before heading west, Bhatu had sent scouts and spies ahead, learning much of the lands there. He knew far more about them than they did about him.

Bhatu was eating a meal laid out on top of a large wooden box. Inside were a trio of Teutonic princes slowly suffocating to death. Their pleas and moans were music to his ears as he would slide his gold plate over the one tiny airhole, leaving it in place for various lengths of time. As far as Bhatu was concerned, he was showing the princes honor, for Mongols believed that the blood of noblemen captured in battle should not be shed. Suffocation was a sign of respect, although it is doubtful the men inside appreciated the subtlety.

The curtain to the tent twitched open and Bhatu's chief adviser slipped in. "A lone emissary from the west has crossed the river and asks for an audience with the Great Bhatu Khan."

"With no guards?"

"No, Khan."

Bhatu forgot his meal momentarily. A man who would ride into the camp alone drew his interest. He signaled for the emissary to be allowed in. The man who came through the entrance was richly dressed, cloaked in robes sewn with gold. A thin band of silver encircled the crown of his head, a large gem set in the center. He carried a staff shaped like a tall narrow cross, the gold encrusted with jewels. How could he have gotten through the Mongol lines without being killed and robbed? Bhatu wondered.

The man bowed slightly at the waist. "Greetings, Great Bhatu Khan, Emperor of the East."

The man spoke Mongol, another surprise to Bhatu. "Soon to be Emperor of the West," he said as he took a piece of meat off his plate and threw it to one of the dogs that lay nearby.

"It is that issue that brings me here."

"Whom do you represent?"

"The Priory, great lord."

Bhatu stood. "Out!" he bellowed, sending lackeys and officers scurrying from his tent. "Everyone out!"

When the tent was empty of sycophants, Bhatu sat back down. "What are you called?"

"I am Hieronnymous, lord. You have traveled a long way from your home."

"I travel where I wish and kill whom I please."

"There are whispered rumors that you seek my people," Hieronnymous said. "Why is that?"

"My grandfather ordered me to find you. He said your people had great wealth and power."

Hieronnymous nodded. "That is true."

"Your people sent the army I just defeated against me, didn't they?"

Hieronnymous smiled. "You could not expect us to surrender easily, could you, Great Bhatu Khan?"

"Then I have dealt with your power," Bhatu said.

Hieronnymous's fingers curled over the top of the staff, the knuckles white. "Perhaps you could be persuaded in a more civil manner to not cross the river?"

" 'Persuaded'?" Bhatu leaned forward, his elbow covering the airhole.

"As you've noted, the Priory has great wealth. We would be willing to share it with you."

"Why don't I just take it now that your army has been destroyed?"

"Our wealth is well hidden. You might find some after much time and trouble, but not as much as we are willing to share freely. And, as you've also noted, we have influence with all the kingdoms on the other side of the river. You destroyed a great army, but there are other armies. There is much land and many more kingdoms to the west of here. We could have the pope in Rome raise a crusade against your forces. He is already considering it, as he shakes in fear inside the Vatican."

Khan's spies had already warned him of that. They had given him detailed reports of the crusades the Christians had sent against the Islamic empires in the Middle East year after year. It was not the sort of war he wished to get involved in, especially as he was very far from home. His goal was not to conquer land but to gain riches. He had no plans to hold the lands he had ridden through.

"What do you offer me?"

Hieronnymous pulled a piece of rolled parchment from inside his cloak and slid it onto the top of the crate. The faint pounding of the suffocating princes could be heard, but both men ignored it.

Bhatu unrolled the parchment and read. The amount of gold and silver listed astounded even him, who ruled from the Pacific and across Asia. "You can bring me this?"

"Yes. In one week's time, all that can be yours. But only if you agree not to cross the river. I have been told a Khan's word is his bond."

Bhatu leaned back in his splendid chair, letting air into the box once more. He ran a finger along the edge of a gold-encrusted dagger as he considered the offer. He was far from home and his men had been fighting all their lives. It was what they lived for, but even a Mongol needed rest. And he had received reports of rebellions in China and– His eyes narrowed.

"Your people are stirring up revolt in my kingdom, aren't they?"

Hieronnymous spread his hands in a sign of innocence. "Lord, we–"

Bhatu slammed the point of the dagger into the top of the box. "My word is my bond. But I must have the truth from you in turn or I cannot trust you. Those I do not trust die before me."

"We have a long reach, great Bhatu Khan, but I did not think it would be respectful to inform you of that."

"A long enough reach to stir up revolt in my kingdom?"

"Yes, lord." Hieronnymous took a step closer. "Your grandfather, the Great Genghis Khan, was lied to. We are not your enemy. We only caused trouble in your kingdom after you began your march in this direction. Before that, there was no influence from us. We have no desire to fight you."

Bhatu's generals had already begun talking in council about turning back. Great victories had been won, but they were realists. Much of winning battles was skill, which the Horde had in abundance, but there was also an element of luck, and there was fear theirs might be running out.

"One week," Khan said. "If this is not delivered"—he tapped the parchment—"I will lead my men across the river."

"Agreed."

"And you will stop supporting the rebels in China."

"Agreed."

"You will give me the names and locations of all the rebels you have supported and those in my kingdom you have suborned."

Hieronnymous nodded. "As long as you give your word not to march on us again."

Bhatu had never really understood his grandfather's obsession with uncovering and destroying this Priory. He had agreed to do it as a respectful grandchild would, but that was years ago and thousands of miles to the east. What this man offered would allow him to run his kingdom for the rest of his days.

Bhatu Khan pressed his palm over the hole, the sounds from inside the box growing fainter. He looked at the man on the other side. "If you give me more wealth, I will destroy the strange ones in the high mountains that my grandfather told me about."

"We heard that they sent your grandfather after us. We knew that he or his descendants would eventually come this way. They are our old enemies. If you could destroy them, we would indeed bestow great riches upon you. But, unfortunately, you cannot fight them. You, like us, are of the earth. They are not. You might consider them people of the sky. To fight them would be like trying to kill a cloud."

"These strange ones in the high mountains—who are they?"

Hieronnymous leaned on the gold cross, appearing weary for the first time. "You would not understand if I tried to explain what they are. We were once one people, many, many years ago. But we have been apart so long . . ." Hieronnymous fell silent for a moment before continuing. "They cannot fight us with swords and we cannot fight them in the way they are. So they use others with swords against us. One day, though, we will have the means, through others as they do, to fight them. And when that day comes, we will destroy them."

Khan smiled. "Or perhaps they will destroy you first."

"Perhaps," Hieronnymous acknowledged, "but it will be a wonderful battle that will cover the entire world."

The Present

Chapter One

Sergeant Major Jimmy Dalton stood astride the Continental Divide, just south of Rollins Pass, with a wooden box containing his wife's ashes in his backpack. Far to the east, through the mountains and hills he had just driven up, he could just barely see the high plains of eastern Colorado, a brown and golden flat haze fifty miles away. To the west, more white-capped mountains stretched as far as the eye could reach.

He was a solidly built man, as sturdy as the pines below that took the brunt of the wind coming off the high peaks. His face was weathered and his short, dark hair liberally sprinkled with gray. He wore camouflage fatigues, a Special Forces patch on each shoulder, the left indicating current assignment to a Special Forces Group, the right combat service in the past with the same unit.

He'd left his Jeep just before Needle Tunnel where the dirt road that followed the old railroad bed was blocked by large boulders. From there he had hiked upward. The divide was his favorite place, and the green valley below had been Marie's favorite. They'd found it shortly after the 10th Special Forces Group—and Dalton with it—was moved from Fort Devens, Massachusetts, to Fort Carson, Colorado, during a round of base closings.

They'd driven up into the mountains on a fall weekend. Dalton had noticed the small sign indicating Rollins

Pass on the side of the Peak to Peak Highway and turned onto the dirt road. It was something they often did, taking new roads to see where they might lead.

Marie had fallen in love with the valley, the hills on either side sprinkled with aspens just turning. Dalton had been fascinated with the rail line, which ended at Moffat Tunnel, the highest railroad tunnel in the world. Even more intriguing to him was the old railroad bed that wound its way two thousand feet higher, over the Continental Divide, where the original rail line from Denver to Salt Lake had gone before the Moffat Tunnel was built. Nearby were piles of weathered timber, the remains of a three-mile-long shed that had been built over the rail line over a hundred years ago to protect it from the snow that covered the ground here three quarters of the year.

The wind was out of the west, piercing his Gore-Tex jacket with icy needles of cold. The leathery skin on his face felt the bite of the late fall air, but he had been in such extremes of weather throughout his military career—from the brutal heat of the Lebanese summer to the freezing of a Finnish winter—that he took little notice. He'd driven above the tree line two thousand feet below. The terrain at this altitude was rock strewn with patches of snow even at the height of summer. A few stunted bushes struggled to grow among the stone and snow.

Marie had always laughed at his wonder that at this exact location two drops of rain or two flakes of snow less than a foot apart on either side of the Divide would end up in oceans three thousand miles apart. Her laughter had been one of the many things he had loved about her. The last time they had come here together, as the amyotrophic lateral sclerosis was just beginning its deterioration of her body, they had both known she would never be able to make the climb. They'd simply sat in the Jeep and looked out over the countryside, a thousand feet short of the Divide. It was a bittersweet memory, the beginning of the end.

He grimaced as he took the small backpack off his right shoulder, the pain from the bandaged wound in his left shoulder a sharp reminder of recent events. He set the pack down and unzipped it. The only thing inside was a small teakwood box. Carefully he took the box out. Protecting it from the wind with his body, he carefully opened the lid and removed a faded letter from an insert on the top. The paper was thin and worn, the creases sharp from years of being carried.

> *Washington, D.C.*
> *July 14, 1861*
>
> *Dear Sarah,*
>
> *The indications are very strong that we shall move in a few days, perhaps tomorrow, and lest I should not be able to write you again I feel impelled to write a few lines that may fall under your eye when I am no more.*
>
> *I have no misgivings about, or lack of confidence in, the cause in which I am engaged, and my courage does not halt or falter. I know how American civilization now leans upon the triumph of the government and how great a debt we owe to those who went before us through the blood and suffering of the Revolution.*
>
> *And I am willing, perfectly willing, to lay down all my joys in this life to help maintain this government and to pay that debt.*
>
> *Sarah, my love for you is deathless. It seems to bind me with mighty cables that nothing but omnipotence can break. And yet my love of country comes over me like a strong wind and bears me irresistibly with all those chains to the battlefield.*
>
> *The memory of all the blissful moments I have enjoyed with you come crowding over me. And I feel most deeply grateful to*

God, and you, that I've enjoyed them for so long. And how hard it is for me to give them up and burn to ashes the hopes and future years when, God willing, we might still have lived and loved together and see our boys grown up to honorable manhood.

If I do not return, my dear Sarah, never forget how much I loved you nor that when my last breath escapes me on the battle-field it will whisper your name. Forgive my many faults and the many pains I have caused you. How thoughtless, how foolish, I have sometimes been. But oh Sarah, if the dead can come back to this earth and flit unseen around those they love, I shall always be with you in the brightest day and the darkest night. Always. Always.

And when the soft breeze fans your cheek it shall be my breath. And the cool air at your throbbing temple, it shall be my spirit passing by.

Sarah, do not mourn me dead; think I am gone and wait for me. For we shall meet again.

Sullivan Balue

Tears rolled down Dalton's face, as they did every time he read the copy of the letter. Even though he knew the words by heart, he read them again, just to see the hand-writing, to bring back the memories. Marie had sent him a copy of the letter when he was a prisoner of war in Vietnam. She'd sent it with every letter she wrote, hoping one of them would get through, knowing that it would touch his soul. It was written by a Union officer from Rhode Island to his young wife a week before the Battle of the First Bull Run. He was an officer who was killed in that first major battle of the Civil War.

Marie knew Dalton had always had a fascination with the War Between the States, brother against brother in savage fighting. A war with many causes, some noble, some not so noble, but still in Dalton's opinion a good war—as good as any war could be—given the root issue of slavery. A good war—Dalton shook his head. He wished he had served in a good war, but he doubted he had. Even in the Civil War the soldiers had been the ones to pay the price of the folly of those who led them. The vast majority of Southern soldiers were poor farmers who didn't own slaves; in the Northern army, the rich bought their way out of service, hiring the poor to replace them in the ranks. The cause may have been noble, but the methods weren't, and it was the foot soldier who paid the price.

Decades earlier, Dalton had been held prisoner of war for five years in the Hanoi Hilton, and Marie had waited for him then, as she had during all the subsequent deployments. He'd fought in El Salvador, Grenada, Lebanon, Somalia, and Iraq. And now, most recently, the strangest battle of all, as a Psychic Warrior assigned to the highly classified Bright Gate project. He had helped destroy a rogue Russian Psychic Warrior who had threatened the world with nuclear destruction. In the end, it had turned out as all previous battles had, with man against man, face to face.

Even this last fight, though, had been bittersweet. He had lost most of the team he had led, and the opponent, a Russian named Feteror, had turned on his own country due to the barbaric treatment he had endured, being enslaved to a computer, his body surgically whittled down to the mind and little more. When Dalton had learned the true nature of Feteror's condition, he'd had a greater understanding of the Russian's actions.

There was another aspect to the letter, though, that had been an integral part of their marriage—their inability to have children. They'd been tested many times over the years, and it always came down to the fact that injuries Dalton had received during torture while being held prisoner had removed his ability to father a child. They had discussed adoption, but with all his deployments it had never seemed like quite the right time and the years had gone by. He felt as if he had taken everything from Marie and given her little in return.

Dalton turned his face to the east, toward the valley she had loved, the letter in his hands. "I never thought you would be gone first," he whispered.

He kicked a rock, sending it tumbling down the scree and boulders to the west. Anger stirred, followed by guilt. And then something else touched his mind, the gentlest of touches, like a single snowflake landing on warm skin and vanishing quickly. It was so brief he wondered if it had been real.

Dalton closed his eyes. The wind gusted. He folded the letter and slipped it in the lid, then picked up the box. The strange feeling came again, stronger, and this time he had no doubt. Thirty-two years of marriage, even with all his deployments, had built a bond between him and his wife that not even death could completely sever. He'd felt this before, when he was being held prisoner in Hanoi. And he had seen her spirit, her essence, when he visited her in the hospital while operating on the virtual plane as a Psychic Warrior. He had let her go then, let her out of her misery.

He could sense her again. She was here.

Sergeant Major Dalton opened his eyes and smiled, guilt and anger forgotten. "Marie, I feel you."

He opened the lid and the wind took the ashes, blowing them out over the valley. He watched them until there was nothing left to see.

"I'll always love you."

Dalton turned to leave, but paused as something else touched his mind. Marie, once more. He was puzzled for a moment, not quite understanding. Then he realized she was warning him. Of treachery and betrayal. He stood still for several minutes, hoping there would be more, but all he felt was the wind. He shivered, then pulled the collar of his jacket up around his neck and headed toward his Jeep.

It was already dark over the East Coast of the United States while the sun set on Jimmy Dalton as he drove down from the mountains. The deep blue of the water off Florida's east coast was far removed from the white snow of the Rocky Mountains.

Slicing through that water, the United States Coast Guard cutter *Warde* kicked up a phosphorescent wake. With a ten-person crew and a length of eighty-two feet, it was one of the Guard's smallest patrol boats, but more than adequate to handle the tasks that confronted it. The crew was experienced at their job and knew the waters between Florida and the islands off its east coast quite well. There were two main types of incident they dealt with— refugees from Cuba and drug runners from South America and the islands in the Caribbean.

In the small bridge set back from the ship's main armament—a twenty-five-millimeter cannon—Lieutenant JG Mike Foster stood just behind the helmsman, scanning the surrounding ocean through night vision goggles. The lights on the control panels were dimmed so that they wouldn't interfere. He turned as a bright green glow almost overloaded the light enhanced in the goggles. His radar operator—Rating Second Class Lisa Caprice—had lifted her head up from the eyepiece.

"Target, bearing two eight zero degrees, range five thousand meters, sir."

"Size?"

"Looks like a forty footer. No beacon." She put her head back down and peered into the eyepiece.

Foster shifted the goggles in the direction she had indicated. "Heading?"

"Also along the coast, heading north, sir."

There was nothing out there that he could see. At five thousand meters he should be able to easily pick up the ship's lights with the goggles, which amplified ambient light.

"She's running dark," Foster informed his bridge crew. "Wake up the off-shift. I want everyone on station." He ordered the helmsman to make for the other ship.

Foster grabbed the radio handset. "Unidentified vessel, this is the United States Coast Guard cutter *Warde*. Please stand by and prepare to be boarded. Over."

He waited but there was no response.

"Range four thousand meters," Caprice said.

Foster could see the other ship now, a darker object against the black ocean. An expensive pleasure yacht with sleek lines, cutting through the water, all running lights out. He picked up the handset, but as soon as he clicked the Send button, a burst of static came out of the speakers.

"What the hell," Foster muttered. He switched frequencies, then moved to another radio and picked up the handset for the satellite radio.

"Key West CG station, this is the *Warde*. Over."

"Warde, this is Key West. Over."

"We are in pursuit of an unidentified vessel that refuses to respond to our hails." He then gave his location and heading, and his headquarters in Key West acknowledged. "We seem to have strong interference on our FM bands," he added.

He picked up the other handset and tried once more, but the result was the same. He tried to raise his headquarters in Key West again, but the radio couldn't break through the wall of static that had descended upon them.

"Could they be jamming us?" he asked his electronics specialist.

"I haven't heard of anyone doing that," Caprice said. "But you never know what these people will come up with next."

They had encountered many strange ruses and tricks

used by drug runners over the years. One trend had been the increase in both equipment and sophistication. Foster wouldn't be surprised if the ship in front of them was using some sort of jammer.

Foster could see two of his crew manning the forward twenty-five millimeter. "What they're going to get next is a boot up their ass."

He didn't like the idea of a confrontation. This was their last day on a weeklong patrol. The boat was due for overhaul and the crew would have a well-deserved month off. Caprice was getting married on Saturday and the entire crew would be attending the wedding. All those things combined to give him a bad feeling about the situation, but it was their duty to stop the boat.

"Range three thousand meters."

Foster reached up and turned on the forward spotlights, fixing the other boat in their harsh glare. There was no one visible on deck. He leaned out the open side window. "Warning shots," he ordered.

The twenty-five millimeter spit out a burst of rounds, the tracers arcing across the front of the other boat.

Foster exchanged the night vision goggles for a set of powerful binoculars. He trained them on the other boat. He could make out the name stenciled on the bow. *"Aura II,"* he read aloud.

Caprice had already accessed their onboard computer registry. "It's not listed, sir."

"Why doesn't that surprise me," Foster muttered.

The yacht had not slowed or changed course, despite the warning shots. They were now less than two thousand meters from the other boat and closing. He scanned the boat once more. Something was strange about the silhouette. There was what appeared to be a large SATCOM dish just aft of the bridge, but instead of pointing up to the sky, it was level, pointing right at Foster.

The captain once more keyed his SATCOM handset. "Key West, this is *Warde*. Over."

There was just static, but he transmitted anyway. "Identity of vessel is the *Aura II*. Not listed in registry. We are—" There was another sharp break in the transmission and Foster almost dropped the handset as a shock went up his arm. "What the hell?"

"Sir—" Caprice was next to him.

"What?"

"Something's wrong. Don't you feel it?"

" 'Feel it,' " Foster repeated. "What do you mean?"

"There's something—" Caprice began but then they all felt it.

Just above the slight swell of the blue Caribbean Sea between the *Warde* and the *Aura II*, immense power rode on electromagnetic waves at the speed of light. It washed over the *Warde*, penetrating the hull and every person on board.

Caprice dropped to her knees, hands pressed against her ears, mouth opened in a silent scream. Foster staggered back, feeling a spike of red-hot pain ripping through his brain. Blood seeped out of his ears, nose, and eyes. Within seconds, he collapsed on the steel plating. The body twitched once, again, and then was still.

With a dead crew, the *Warde* continued straight on course, cutting across the wake of the other ship and disappearing into the darkness.

The *Aura II* slowed to a halt. Two Zodiacs were lowered over the side, each filled with a load of cocaine. The rubber boats headed directly for shore. As soon as the boats were clear, the yacht's engines powered up and it cut a wide turn, heading back to the southeast.

There was no where, no when, no form, no substance. Time and space, the two linchpins of human existence in the real world, were a vague memory, like the taste of an exotic food that he could not recall the name of and didn't know whether he had really tasted or merely dreamed of.

The entity that was the psychic projection of Jonathan Raisor was trying to form something that he might call self. It was one step worse than that feeling of being between sleep and consciousness, when one was somewhat aware of the outer world, but commands from the brain couldn't make it through the nervous system to move the body, and the mind, the self, was frozen in place unable to influence the real world. Raisor was having a difficult time connecting the scattered images to form a cohesive thought to even begin to send a command. And where would he send it, with his body frozen in its isolation tube back at Bright Gate?

All he knew was gray, stretching in all directions around him. Even his psychic essence was gray—a formless fog of gray inside a limitless cloud of gray. Where did he end and the outside begin? And what was the outside in this virtual plane? And where was the real world—beyond, below, outside, inside of—with respect to the virtual?

The one thing Raisor's psychic essence clung to, one overriding emotion, was revenge. This had been done to his sister. His body, like hers, now floated inside an isolation tank at Bright Gate. If he still existed, and there were moments when even he doubted it, that meant she still might exist somewhere on the psychic plane.

The way he was, he knew he could not do what he needed. He had to find Bright Gate. That was one firm thought that echoed in his psyche. But to find Bright Gate, he needed Bright Gate's power and computer to give him form and substance, and for the ability to move along the virtual plane and then reenter the real world.

He went back to the only thing keeping him from dissipating: He had been betrayed, his power and connection to Bright Gate cut off. As his sister had been betrayed. Revenge was the one thing keeping what there was of him intact, an emotion more powerful than the dullness of the psychic plane he floated in. Without it, he felt that he would blow away, like fog in a stiff breeze, until there would be nothing of him left.

Every so often he sensed something in the grayness. Something or perhaps even someone. But always at a distance, as if avoiding his presence. Perhaps the disembodied psyches of others like him, spirits lost without being able to get back to their bodies; maybe even his sister. Or perhaps Psychic Warriors from Bright Gate, going about their business. But somehow he picked up that these distant presences were something entirely different. And that they sensed him and avoided him deliberately. The remote viewers at Bright Gate had reported such presences from the very beginning of the program.

Like a high-power searchlight, a beam pierced the gray. Raisor turned toward it, willing his essence to move, uncertain if it was possible. He wrapped himself around the hate he felt for those who had abandoned him. For those who had betrayed his sister. He was unable to judge the distance, but almost imperceptibly the beam of light drew closer.

Just as quickly, the light was gone and he was in the gray once more. If he had lungs and a mouth, he would have screamed his dismay, but he could only feel the despair. Whatever it was, the beam was the only change he had experienced in however long he had been lost here.

If it had come once, it would come again. Raisor's entity had nothing other to do than to wait and be ready. He was a man lost at sea waiting for a life preserver that had come tantalizingly close.

Chapter Two

Against the darkness of space, a sliver of light appeared as the payload doors of the shuttle *Endeavour* began opening. On the seventh day of an eight-day mission, the crew of the *Endeavour* had already accomplished all the tasks that NASA had publicly announced for it prior to the flight. However, NASA had not yet told the public that. The press releases issued each day by the agency spread out the announced missions to cover all eight days, allowing the last two days to be used on the unannounced, classified assignments. It was the way most shuttle flights were conducted. Without the influx of money from the Pentagon, NASA would hardly be able to launch a third of the flights that it did. And the last thing the Pentagon wanted was publicity for the missions it assigned to the shuttles.

Each cargo bay door was sixty feet long and fifteen in diameter. They locked in the open position, opening the bay to space. The bay was practically empty, the three civilian satellites the shuttle had brought into orbit with it already deployed.

In the airlock at the lower bottom of the flight deck, a single man was donning an EMUS–Extravehicular Mobility Unit Spacesuit–with the assistance of one of the crew. The man climbing into the suit was not officially listed on the shuttle's crew; he was known only by the code name Eagle Six. He had boarded the shuttle the night before the launch, hidden among the swarm of workers making last-minute preparations. When the official crew made their way to the shuttle under the glare of TV cameras, he was already on board, ready to go.

Eagle Six was the most experienced astronaut at EVA, extravehicular activity, in the United States, having done twelve similar missions, yet he wasn't a member of NASA. Officially, he was a member of the National Security Agency, at least according to government records.

Once Eagle Six insured that all the seals were secure, his assistant placed the PLSS–Primary Life Support System–on his back. Once that was working, the astronaut cleared the airlock, sealing the door to the crew compartment behind him. He was breathing pure oxygen now, and would for several minutes. He waited patiently, reviewing in his mind the actions he would be taking. He had learned the importance of being certain of every movement he was going to make before he made it. Space was a completely unforgiving environment.

The pilot, on the upper flight deck, had their target in sight. The first thing he had spotted was the large solar panels. As they got closer he could make out the main body of the long, rectangular satellite perpendicular to the panels. It was dotted with several circular parabolic antennas pointing earthward along with other types of antennas.

With delicate touches on his maneuvering thrusters, the pilot edged the shuttle closer and closer to the satellite, at the same time orienting the craft so that the bay would face it. It was a slow and intricate process, the last fifty meters taking fifteen minutes of tiny adjustments.

When he was done, the satellite was directly "above" the shuttle cargo bay. Inside the airlock, Eagle Six depressurized the bay and opened the door to the cargo bay. He took a moment to look up at the satellite, then turned to his right. In the front, port side of the bay was the FSS—Flight Support Station—which held the MMU, or Manned Maneuvering Unit.

He stepped up on the platform, sliding his boots into the loops at the base of the FSS. The PLSS on his back pressed against the MMU. Carefully he belted himself into the MMU. Then he ran through a system check. The MMU was a larger system that fit over the PLSS, with control arms coming out around his sides. It was a propulsion system that held two nitrogen-under-pressure fuel tanks. There were twenty-four holes on the exterior of the MMU, which the nitrogen could be directed through to provide thrust.

The hardest thing about EVAing was the three-dimensional aspect, along with the two types of movement involved—translation and rotation. Translation was straight line movement, while rotation was a spinning movement. It got complicated when the two were combined, because he had three types of translation: up or down; forward or back; and right or left. And then he had three types of rotation: pitch, yaw, and roll. Three times three equaled nine ways of movement. It confused many who entered the astronaut program and was the cause of numerous washouts of otherwise highly qualified candidates. In the weightless-environment training facility in Houston, he had watched trainees get confused and disoriented in the pool by the multiple movement options.

His left hand controlled translation while his right dictated rotation. He had trained with the MMU so often in the pool that his movements, like those of a helicopter pilot, had become instinctual. If he stopped to think, he would be lost.

All was go. He released the MMU from the FSS. He was no longer an astronaut but a satellite. He was free of everything, of Earth, of gravity, of the shuttle. It was as close as a human could come to being God, at least that is what he thought, floating high over the planet. He could move in any direction with just a slight movement of his hands. Despite the sense of power, there was also an almost overwhelming feeling of being very, very small against the vastness of space. This mixture of opposing feelings could overwhelm at times. He'd learned that when moving he had to keep his focus entirely on his goal.

He jetted down the bay to a large box strapped to the floor. Carefully, he removed the straps, then attached a leash to his boot. With a twitch of the controls, he headed away from the shuttle bay and toward the satellite. There wasn't much thrust from the holes in the MMU, just the equivalent of 7.56 Newtons of power, but in space it was more than enough.

As he got closer he could see the letters stenciled on the side: MILSTAR 4. After working on a dozen deployed military satellites, he still couldn't understand who bothered to put the name on each. It wasn't like anyone else was going to stop by and check it out or that Space Command would lose track of one of the many satellites and they wouldn't be able to find it.

He was between the shuttle and the satellite when he halted, locking the automatic attitude control with his right hand. Below him was the Earth. The entire blue-white orb. In this way Eagle Six was no different than the NASA crew members: no human could fail to be awed by the spectacle of the planet in its totality. There was a storm over the Pacific, a swirl of white clouds over the blue, and he watched it for several moments. It was hard to imagine that people were beneath that, being battered by wind and rain.

Forcing himself to concentrate on the mission, he continued on his way. Eagle Six had watched NASA astronauts do work in space using the MMU, particularly the

Hubble repair, and he knew he could have done the labor in half the time, given his experience. Working in a suit was difficult, and flying the MMU compounded that. The good part was that every part of the MMU had a built-in fail-safe. No single failure could cause a system failure, which, given the parameters of the environment, would be fatal. Compensating for the box attached to his foot made it much more difficult—if NASA was doing this mission, there would have been two astronauts, hauling the box between them.

He arrived, braking with small blasts of nitrogen as he got closer. He felt the tug on his foot as the box went past. He was ready for it and prevented himself from tumbling with a few expert movements. He unleashed the box from his foot and attached it to the satellite.

He had enough energy and oxygen to last six hours. He'd done this exact mission three times before. The first time, it had taken almost five hours, but the last one had been just under four, so he felt confident he had plenty of time.

He opened the top of the box, revealing a set of tools and another lid below the first. Taking out what he needed, he unbolted the panel on the front of the satellite and made sure each bolt, and the panel itself, were secure, using magnets on the side of the box. He reached into the satellite and unhooked a computer and then a transmitter, securing both on tethers.

Then he flipped open the next lid on the box, revealing a new computer and transmitter. He slid them into place, making sure all the connections were secure. He ran a systems check and everything came back green.

Eagle Six had been out for just over three hours. Collecting everything he'd brought with him, he made sure it was secure inside the box. With a deft touch of the controls, he spun about, facing the shuttle. He moved away from the satellite until he was once more halfway between it and the craft. Then he changed his attitude until he was facing Earth. He unhooked the box and gave it a shove, sending it slowly tumbling "downward" into Earth's gravity well. Of course, the shove sent him "upward" in reaction, and he stilled the movement with a burst of the jets on his back.

He stayed still for minutes, watching the box slowly disappear, savoring the absolute solitude of his location and the beautiful vista of the planet below. The Pacific was below and he could see lightning flickering in the large storm cloud over the ocean. Letting go of the controls, he reached both hands out, framing the storm between his gloves.

Reluctantly, he returned to business. He activated his secure communications channel to the MILSTAR satellite, bypassing the crew and NASA. "Boreas, this is Eagle Six. Over."

The reply was instantaneous. "This is Boreas. Over."

"How do you read me. Over."

"Read you six by six. Over."

"MILSTAR 4 has been upgraded. Over."

"Wait one while we check it. Over."

The astronaut didn't mind waiting. To the right of the Pacific, he could see the edge of the west coast of the United States, sweeping from Baja up to Alaska. He knew everything he could see, MILSTAR 4 could reach with its transmissions. The MILSTAR system was cutting-edge communications technology for the American military, consisting of a series of satellites that could exchange secure communications with each other and the planet's surface at bandwidths and speeds previously thought impossible.

The speaker in his helmet came alive with sound. "Eagle Six, this is Boreas. We read MILSTAR 4 on-line for

HAARP transmissions and upgraded. Good job. Out here."

Eagle Six's hand flicked the control and he spun about, facing the shuttle. He jetted toward the cargo bay. He landed smoothly and backed the MMU into the FSS. He unbuckled from the maneuvering unit and made his way across the cargo bay to the airlock. Above him, the cargo bay doors slowly began to swing shut.

He entered the cargo bay and cycled through. As soon as he got into the lower level of the crew compartment, one of the shuttle crew was there to help him remove his suit. He stripped down to his underwear as the crew went about its business preparing to conclude the flight.

As he zipped up his flight suit, the collar flipped up for a second, revealing a small pin in the shape of an elongated cross. He quickly covered the pin up, then went to his seat as the shuttle maneuvered for reentry orbit.

Behind the shuttle, the antennas and dishes of MIL-STAR 4 looked over the planet.

Chapter Three

The windshield was streaked with mud, the wipers pushing aside as much of it as they could. Dalton had taken the road down from Rollins Pass much too fast, almost skidding off twice. His reckless driving hadn't stopped on the Peak to Peak Highway or the other roads on the way to Fort Carson as he outraced his headlights. Instead of getting on I-25, he took the more dangerous roads in the foothills until he arrived at the post.

He was almost disappointed to have made it. There had been times when the grimy windshield, winding mountain road, and excessive speed, combined with tears blinding his eyes, should have sent him flying off into the darkness to crash hundreds of feet below in a mangle of flesh, blood, and metal. But each time the Jeep veered toward oblivion, there was a sense of Marie guiding him, causing him to jerk his hand and skid back on the road.

He pulled into the driveway of his quarters and turned off the engine, sitting alone in the dark, listening to the ticking noises of the engine cooling. The small house was dark, not even the light on the porch on. He felt his chest constrict. That had been Marie's ritual every evening. As soon as the sun began to set behind Cheyenne Mountain, she turned on the porch light, then the living room light next to the front window. And when Dalton drove home from work, the glow would be there to welcome him. It had been that way in all the quarters on all the army posts they'd lived on through his career.

There were no more tears to bring forth. His eyes were red and bloodshot. He leaned his head back. The garden. He'd have to spray it to keep the deer from eating Marie's flowers. It had been one of the biggest sources of irritation when they'd moved in seven years ago. The deer ate everything and it had taken Marie two years to come up with a solution to keep them away—eggs mixed with water, sprayed all over the yard. Another ritual she had performed every evening before they went to bed.

There were no more rituals. The jagged reality of that was finally settling into Dalton's chest like a cold fist surrounding his heart and squeezing tight.

Headlights coming down the street cut into his despair. His quarters were the last on a cul-de-sac, so someone driving on the street this late was unusual. The car turned in behind his Jeep, silhouetting him in his seat.

Dalton always kept his pistol in a clip holster attached to the inner side of the seat when driving. He removed it and slid it into the holster in the small of his back as he got out, shielding his eyes against the glare with his left hand.

The headlights went out and he could hear a door opening. He blinked, eyes adjusting. A man in uniform was all he could make out at first.

"Sergeant Major Dalton?" The voice was deep, one used to command.

"Yes?"

"I've been waiting for you. I was just down the street all evening." The figure came forward, a hand extended in greeting. "General Eichen."

Dalton stiffened and began to salute.

"At ease," Eichen said, waving a half-salute in the dark. "We need to talk."

Dalton had never heard of Eichen but in the moonlight he could just make out the three black stars sewn on the general's fatigue collar. A lieutenant general approaching in the dark—all Dalton could assume was that this strange visit had something to do with Psychic Warrior and the mission he had accomplished in Russia.

"This way, sir." Dalton led him to the house and opened the door.

"Leave the lights off," Eichen said as Dalton reached for the switch.

Surprised, Dalton did as Eichen asked. Eichen went over to the chair next to the front window and turned it so that it angled between the room and window, then he sat down. Dalton sat on the couch and waited.

"I work for INSCOM," Eichen began.

Dalton knew the acronym. Intelligence Support Command.

"Technically speaking at least," Eichen continued. "In reality I work directly for a special branch of the National Security Council. Which works directly for the President. It's a very small group that goes by the code name Nexus."

Dalton was now certain this had to have something to do with the mission into Russia. The government had tried to keep the events under wraps, but all the world knew that a nuclear weapon had detonated in Moscow. However, the existence of Russia Special Department Eight (SD-8)—their equivalent of Bright Gate—and of Feteror/Chyort, the Russian avatar, was something the Russian government was keeping highly classified, a decision the present American administration had agreed with wholeheartedly. The nuclear explosion was being blamed on dissident right-wing terrorists, which also allowed the Russian president to crack down on his rivals, another thing which the administration agreed with.

"Did you know that the President was not aware of

the existence of Bright Gate and the Psychic Warrior program up until five days ago?" Eichen asked.

Dalton stiffened. "No, sir, I didn't."

"Did you know that the President did not sanction the Psychic Warrior mission to stop the Russian Mafia from trying to steal the nuclear weapons?"

Dalton felt a twinge of pain in his back from an old wound. "Sir, we were told we had authorization from the National Command Authority to conduct the mission."

Eichen's hand fluttered in the dark. "Don't worry, I'm not accusing you of anything. I'm informing you of the facts. Hell, if the President had known of Psychic Warrior and the pending interception of those nukes by the Russian Mafia, I'm sure he would have authorized the mission. The problem is that someone did authorize the mission without his sanction. Someone's been running Bright Gate without his knowledge. The real problem is, Sergeant Major, who the hell *is* behind Bright Gate?"

Dalton was at a loss. He'd had his orders and he'd done as they indicated. The entire operation at Bright Gate had appeared to be legitimate. The orders and calls his battalion commander had received from the Pentagon sending Dalton and the team to the secret base to train as Psychic Warriors had also seemed quite valid. Before leaving for Russia, he'd been assured he had National Command Authority sanction for the mission.

"Sir, we were training in 10th Group on the precursor to Psychic Warrior, in a program called Trojan Warrior, *two years* ago. How can something have been hidden that long? Or not come to someone's attention?"

"I'm sure the orders were legitimate in that they came down the chain of command," Eichen said. "But where they started in the chain of command is another issue. This has been going on a lot longer than two years.

"Let me give you what little background we do know.

Bright Gate was the brainchild of a scientist named Professor Souris. She worked at a facility called the High-Energy Research and Technology Facility—HERTF is what those who work there call it—located on Kirtland Air Force Base. That we *did* know about. It was built to test directed-energy weapons, particle beam technology, and radio and microwave frequency potentials for combat.

"I've been there. The facility is located in a canyon in the Manzano Mountains. The walls were built four feet thick to contain some of the results of what they are working on. We budgeted twenty million dollars to build the place and quite a bit to keep it running. And then we staffed it with the brightest minds we could find, Souris among them.

"Apparently, as near as we can piece together now, Souris began doing some speculative work on her own. Work trying to cross the boundary from the real into the virtual plane. That she succeeded we now know, given the events of the last couple of weeks and the existence of Bright Gate."

"How did Bright Gate get established then?" Dalton asked.

In the dim light reflected through the windows, Eichen appeared old and worn. "Let me give you the big-picture background and you'll have to bear with me, Sergeant Major, as some of what I'm going to tell you is going to sound quite fantastic, but I assure you, it is the truth. I had a hard time accepting it all when I was first approached to be part of Nexus, but as the years have gone by, I've learned more and more and my belief has grown to be absolute.

"Nexus was founded by General Eisenhower when he was President. After a couple of years in office, Eisenhower realized that things were not as they appeared to be, that there were actions going on that he wasn't being briefed on.

And it appeared that key members of his administration, especially in the military and intelligence agencies, along with leading members of industry, were working with a different agenda. What that agenda was, he had no idea. He tried to make it as public as he could; I'm sure you know about his warning in a speech to the country regarding the military-industrial complex, but it was much darker than that. And he was threatened."

Dalton stirred uncomfortably. "The President threatened?"

"Eisenhower took the threat quite seriously," Eichen said. "Kennedy didn't."

There was a long period of silence as Eichen let the implications of that last sentence sink in. Dalton didn't know what to say or think, so he remained quiet until Eichen continued. "Eisenhower didn't roll over though. He formed a group to watch these people and to figure out what they were up to. The group was called Nexus. He kept it very small and limited to people he absolutely trusted. Over the years, that trust has been handed on to each successive member. It's more than forty years later and we've learned little."

Eichen fell silent and Dalton waited.

"What do we know?" It was as if Eichen were really asking himself that question. "We know that there is some sort of international group that manipulates governments, industry, religion, the media—hell, damn near every aspect of our life. Who they are, we don't know yet, although we do know they have been called the Priory. How many members, what their objectives are, where they're located—those are still all uncertain. They've always used other organizations as fronts for their work.

"Using the work she developed at HERTF and our own government's secret infrastructure, Souris founded Bright Gate with the blessing of the Priory. I'm sure you can imagine how easy it is using compartmentalization and security classifications to keep something secret inside our own government's bureaucracy.

"We think Bright Gate didn't turn out as well as she— or more accurately, the Priory—had hoped. We're not exactly sure what happened, but after a year at Bright Gate, she left and founded another secret base in Alaska called HAARP. I'm going to Alaska shortly to find out what the hell is going on there. You've been ordered to report back to Bright Gate, haven't you?" Eichen asked.

"Yes, sir." Dalton was still trying to assimilate everything he'd just been told.

Eichen reached into his breast pocket and pulled out a folded piece of paper. He handed it across the coffee table to Dalton. "Read it. You can turn on the light."

Dalton switched on the small lamp next to the couch and unfolded the paper. The letterhead at the top read WHITE HOUSE with the presidential crest below it. The note was handwritten:

> TO: *Sergeant Major James Dalton*
> FROM: *The President of the United States*
> *You are reassigned effective receipt of this letter to work directly for Lieutenant General Eichen, who works directly for my office. You are to share information of this reassignment with no one.*

Dalton noted the signature and the imprinted seal at the bottom of the page.

"Turn off the light," Eichen ordered. He reached out. "I need that back."

Dalton handed him the note, and in exchange, Eichen gave him what appeared to be a compact cell phone.

"That's a SATPhone with a direct link to me," Eichen explained. "You flip it open and punch in number one and my phone will ring. I *always* have mine with me and you will always have that with you. I want to know what's going on at Bright Gate."

Dalton took the phone and slid it into a pocket. "Anybody could write that, General," he said, indicating the pocket Eichen had slid the note into.

"True," Eichen acknowledged.

Dalton was tired. He leaned back on the couch. "And, sir, the last orders I followed like that were obviously illegal. What's different now?"

"You can call the President on the phone I just gave you."

"And have someone imitate his voice."

Eichen's teeth shone briefly in the dark as he smiled. "It's good you're starting to get paranoid."

"Sir, I've been paranoid my entire career. That's why I'm still around."

"You weren't paranoid enough when you were assigned to Bright Gate," Eichen noted.

"I *was* paranoid, but I received a legitimate order from my chain of command to report there," Dalton said. He was stung by the implied criticism.

"What can I do to prove to you this order is legitimate?" Eichen asked.

"Tell me what's going on, General. I'm tired of people withholding information from me, thinking I'm too stupid to understand. Why was Bright Gate developed? What is the goal of this Priory group you mentioned? What's the goal of Nexus, who you work for?"

" 'What's going on'?" Eichen repeated. He sighed and leaned back in the chair. "That's what we're trying to find out. All I can tell you is that the Priory has been manipulating our government—and others—for a long time. How long, we don't know, but—" Eichen paused, searching for the right words. "Let me put it this way. As near as we can tell, as long as there has been recorded history, the Priory has been in the shadows. We've discovered little snippets of information here and there that indicate that.

"How powerful they are, we don't know, but we do have evidence they are very powerful indeed but also very small. They use others to work for them. Bright Gate and Psychic Warrior are just one area they have manipulated. There are many others; how many I'm almost afraid to find out.

"We think SD-8 in Russia was the same thing—a research facility that was founded by the Priory—and that those in Moscow never really had a clear picture of what was going on there."

Dalton considered that. "If the Priory has such power to start with, why did it need SD-8 and Bright Gate?"

"That's a very good question," Eichen said, "which we don't know the answer to."

"Is Dr. Hammond working for the Priory?"

"Not that we know."

Something clicked then for Dalton, an unresolved issue he had puzzled over ever since finding out about it. "The first Psychic Warrior team that was lost. Raisor's sister was your agent, wasn't she?"

Eichen nodded. "We got her in there after Souris left and the Priory's attention had shifted to HAARP. We wanted her to use Bright Gate to check out HAARP. Apparently someone else didn't want her to. Hammond's predecessor, Dr. Jenkins, pulled the plug on her team. Jonathan Raisor pulled the plug, so to speak, on Jenkins."

"Did Raisor know his sister was your agent?"

"No."

"But Jenkins worked for the Priory?"

"He was Souris's replacement. The one who took her theoretical work and made it practical in the form of Psychic Warriors. When he was killed, we managed to get

Hammond into the slot there before the Priory could send someone they had corrupted. It's like playing a chess game in the dark, each side trying to take control of a square before the other can."

"And sometimes pawns have to be sacrificed, right?"

"You're a soldier. You know how it is."

Dalton had no doubt about his status as a piece on the board. "So the Priory doesn't have control of Bright Gate right now?"

"There isn't much left there," Eichen noted. "But I have no doubt that a new Psychic Warrior team will be reconstituted. And it's very likely someone on that team will be working for the Priory."

"Jesus," Dalton muttered. "What a mess. We're fighting ourselves."

"Not just us," Eichen said. "This is worldwide. We have members in Nexus from other countries. It turns out Eisenhower wasn't the only world leader threatened by the Priory. Most go along, but some, men and women in positions of power who see the threat from the shadows, are putting everything they have on the line."

"But you don't even know exactly what the threat is or what the Priory's goal is," Dalton noted. "For all you know, the Priory might have a good reason for doing what it does."

"I doubt that," Eichen said.

"Why, sir?"

"Why hide if their motives are good?" Eichen asked in turn. "Trust me on this. The Priory is our enemy. I've looked at your service record, Jimmy," Eichen said. "You appear to be a good soldier. You've served your country a long time, and now we're asking you to serve once again."

Dalton didn't take the bait. "You know more than you just told me."

"Not much more. And you're going to be out there,

exposed. What I have told you won't compromise much of our organization. The Priory knows Nexus exists, as we know it exists. I'm your cutout."

Dalton knew what the general was saying: If he was compromised, he could only give up the little he knew, which was basically his cutout, or intermediary—the general who was his only link to Nexus. The rest of the organization would be safe.

"What is Nexus's agenda?"

"We fight the Priory, try to stop it from taking actions that harm our country."

Dalton thought that overly defensive and reactive, but kept that opinion to himself. "What do you want me to do?"

Eichen stood. "Go back to Bright Gate. I want you to see if you can find out what Eileen Raisor discovered before she was cut off."

"How will I do that?"

"Use the master computer there—Sybyl. There should be some sort of record of Ms. Raisor's mission. There might be nothing. I don't know. But I'd like to know as much as possible before I go to Alaska. Then try to find out who was running things there—who was behind Jenkins and Souris before him. Find *their* cutout if you can. Maybe we can work our way up their organization. Anything you find out, you report back to me."

"What happened to Souris?" Dalton asked. "Is she still at HAARP?"

"That's another strange thing," Eichen said. "She disappeared two years ago. We haven't been able to find her since."

"Killed?"

"Perhaps. Or maybe she's working on something else for the Priory now. We don't know."

Dalton had worked in the gray world of covert operations for most of his career, but this was the most bizarre thing he had ever heard.

"Are you with us, Sergeant Major?"

Dalton didn't ask the question that popped into his mind—what would Nexus do to him if he said no? "Yes, sir."

Eichen turned for the door, but paused, hand on the knob. "I am sorry about your wife. I know this is a difficult time to ask this of you."

The door swung shut behind the general. Dalton saw the headlights go on and the car drove away, leaving Dalton once more alone in the dark in the house filled with memories.

Henry Kissinger had once stated that power was an aphrodisiac, but Linda McFairn thought that too narrow and foolish a definition. She cared little about bedding younger, good-looking men, unlike the majority of her male colleagues high in the echelons of government, who spent much of their free time pursuing young, nubile women. To McFairn, power was a lever that could be used to produce desired results. Sex, unless it served a specific purpose, was a waste of energy and, in a town where slander was thrown about with ease, a potentially damaging act, more so for a woman than a man, naturally.

She'd learned that over thirty-eight years ago when she started as a Russian linguist at the National Security Agency. She spent twenty years working her way around various slots in the Operations Directorate, then got her big break as Executive Assistant to the Deputy Director. It took another eighteen years of various assignments for her to make it from the outer office to the inner office.

As Deputy Director she was second only to the Director, a three-star Air Force general. In reality, her decades in the Agency, as opposed to his recent assignment, made her more experienced by far in the power workings of Washington and inside the Agency. The Director was always a military man, as the NSA fell under the jurisdiction of the Department of Defense, which meant she had gone as high as she could possibly go in the Agency. The fact that she had never married had produced more than a few subtle and not so subtle charges that she was a lesbian, something she found typical of male thinking. She'd discovered there were two basic reactions by most men to women in power—if they could screw her, they'd tolerate her but not respect her; if they couldn't bed her, then she was a lesbian and they still wouldn't give her respect. She had learned that while they might not respect her as a person, they would respect the power she wielded.

The NSA was in charge of all electronic intelligence activities for the United States, which meant its domain was information. And information, used properly, was power.

Her office was on the top floor of the "Puzzle Palace" at Fort Meade, a large glass building that dominated the landscape. It was directly at one end of the main corridor, the Director's at the other end. She made the trip to his office once a day to sit in on the daily intelligence briefing, if both he and she were in town. He was currently overseas, leaving her in charge.

Her desk was teak and quite large, over eight feet wide by four across. A twenty-inch flat-screen monitor was perched to her left, the keyboard and mouse on a moveable shelf just under the desktop. The in-box was to the far right, the out-box to the far left. Her policy was never to leave anything in the in-box when she locked up to go home, which had caused her to spend many a late night in the office, once in a while causing her to catch a nap on a plain leather couch on the far side of the room and not go home. The fact that she was here at two in the morning was not an unusual occurrence.

On the wall next to the door, directly across from her desk, a quote in large letters was framed: ALL WARFARE IS BASED ON DECEPTION. It was from the *The Art of War* by Sun Tzu, a book that McFairn kept in the top drawer of her desk and read from every day.

Double doors led to the main corridor. Behind her, thick bulletproof glass windows overlooked acres of parking lots surrounding the building and the main post of Fort Meade. Two pieces of paper rested on the desk in front of her. One was a transcript of a SATCOM transmission that the NSA had intercepted—it intercepted and attempted to decode *all* satellite transmissions worldwide. The other was an internal classified Defense Intelligence Agency memo, hot off the wires.

She turned slightly as one of a row of phones inlaid to her right buzzed. She knew from the distinctive sound that it was her personal secure line. Only a handful of people had that number, but she knew even before she answered who would be on the other end.

She hit the intercom. "Yes?"

"This is Boreas. HAARP picked up an anomaly on the virtual plane. It lasted about fifteen minutes and then it disappeared."

She glanced down at the two documents and leaned forward slightly. "Bright Gate?"

"No. Bright Gate wasn't active."

"The Russians?"

"Since SD-8 was shut down, things have been quiet on that front."

"Then who?"

"I believe it was the same source as last time. Our friends from south of the border. The Ring, using Aura."

McFairn knew about the Ring: a group of drug lords from Colombia who had banded together to form a coalition. "Were you able to pinpoint the source?"

"Pinpoint? No. You know we don't have that capability without a second receiver."

"I think I know the location where the transmission was received, but not the source," McFairn said. This time it was Boreas who waited on her. "Off the southeast coast of Florida. We intercepted a satellite transmission from a Coast Guard cutter—the *Warde*. It was chasing a vessel when its transmission was abruptly terminated and the ship couldn't be raised again. Just thirty minutes ago, the same cutter was discovered run aground on the coast of Florida, on Key Largo. The crew was dead. Cause of death currently unknown but the initial report indicates bleeding from the nose, eyes, ears, and mouth. The scene has been sealed."

"That means Aura works," Boreas said.

"We knew it would work," McFairn snapped. "*Yours* works, why wouldn't theirs? They got it from your group in the first place. From Professor Souris."

"But if your information is correct, that means Aura is directional. And we don't know how *far* the transmission was sent if we can't lock down the source."

"It's got to be line of sight," McFairn said.

"HAARP is line of sight," Boreas corrected. "What if Aura isn't? What if Souris has improved it? She's had the time and the support to do a lot of work. It might even be mobile, which means she's cut down the transmitter antenna size and the transmitter itself. She was working on all of that before she left."

McFairn leaned back in her chair and closed her eyes as she thought. "What do you want me to do?"

"You have to target and terminate the Aura transmitter field, wherever it is. And eliminate Souris."

"We already agreed on that course of action. The problem is, how do we find it and her? I've had my people searching but no luck so far."

"Psychic Warriors out of Bright Gate ought to be able to help us pinpoint Aura if it activates again."

"You tried that once. You screwed it up and I had to clean up the mess."

"I didn't screw up," Boreas argued. "That was Ms. Raisor. From your end."

"Ms. Raisor wasn't one of my people. She was from Nexus."

"Nexus—" McFairn could hear the disgust in Boreas's voice. "Children running in the dark, looking under rocks for the truth. There's an old saying: Look under enough rocks and you'll eventually find a snake. They've looked under too many rocks and now it is time for them to get bit."

McFairn remembered the thump on the top of her limousine the previous week; the marks left behind by an avatar. She knew whose avatar that was now—Jonathan Raisor—the brother of the woman who had made the initial discovery of the existence of Boreas and HAARP. Boreas had had Dr. Jenkins at Bright Gate terminate that team, abandoning them on the psychic plane. And then Raisor had terminated Jenkins. She wondered if Jonathan Raisor had worked for Nexus like his sister.

Knowing Boreas was waiting for an answer, McFairn made her decision, not that she felt she had much latitude. "All right. We'll try to track down Aura and terminate Souris."

"Bright Gate is not currently at an operational level," Boreas noted. "The recent events in Russia took their toll."

"They still have some people left who can go over." She glanced at the other piece of paper on her desk. "We have to be careful. Someone is already starting to ask questions."

"Who?"

"Someone inside the Department of Defense. They're

sending a representative on a fact-finding trip to your location. A General Eichen from the oversight committee on intelligence."

"I can't allow that. We're too close to the final resolution."

McFairn was tempted to ask what exactly that resolution was. "I don't think it's a coincidence. Could Eichen be working for your enemy?"

"It's possible. Or he could be working for Nexus."

The fact that Boreas didn't consider Nexus his primary enemy was something McFairn found interesting. "What are you going to do about him then?"

"I think this is a good opportunity to test HAARP."

"Killing Eichen will draw attention."

"Eventually," Boreas said. "At first it will look like an accident, which will gain us the time we need. And if he is from Nexus, it will send the proper message to them."

"I don't think I can allow—" McFairn began, but she was cut off.

"You have no choice in the matter."

"Perhaps if you told me why you are doing all this," McFairn said, "we could work together better."

"You've gotten what you wanted from us," Boreas said. "Now we're asking for repayment. I assure you that HAARP poses no danger to your interests or your country's security. In fact, it will add a very powerful weapon to your country's arsenal."

"You just said you were going to use it against Eichen," McFairn noted.

"To protect it for a little while longer."

"How about telling me who your real enemy is if you find Nexus only a nuisance?"

"For now, all you need to know is that the Ring is the face of my enemy but not the controlling entity." Boreas changed the subject. "We need to regain control of Psychic

Warrior. I want a team. Destroying Aura might not be the best solution if Souris has made improvements over what I have here at HAARP. I want to at least get an idea what she's done, and Psychic Warrior would be the most efficient way to do that. Could you get your friends south of the Potomac to reconstitute another Psychic Warrior team?"

"Do you mean the Pentagon or the CIA?" McFairn didn't wait for an answer. "I think both are a bit leery of Bright Gate, given each one's respective team was decimated." She leaned forward, palms flat on the desktop. "I was prepared for this possibility. I have a better option closer to home, constituting a team from within the ranks of my own Agency. But it will take time to train another Psychic Warrior team," she noted.

"Pick someone opportunistic to lead the team," Boreas said. "Someone like you, who understands the nuances of loyalty when weighed with self-advancement."

McFairn didn't respond to the barb.

"What forces does the Department of Defense have in Colombia?" Boreas asked.

"Task Force Six," McFairn said. "The covert counter-drug teams."

"All right. Use them to draw out Aura. The more we make the Ring use it, the closer we can get to the transmitter and Souris."

McFairn pressed her hands against her temples, trying to keep the pain she felt from building further. "I'll contact the Pentagon and get things moving. I'll let you know the schedule."

She hit the Off button. She called the Pentagon and passed on the speculation about the attack on the Coast Guard cutter originating from the Ring.

Then she checked her Fort Meade directory and found the name she was looking for. She made that call, getting

the personnel she wanted moving. After hanging up the
phone, she went to the wall to the right of her desk.
Pressing the proper code in a keypad caused a panel to
slide up, revealing a steel door and a retina scan. She
leaned forward, placing her right eye against rubber.

The safe door opened with a click. McFairn removed a
thick three-ring binder with TOP SECRET stamped on the
cover and carried it back to her desk. Taking a pad of paper, she wrote down a summary of the conversation she
had just had with Boreas. She three-hole-punched it and
placed it in the rear of the binder, the most recent addition.

She paused before taking the binder back to the safe.
She flipped through the hundreds of pages until she was
back at the cover page. Two words stood out against the
white paper:

THE PRIORY

She turned that page and looked at the first entry,
which she had made over twenty-five years ago when she
had first been contacted by someone representing that
group. Despite the thickness of the book and the years between, she knew little more about the shadowy organization than she had in the beginning.

What she did know could be summed up succinctly: It
was powerful. It was international. It had existed for a very,
very long time. And now for some strange reason, it
wanted HAARP operational worldwide.

She'd made a deal with the devil and now it was collecting.

There was a second binder in the safe. It was much
thinner than the first one. It too had a cover page:

THE PRIORY'S ENEMY

Opening that binder, the most recent entry was labeled The Ring. She knew something about the consortium of drug cartels that had been formed in Bogotá over

twenty years ago. It had been the focus of much attention from the various American intelligence agencies over the years, although little had been discovered about it.

The problem was, she knew that the Ring was just a front for the Priory's enemy, just as she—and her agency—were working for the Priory. The fact that the Priory's enemy used drug dealers made her feel somewhat better about her alliance with the Priory. The enemy of her ally was indeed her enemy.

That the Ring was developing a weapon along the lines of HAARP was very disturbing, but they'd known that would be a problem when Dr. Souris disappeared from the program two years ago and was rumored to be working for the Ring. McFairn didn't think it was a coincidence. She had a feeling whoever was pulling the strings behind the Ring had suborned Souris just as she herself had been suborned by Boreas and the Priory.

She controlled the most powerful intelligence-gathering organization on the face of the planet, and in the past three decades she had not been able to even come up with a name for this group that opposed the Priory or even the identity of a single agent of it. That made her very nervous indeed

Chapter Four

At 14,005 feet in altitude, the Mount of the Holy Cross joined by sixty inches the fifty-four peaks in Colorado known as fourteeners. South of Vail and Interstate 70, it was in the center of the White River National Forest and far removed from the nearest paved road. The mountain had gained its name from the cross-shaped snowfield on its north side—away from the sun—that was present year round.

It was an impressive peak and Sergeant Major Dalton's new home. Two thirds of the way up the rocky east face, a camouflaged door was sliding up, revealing a metal grate that slowly extended outward fifteen meters from the side of the mountain. The pilots of the Blackhawk helicopter edged their craft perilously close to the rock face, blades less than a foot from striking, and did a perfect three-point landing on the grate.

Dalton slid open the door and handed out several crates and boxes to the administrative crew who were there to greet the chopper. This was the only way in or out of Bright Gate, and every flight had to carry resupply.

He threw the last box over his shoulder and headed into the dark cavern as the helicopter departed, going back to Fort Carson, outside of Colorado Springs. The grate began to move into the mountain, causing him to almost lose balance for a second, and the door came down, cutting off the light from the outside.

"Sergeant Major."

Dalton nodded a greeting. "Lieutenant Jackson."

She was standing next to the vault door that led to the interior of the mountain and Bright Gate. She wore a dull green one-piece flight suit, a silver bar on the shoulders. She was a tall, slender woman in her mid-twenties, and her blond hair was cut shorter than required by military regulations, a matter of practicality when operating as a Psychic Warrior in the isolation tanks that were their home during a mission.

"Are you all right?"

Dalton considered the question, knowing that it was more than just a pleasantry. Honesty dictated a long, involved answer, practicality a shorter, more direct one. "I'm functional."

A look crossed Jackson's face, something he couldn't make out, and he didn't get a chance to see it again as she turned to the door and punched a code into the keypad on the side. The circular door was eighteen feet in diameter with rings of black metal on the polished steel surface. Dalton knew those rings were part of the psychic fence guarding Bright Gate and extended on either side of the door, and through the bottom floor and top ceiling, completely surrounding the facility.

The door rolled sideways into a recessed port, revealing a corridor lit with dim red lights. It was cut out of solid rock and descended slightly. The admin personnel entered, carrying their loads, Jackson letting them past. Once Dalton was through, she used the keypad on the other side to shut the door. The psychic fence was engaged once more.

"You can dump that here," Jackson told Dalton as they paused next to a cross corridor the admin personnel had turned onto. "We just received a call. Raisor's replacement is due in shortly."

" 'Raisor's replacement'?" Dalton repeated. "Is Raisor really gone?"

Jackson didn't answer, leading the way toward the team quarters.

Dalton stopped her. "I want to see my team."

Jackson nodded and changed direction. The door she stopped at also had a keypad next to it. She punched in a code and it opened with a click. Dalton walked in slowly, taking in the bodies suspended in the tubes. Two teams of Psychic Warriors—twenty people.

"They're alive," Jackson said. "Hammond ran CAT scans and there is brain activity. Very low level and not normal, but since we're dealing with abnormal from the very start, she doesn't know what it means. It might just be a reaction from the autonomic nervous system in response to the isolation tubes keeping the bodies alive."

Dalton walked among the tubes, seeing the members of his Special Forces unit who had been "killed" on the psychic plane by Chyort/Feteror, the Russian avatar. And beyond them, the tubes holding the first Psychic Warrior team, the one he hadn't been told about when first recruited to the PW program. He stopped in front of one of them containing a woman. He could see the resemblance to Raisor, whose body floated six tubes further down. The nameplate on the front of the glass read Eileen Raisor. Where Jonathan Raisor had gone on the last mission, when he broke off from Dalton's team, was a mystery, and since General Eichen's visit the previous evening, something Dalton saw in a different light. The fact that Eileen Raisor had been recruited by Nexus and ended up being betrayed was something Dalton planned on keeping foremost in his mind to keep from suffering the same fate.

"Does the first team have the same CAT scan signs?" he asked.

"No. They're flat."

"Ah, crap," Dalton muttered. He turned and left the room, heading for the control center.

Dr. Hammond was at her normal place, behind the main console, surrounded by computer terminals that gave her access to Sybyl, the master computer that controlled the entire facility and the Psychic Warrior program.

"Sergeant Major," she said, nodding in greeting.

"Doctor." He grabbed a seat and rolled it over next to her as Jackson did the same on the other side. "Anything on our people?"

"Nothing. We're keeping the bodies alive, but their psyches..." Hammond trailed off.

"Let me ask you something," Dalton said. "Sybyl tracks us when we go over to the virtual plane, right?"

"Track isn't the right word," Hammond said. "Sybyl has to supply your avatar with both power and form, so it is always in contact with you, but the computer really can't tell exactly where you are. We don't really know what space and distance is on the virtual plane."

"Does the computer track where we come out in the real world?"

"No, because the link is through the virtual."

"Is there *any* sort of record of our trips when we go over to the virtual?" Dalton asked.

"Sybyl records all data on the link, both reported and requested," Hammond said.

"Could you pull up the data for the first team?" he asked.

Hammond turned to the computer and typed in a rapid series of commands. "Here it is."

Dalton looked over her shoulder but could make little sense of the words. "What does that mean?"

Hammond pointed. "Real time is recorded here. This

is power data. This is communication's linkage. The first team was over for, let's see . . ." She scrolled down. "Forty-two minutes in real time before the linkage was cut."

Dalton saw something on the right side of the screen. "What does this mean?"

Hammond read what he was pointing at. "One of the team members, Eileen Raisor, was requesting information from Sybyl about a location."

"What location?"

Hammond moved the mouse and clicked. She read the letters out loud. "A-F-S-M-S-C."

"Which stands for?" Jackson asked.

"Air Force Space and Missile Systems Center," Hammond answered.

Dalton wondered what that had to do with HAARP.

"She wanted to know where it was and what it did," Hammond continued. "Sybyl gave her the data. The team was cut off less than a minute later." She continued to use the mouse and keyboard, searching further into the data, when she suddenly stopped. "Oh my."

"What?" Dalton asked.

Hammond's eyes shifted about, as if afraid of being overheard even though there was no one else in the room. "Sybyl's been infected."

"Infected?" Dalton repeated. "With what?"

"A bug."

"From where?" Jackson asked.

Hammond frowned as she looked at the data on her screen. "That's the weird thing. I think the bug has been there all along. An integral part of the master program."

"A time-delay activation?" Jackson asked.

"It's been active all along," Hammond replied.

It was Jackson's turn to look confused. "What does the bug do?"

"As far as I can tell by looking at this, it tracks Sybyl's

activity and notes whenever the virtual plane is accessed here. I think there's more to it than that, though—it's going to take me a while to break down the lines of code. But someone had access to this data real-time as that first team was on the psychic plane."

"So whoever it was knew about the request reference AFSMSC by Eileen Raisor?" Dalton asked.

"Yes."

"Who could have put the bug in there?" Dalton wanted to know. "And why?"

"It had to have been someone here inside Bright Gate," Hammond said. "We're secure to the outside world."

"No, you're not," Dalton said. "I don't know much about computers, but you just told me someone's monitoring Sybyl, which means that information is getting out of here in some manner, correct? And if information from the computer can go out, then someone on the outside can get into Sybyl, right?"

"No." Hammond was shaking her head. "We were tested by the NSA. We're secure from hackers."

"Unless the NSA did the hacking," Dalton said. He thought of what Eichen had said about the government being infiltrated and about Jenkins, Hammond's predecessor. "Raisor said the first PW team was betrayed by someone in our own government."

"But why would someone outside of here want to know when Sybyl is active on the virtual plane?" Hammond asked.

"To hide something from Psychic Warriors when they're deployed," Dalton said. He thought about it. "We've got two problems. One is we don't know who is doing this surveillance. The second is we don't know what's being hidden from us."

"I think—" Jackson began, but suddenly stopped.

"Go ahead," Dalton urged her.

"I shouldn't say anything. I don't really know for sure, anyway."

"Know what for sure?" Dalton asked.

Jackson glanced at Hammond. "You weren't with the original Bright Gate program, were you?"

Hammond shook her head. "I was brought in after Professor Jenkins died in a car crash."

"Who brought you here?" Jackson asked.

"I was working for the Department of Defense at Livermore. A General Eichen approached me."

Dalton considered that. Since she mentioned Eichen's name so easily, Dalton assumed that she was an unwitting participant and not reporting back to him. "So you weren't NSA or CIA?"

"No, why?"

"Because the NSA and the CIA started Bright Gate," Jackson said. She shook her head. "It's nothing. Really." She quickly walked out of the room, leaving Dalton alone with Hammond.

"She's right," Hammond said.

"Right about what?"

"There's something really strange about this place, this program. All of it. Beyond the technology. I was working on quantum physics at Livermore when Eichen tapped me to come here and take over, and we had no clue about any of this level of advancement in physics. It's like it came out of the blue."

"The Russians had the hyperspace howitzer way back in the early sixties," Dalton noted.

"Yeah, and where did they get *that* from? I've been studying the data the Russians recovered on that, and it's definitely too far advanced for the time it was developed. Hell, it's too advanced for us *now*. I don't think we could duplicate the howitzer even with what we know. It's good it was destroyed."

Hammond leaned back in her chair, exhausted. "There's something else. I've been looking at some of the information you brought back from the Russian SD-8 base."

"And?"

"Chyort—the devil avatar—he was..." Hammond trailed off into silence.

Dalton waited a few moments. "Tell me."

"Even with what they did to his mind—making a direct interface with the computer—he was more than the sum of his parts."

"Meaning?"

"Meaning I don't understand this." Hammond shifted her tired gaze to Dalton. "You've constantly accused me of not knowing what I'm doing, and I'm admitting to you now that I agree with you. All of this"—she waved her hand to indicate the Bright Gate control center—"it's based on concepts we don't really understand. I don't think the Russians really had much of a clue what they were doing either."

Dalton was trying to follow what she was getting at. "But you said it didn't matter if you understood the concepts as long as you can use them."

Hammond gave a weary smile. "I did say that, didn't I? But I've been thinking about that, and the best analogy I can come up with is that it's like saying we didn't understand the concept of the internal combustion engine, but we built one and used it in a prototype car. The question is, who *did* understand the concept enough so that we could build it? Who was able to invent and build a mind-computer interface at SD-8 so well that the results were far beyond what we could have imagined?"

"Have you heard of a Professor Souris?" he asked.

Hammond indicated she hadn't. "Who is that?"

"She's the first one to work on Bright Gate."

"That's strange," Hammond said. "There's no record of her anywhere here."

"Couldn't all this"—Dalton indicated the control center—"be the result of an intuitive leap on one person's part? I mean, where do scientific breakthroughs come from to start with?"

"If that's true and Souris did this," Hammond said, "I would expect to see some documentation. More data. We've got the equipment, the computer, the system, but we don't have anything detailing the supporting theories. That doesn't make sense. That's not how a scientist works."

To that Dalton had no reply.

Hammond rubbed her eyes. "Oh well. I guess I ought to get working on the program to see what the hell is going on."

Dalton left her and went to the bunkroom. Jackson was lying on her back, hands behind her head, staring at the ceiling. Hammond's words bothered him. He had assumed from the very beginning that Bright Gate—and the Russian's SD-8 when he'd learned of it—had been the result of brilliant scientific work. But to have the current lead scientist here say she was baffled was disturbing. He knew he'd have to call this in to Eichen at the first opportunity. His mind went back to what had been said before Hammond talked about that, and he sat down across from Jackson.

"Sergeant Major?" Jackson was sitting up.

"It's Jimmy," he said without thinking. He saw the surprise on her face. "That's the way we operated in SF. Between a team leader and a team sergeant. Who respected each other. But only when they were alone, not in front of others. If that's all right with you, ma'am," he added.

Jackson stuck her hand out. "Ljala."

Dalton's eyebrows arched. "Excuse me?"

Jackson laughed. "Ljala. When I was a kid, my friends called me Jerry."

"Ljala," Dalton repeated. "I've never heard the name before."

"It's Roma. From my mother's side. My surname is from my father's."

"Italian?"

"No." Jackson got up and sat down on the bunk across from him. "Outsiders call us Gypsies. Roma is what we call ourselves. You're a *gadje,* an outsider."

Dalton untied his boots, pulling the laces, easing the tightness. "You're a Gypsy?"

"Roma," she corrected him. "The term *Gypsy* comes from early beliefs that my people came from Egypt. We didn't. And most Roma don't like the term *Gypsy,* as it's usually used in a derogative manner."

"Roma," Dalton amended. "Where *did* your people come from?"

"That's a long story that we don't share with *gadje,*" Jackson said. She smiled. "I don't really consider myself a true Roma, though. I'm sorry if I was short with you. I haven't talked about it in a long time. My mother was a true Roma. That's why I got picked to be part of Grill Flame."

Dalton had worked briefly with the classified CIA program in the eighties and early nineties that used psychics to remote view. "Because your mother was a Roma?"

Jackson smiled, leaning back on the bunk. "You know, crystal balls inside the dark tent, telling someone their fortune. Laying out tarot cards and reading them. It's in the blood. Makes sense, doesn't it?"

"Maybe," Dalton said.

"There's a little bit of truth in myths and legends," Jackson said. "My mother was a true reader, as was her mother before her and the maternal line through the ages. They could see what others couldn't. A person's lifeline in their palm. The future in the cards. The sense of the spirits of the dead. And it was real, what they saw."

"You believe that?"

"Don't you now?"

Dalton nodded. "Can you read, sense the spirits?"

Jackson's smile was gone. "I rebelled against it. My mother embarrassed me. My father was so solid, so straight and narrow, I didn't see why he had gotten involved with my mother. He was *gadje* also, the son of a preacher, a manager in a lumber mill. My mother—I didn't understand why she gave up the road for him and turned away from her people. Maybe because he was so solid and steady. She, on the other hand, was beautiful and wild. Maybe opposites do attract, who knows? My mother drove me crazy. My friends thought she was nuts. The clothes she wore and the way she acted. Setting up a room in our house and reading fortunes.

"So I went as far from it as I could. To the Academy. The Army. And then they dragged me into Grill Flame when I took a test everyone in my Intelligence unit was required to take and I scored high on what they were looking for. I've thought a lot about it, since being here at Bright Gate. I ran from my heritage to be drawn directly into it."

"And your mother?" Dalton asked. "How does she feel about it?"

"She passed away my yearling year at the Academy."

Dalton hesitated, then asked, "Do you feel her?"

Jackson slowly nodded. "Sometimes. Sometimes here in the real world. And sometimes when I'm out on the psychic plane, I feel her spirit. It's not like we can carry on a conversation; more like I can pick up her emotions, her feelings."

Dalton's voice was low. "I feel Marie just like that at times. I know she's out there."

Jackson leaned forward and reached out with her hand, grasping Dalton's in hers. "She is. She's out there and she'll always be with you. The world is a much bigger place than that which we pick up with our five senses. You and I—we have the inner eye."

"I've been learning that," Dalton said. "So what didn't you want Hammond to hear?"

Instead of replying, Jackson asked a question. "What do you think happened to the first PW team?"

"They got cut off."

"But why?"

"I don't know," he lied.

"I think it's because they saw something they weren't supposed to see," Jackson said.

"What did they see?"

"If we knew that, we'd have a chance of knowing who did it to them."

"Raisor said he knew."

"And look where he's at now," Jackson pointed out.

"I'd say the fact someone was monitoring Sybyl and they got cut off right after asking for information about the Air Force Space and Missile Systems is significant," Dalton said.

"I agree."

"I've got a feeling you know more than you're telling me." Dalton sat down on the footlocker at the end of her bunk. He felt bad knowing that the opposite was true. He knew exactly why the first team had been cut off, but he knew that telling Jackson about Nexus would endanger her. Of course, he also realized *not* telling her could be just as dangerous. But if she came to some conclusions on her own, certainly that couldn't hurt. Besides, Dalton wasn't one hundred percent sure he believed what Eichen had told him.

"It's foolish," Jackson said.

"Why don't you let me determine that?"

Jackson shook her head. "Old tales. That's all I was thinking about. They have nothing to do with this." She lay back down on her bunk. "I'm tired. I need some sleep."

Dalton stood and walked out of the bunkroom to the male latrine. He felt like a low-rate spy as he went into one of the stalls and sat down. He opened up the phone. There was a short buzz. A second. And then Eichen's voice:

"Go ahead, Sergeant Major."

He updated Eichen on the current inactive status of Bright Gate, Eileen Raisor's request for information about the Air Force unit, Hammond finding the virus in Sybyl, and Hammond's concern about the development of the Bright Gate technology, which echoed what Eichen had told him the previous night.

"All right. I'll check out the Space and Missiles Systems Center. Keep an eye out there for anything else."

"What about whoever is replacing Raisor? Is he or she one of yours?"

"Negative. I have no idea who is coming to take over Bright Gate, but I'm relying on you to keep things under control there."

"What about Lieutenant Jackson, sir? Can I bring her in on this?"

"No. The fewer who know, the better. And Jackson was with Bright Gate. If I were you, I'd keep an eye on her too."

But you aren't me, Dalton thought. "Yes, sir."

McFairn leafed through the documents she had had her people intercept from the Pentagon. As deputy director of the nation's primary communications security agency, McFairn could access any communications, no matter how highly classified. After all, it was her people who designed the secure systems all government agencies used.

A Task Force Six team was en route to Colombia to interdict a drug shipment and kidnap a cartel member to try to find out what happened to the Coast Guard cutter. Exactly as she had arranged. She hit the autodial for Boreas and faced the windows, noting the large flag on the pole outside the building flapping in a stiff breeze.

He answered immediately and her message was succinct, informing him of the team's itinerary.

"I'll have HAARP on line to help locate Aura," Boreas said in response.

"What makes you so sure that Aura will be used?"

"Because you are going to have one of your agents in Colombia inform the Ring that the team is coming," Boreas said.

McFairn swung her chair around, no longer looking out the window at the flag. "That's treason."

"Come now," Boreas said, "certainly you've sacrificed smaller units before for the greater good. In war, sacrifices have to be made."

"I didn't know we were at war."

"Countries are always at war or preparing for war, which is essentially the same thing. Think of the power we are giving you with HAARP."

"Who is we?"

"I told you long ago not to concern yourself with our identity," Boreas said. "You are to do as you are told."

"I know you work for the Priory."

"But you have no idea what that word represents."

McFairn knew there was no more arguing. She had crossed her Rubicon long ago and there was no going back. She waited until he finally spoke again.

"What about Psychic Warrior?" Boreas asked. "Do you have a new team ready to go to Bright Gate?"

"I've selected the personnel from within my own agency."

"Can they be counted on?"

"Yes."

"I want to meet the team leader before they go to Bright Gate."

"I'll have Agent Kirtley fly in with General Eichen. He can get a feel for what's going on along the way and keep an eye on the general."

"Good. Don't forget to make the call south."

The phone went dead.

McFairn sat silent for a long time. Then she pulled out her dog-eared copy of *The Art of War*. She thumbed to the page that listed the five dangerous faults of a general: The last one was oversolicitude for one's men, which exposed a general to worry and trouble.

She put the book down and picked up the phone, calling her station chief in Bogotá.

Despite the passage, she didn't feel much better when she hung up.

Chapter Five

"Eight thousand people are employed in the various phases of the MILSTAR program."

General Eichen knew that last sentence was designed to impress politicians, the implication being that continued funding of MILSTAR meant eight thousand votes. The colonel giving him the briefing was obviously used to it and was just as obviously one of the MILSTAR employees who had absolutely nothing to do with the actual operation of the program itself, but was more involved with selling the program. Eichen knew this was typical of the entire defense establishment, from contractors to deployed units. The tooth-to-tail ratio of the Department of Defense was ten/ninety percent and shrinking every year.

Eichen was at the Air Force Space and Missile Systems Center in El Segundo, California, a stop he felt necessary to make before moving on to Alaska and checking on HAARP. He'd had his plane detour to California immediately upon receipt of Dalton's call.

"MILSTAR is the future of communications," Colonel Braddock continued as he walked in front of a mock-up of one of the large satellites. "It is a joint service satellite communications system that provides secure, jam-resistant, worldwide communications to meet essential wartime requirements for high-priority military users. The multisatellite constellation will link command authorities with a wide variety of resources, including ships, submarines, aircraft, and ground stations."

Eichen was seated in the front row of the otherwise empty conference room. His rank and his credentials from INSCOM had earned him this briefing, but he really wasn't sure what he was looking for, so for the moment he kept quiet and listened to Braddock's spiel.

"MILSTAR is the most advanced military communications satellite system in the world. Once completely operational, the constellation will consist of MILSTAR satellites One through Four in geosynchronous orbit giving global coverage and a fifth, the system coordinator known as SC-MILSTAR. Each midlatitude satellite weighs approximately ten thousand pounds and has a design life of ten years.

"Each MILSTAR serves as a smart switchboard in space by directing traffic from terminal to terminal anywhere on the Earth. Each satellite processes communications signals and through the SC-MILSTAR can link with the other three MILSTARs. The satellite establishes, maintains, reconfigures, and disassembles required communications transmissions as directed by users. MILSTAR terminals on the surface can provide encrypted voice, data, telemetry, and facsimile transmissions.

"Geographically dispersed mobile and fixed control stations provide survivable and enduring operational command and control for the MILSTAR constellation. The AN-TRC-194 is the designation for the MILSTAR Ground Command Post, which can be at a fixed site or transported by aircraft, ship, or truck. These terminals use extreme-high-frequency, EHF, uplinks, and an SHF, super-high-frequency, downlink."

The colonel was on a roll. Eichen had all this information in the top secret packet he'd been handed by the installation commander upon his arrival. He'd known basically what MILSTAR was before landing, but he listened to Braddock, keeping his mind open, because he had no idea what HAARP was yet, so he had no idea what part of what he was being told was important.

"Each MILSTAR can handle low-data-rate, LDR, and medium-data-rate, MDR, communications. Each transmission, LDR and MDR, is frequency-hopped over a two-gigahertz bandwidth to provide high resistance to jamming. MILSTAR covers a greater width of the electromagnetic band than any transmitter ever made. In addition, the MDR provides thirty-two channels that each operate at data rates up to one-point-five million bits per second. Because transmission security is not one hundred percent at that rate, the satellite has two specially designed nulling spot antennas that can identify and pinpoint the location of a jammer and electronically isolate its signal within a small region of the satellite's two-gigahertz communications spectrum."

"Which means?" Eichen asked.

"That MILSTAR cannot be jammed by any technology currently available," Braddock said.

"These nulling spot antennas are basically counter-jammers?"

"Yes, sir."

"So MILSTAR can transmit on its own?"

Braddock frowned. "In response to an attempt from a hostile source trying to jam it, yes, sir."

"How many ground stations can each satellite handle?"

"The MDR can handle at least two thousand, four hundred user terminals simultaneously."

The colonel waited for another question; when none was forthcoming, he continued with his briefing. "We put the satellites together here, led by the MILSATCOM Joint Program Office, of which I am the executive officer.

Lockheed Missiles and Space Company is the primary contractor. TRW Space and Electronic Systems provides the low-data-rate payload, while Hughes Aircraft provides the medium-data-rate payload. The actual satellite"– Braddock turned to the mock-up–"is made up of components, which allows on-site upgrade."

"What does that mean?"

"We can pull a piece, say the LDR main computer, and replace it when a better one is designed."

"How do you do that when it's in orbit?"

"A space shuttle mission. We've already upgraded the first two MILSTARs with the MDR, which they didn't have in their original configuration. There have been six MILSTAR maintenance missions by the shuttle."

"Six? You said only two needed the upgrade."

For the first time Braddock seemed at a loss. "Well, sir, there have been other upgrades to the system."

"Such as?"

"That's classified."

"I have the highest security clearance possible," Eichen countered.

"Uh, yes, sir, I know you do. But, to be honest, I don't know what the other four missions were. They were compartmentalized."

"Then how do you know about them at all?"

"We have to provide access to a full-scale mock-up for EVA training any time a mission is planned. We've done that six times. Thus I assume there were six missions."

Eichen leaned back in the chair and considered that. "So someone is modifying the MILSTARs and you don't know who it is?"

"No, sir. I mean, yes, sir. That's true. Of course, whatever agency it is, it has the proper clearances and authorizations."

"How do you know that?" Eichen had run into this more times than he cared to remember.

"We wouldn't have given access to the mock-up without proper clearance and authorization."

The stock answer. Eichen was tempted to ask the colonel to reverse that logic, but he held back as he knew it would do no good. "How is the satellite launched?"

"Two methods. So far all have been via *Titan IV* with a wide-body Centaur upper stage. For the SC-MILSTAR, it will be via space shuttle release."

"Why the difference?"

"SC-MILSTAR is going in a geosynchronous orbit over the north pole, while the others are basically above the equator. The next shuttle launch, *Columbia,* is going up from Vandenburg and is set for a polar orbit. It just makes sense to use the available platform rather than having a Titan moved from the Cape to Vandenburg.

"Once the system is fully operational, command and control of it will be given over to the U.S. Space Command at Falcon Air Force Base outside of Colorado Springs."

"Cheyenne Mountain," Eichen said. He didn't like the new name given to the massive underground complex. He remembered when it had simply been called NORAD, before that agency was a victim of the end of the Cold War.

"Yes, sir."

Eichen stood. "Thank you very much, Colonel." He headed for the door, then paused. "One last question."

"Yes, sir?"

"When does the SC-MILSTAR go up?"

"In three days. MILSTAR will be operational worldwide in seventy-two hours."

Chapter Six

The ambush was laid out perfectly. L-shaped, with the heavy M-60 machine gun along the short leg, aimed down the dirt road where it curved to the right. The long leg was comprised of eight men with automatic weapons, each with aiming stakes carefully stuck in the jungle floor to delineate their fields of fire in the darkness. Across from them, on the far side of the road, antipersonnel mines lined the ditch where any survivors of the initial firing would most likely seek cover. Four large antitank mines had been carefully buried in the road, their remote detonator in the hands of the captain in charge of the team.

They'd flown in by chopper from the aircraft carrier *Roosevelt* the previous evening and set the kill zone up that night. According to the intelligence the CIA representative had given them, their target was due through just before dawn, which was less than an hour away.

They were members of the 10th Special Forces Group (Airborne) on loan to a shadowy organization under the umbrella of the CIA with the unassuming code name of Task Force Six. TF-6 had been formed in the mid-nineties to take the drug war from the streets of America to the sources, whether in South America or in the Far East. Twelve missions had been conducted over the intervening years, ranging from raids on labs to assassinations of key cartel or Triad members. All had been complete successes without the loss of a single man or the source of the action being compromised.

"Lucky thirteen," Master Sergeant Garrison muttered.

" 'Tomorrow let us do and die,' " Captain Scott replied in the same low voice, eyes peering through night vision goggles, noting the distant glow that indicated headlights coming their way.

Garrison nodded, seeing the same thing and recognizing the quote. It was their routine just before action. " 'Cry "Havoc!" and let slip the dogs of war.' " He keyed the FM radio. "Target ETA four minutes. Give me a check by the numbers."

Each man reported in, their voices subdued and tinny in the small earpiece.

Garrison checked the action on his MP-5 one more time. " 'You can go where you please, you can skid up the trees, but you don't get away from the guns.' "

Scott took his attention away from the coming lights. "That's a good one. Twain?"

"Kipling. Read it last week. It was in . . ." He paused.

"What?" Scott was alert also, both men sensing something, even though the car was still two miles away.

Garrison rolled onto his back and looked up at the branches above, the night vision goggles revealing the scene in shades of green, even the night sky where it peaked through. There was a very dim red sphere high up, above the trees about eighty meters away to the south. Garrison had never seen the like. He knew the goggles would show a cigarette burning as a bright red glow, almost a searchlight, so whatever was there was extremely low level. Then it was gone, blinking out.

There it was! Fifty meters from where it had been. "What the hell—" Garrison muttered. The level in the goggles was so low, he wondered if it was a malfunction.

"The car's stopped," Scott reported.

Garrison twisted his head awkwardly. The glow from the headlights was stationary, a half mile short of the kill zone. "Something's wrong. We need to pull back. Now." He looked up. The unidentified glow was gone once more.

"Maybe someone had to take a leak," Scott reasoned. "Let's give it another minute."

The glow hadn't reappeared but Garrison's apprehension was increasing with every passing second. Their orders were to take no chances, which was rather ludicrous given they were preparing for a combat operation, always a chancy thing in Garrison's military experience. They wore sterile fatigues, no identification or dog tags, but it wouldn't take a genius to figure out where they were from.

"I strongly recommend we pull back *now*, sir."

The use of the official military courtesy startled Scott and gave him an idea how serious the team sergeant was. He keyed the radio. "All elements, pull back to the extraction rally point."

The team was well trained; not a single word of protest or question was heard over the commo net as each man began to slide back from his carefully prepared position.

"Multiple intruders coming in from the north," a voice reported. That was Boyd, their demo man, who had rear security.

"Got some from the east, north side of road, about a platoon," Pinello, the furthest deployed man informed them.

With a sinking feeling, Garrison looked west, behind their position. He could now see a dozen figures moving through the jungle, approaching cautiously. "At least a squad-sized element to the west," he reported.

They were surrounded on three sides. The only way out was through the kill zone they had so carefully prepared, across the open road, through the mined ditch and into the jungle beyond.

"By teams, withdraw to the south," Captain Scott ordered. "On my command, split team one move with demo in the lead. Boyd, deactivate the road mines and point us through the ditch setup."

Garrison grabbed the captain's arm. "It's too obvious."

"Any other way we're sure to be running and gunning," Scott responded. "They can't know for sure we're here."

"Then why do they have us surrounded?" Garrison asked, but there was no more time for discussion.

"Team one, move," Scott ordered.

Five shadowy figures slipped across the road, Boyd leading the way, the only one who knew the escape route through the minefield he had sown—a mistake, Garrison was realizing much too late. That information should have been disseminated; it was a basic rule he'd had beaten into him in Ranger School over sixteen years ago.

A line of tracers seared down the road, intersecting with Boyd and sending his body tumbling, confirming the mistake. The sound of the machine gun ripped through the jungle stillness a millisecond later. The other four men dropped to the dirt and returned fire.

"Boyd," Garrison hissed. "Boyd!"

There was no answer. Another burst of machine-gun fire lit up the darkness with a line of green tracers that passed over the road and barely a foot above Garrison's head. Sergeant Buhler, manning the M-60, sent a long burst of red tracers in the opposite direction.

An amplified woman's voice echoed out of the night. "American soldiers. You are surrounded. Surrender and we will let you live."

The first tinge of dawn was lighting up the sky to the east. Garrison knew there was no way they could break out and make it to the extraction pickup zone without more losses.

" 'War to the knife,' " he whispered to Captain Scott, quoting Palafox's response to a French general's request to surrender at Saragossa in 1808. This was a situation they had discussed, and the team consensus had been to never surrender. To go down fighting. The saying was a code word for a situation that they hoped they'd never be in.

"I'm calling this in," Scott had the handset for the SATCOM radio in his hand.

Garrison couldn't tell which direction the voice was coming from as it spoke once more. He could pick up a slight accent, although he couldn't place it in the distortion.

"American soldiers. There are nine of you still alive. Your dead bodies have the same leverage as your live ones. The only ones who will care about the difference are yourselves and your families. It is your choice how this ends for you."

"How do they know our strength?" Garrison wondered aloud.

"I'm not getting anything on the SAT link," Scott said, dropping the handset in disgust. "Just static."

"We've been set up." Garrison pulled extra magazines out of his web vest and stacked them, ready for use.

"Why? Who?" Scott was bewildered as another burst from the machine gun caused them to duck their heads. The angle of fire had changed, meaning the gun had moved. The four men in the road were no longer in defilade, as rounds struck one of them, ripping into his leg.

"Granger's hit!" the senior medic, Lambier, yelled from the road.

Before the machine gun could fire again, Lambier grabbed Granger and rolled toward the far ditch, preferring the chance of the mines against the certainty of the gun. They landed with a splash in two inches of water, and both men tensed, waiting for the explosion, but nothing happened. The last man trapped on the road, Staff Sergeant Baldwin, low-crawled after them. He dove head-first into the ditch, landing on top of one of the claymore trip wires.

The semicircular mine exploded, ripping Baldwin's body in half, throwing the torso back onto the road. Amazingly he was still alive, his hands scratching into the dirt, trying to pull himself to safety. He made it about five feet, leaving a trail of blood and intestines behind, before he died.

Garrison hit Scott on the arm, shaking his team leader out of the shock of seeing Baldwin's dying efforts.

"Captain—Sir—"

"No more," Scott said. "This isn't worth it." He began to stand, hands upraised.

Garrison jumped up and grabbed his team leader around the shoulders. "Get down!"

They were Garrison's last words, as a fifty-caliber round entered just below his left eye, under the night vision goggles. The massive bullet, over half an inch in diameter and designed in the early 1900s to be used against tanks, carried such weight and velocity that Garrison's head exploded, spraying Scott with his team sergeant's blood, bone, and brain matter.

On top of the ridge, over three quarters of a mile away, Natasha Valika lay perfectly still, the recoil of the fifty-caliber Barrett M-82A1 rifle having gone from the shoulder pad through her body. The warm blast reflected back from the muzzle break had passed over her cheeks like a lover's caress.

"They're surrendering," she muttered into the boom mike in front of her lips as she saw the man next to the soldier she had just shot waving his arms wildly. The

words were relayed to her mercenaries surrounding th
Special Forces team and to a retransmitter in a Lan
Rover nearby that uplinked to a satellite and forwarde
the transmission to a dish on an island in the middle of th
Caribbean.

The SATCOM retransmitter took up only a small part c
the cargo bay of the Rover. The rest was filled with tw
rows of high-power lithium batteries on the floor, on to;
of which sat a series of power converters which wer
linked by cable to the mast on the roof, much like that o
news vans, but in addition to the normal satellite disr
there was a dipole antenna and dish at the very top, ex
tended sixty feet into the sky but angled toward th
ground in the direction of the Special Forces team.

A second Land Rover was right behind the first, con
nected to it with several power cables. The shocks wer
strained to the utmost, as the truck's entire cargo bay wa
dedicated to batteries. Stenciled on the side of the vehicle
in small letters was the name *Aura III*.

The passenger seat in the front Rover faced back
wards. In it was a woman, Dr. Souris, surrounded by nu
merous consoles and gauges governing the equipment, th
human link between Valika and her employer, eight hun
dred miles away. Souris was reclined back in the seat, he
eyes open but unfocused, seeing nothing of her immediat
surroundings. Her head was shaved and various lead:
each ending in a pad a quarter inch in diameter, wer
stuck to her scalp at locations marked by red tattoos.

Her lips moved, whispering into the boom mike i
front of her lips, as she reported in what she was "seeing
"Three of them are dead, one is wounded. There are si
others. I think Valika is going to kill the survivin
Americans even though they are surrendering."

———

On the ridge, Valika centered the reticules of the scope on the man's head, her finger resting lightly on the steel trigger. She was aware of her breathing, her heartbeat. Even the pulse of blood through the vessels in her body could affect the shot. She knew there was a round in the chamber, eight more in the box magazine. The weight of the heavy barrel rested on a bipod, the stock tight in her shoulder.

"We want them alive," a man's voice crackled in her ear.

So much power in the two-pound pull of a sliver of metal. Valika's tongue unconsciously licked her thin lips.

"I said we want them alive," the man repeated. "Put the gun down, Valika, and send the men in."

Valika removed her eye from the scope. "I don't like being spied on, Señor Cesar," she radioed. "Where is the witch?"

A new voice, very low, feminine, echoed in her earpiece. "Where I can see you."

"It worked, Professor," Valika granted. She barked out commands to the mercenaries' lieutenants, ordering them to take the Americans prisoner. "We don't need you anymore, Souris. Turn off the Aura generator."

"This is just the beginning," Souris said. "The world will be ours."

The radio clicked off. Valika slowly stood and looked about, knowing there was no way she could tell if Souris's spirit was still watching her. A chill ran down her back and she shivered.

Reluctantly Professor Souris's left hand reached toward the switch for the Aura generator. She did not want to return to her Earth-bound body. Her spirit was soaring free above the trees, swooping and gliding, unrestricted by gravity, by the foibles of the flesh. To turn off the generator was like asking an alcoholic to smash the bottle at the golden moment of drunkenness when all felt just right; telling a marathoner to stop just as the body reached the runner's high of perfect rhythm and the feet were gliding effortlessly over the road and it felt like one wasn't even breathing.

The hand twitched and tremored, hovering above the switch.

Then it stopped in surprise. Souris's psyche saw something on the virtual plane, a burning essence racing her way. Full of rage and anger, a red-hot form against the gray.

She flipped the switch and the field—and form—disappeared and she was back in the Rover.

Raisor would have screamed if he had a body to produce the sound, as the cone of light was snuffed out and he was back in the featureless psychic plane.

He paused. But it was not so featureless now. He could sense more than before, picking up the faintest outlines of the real world as if through very darkly colored crystal. He was somewhere south of the United States. Over jungle.

He had gained some strength through the effort of moving on his own. He remembered Dr. Hammond at Bright Gate and her explanations of the importance of the avatars that her master computer, Sybyl, generated to allow him and the others to move on the psychic plane. She had said they were useful but not essential to existence on the plane.

Another pause. He was remembering more. There was more of him here than he had thought. He had some power.

And the cone of light. How he knew, he could not articulate even to himself, but he knew the light promised more power, a haven in the virtual world. He would find it again.

Chapter Seven

A metal field was growing in the middle of a brutal Alaskan winter, braving the harsh winds coming off of the Wrangell Mountains. Eighty acres of metal sprouted from a surface of loose gravel and blowing snow–last year it had been only sixty acres. Over 540 towers, each exactly seventy-two feet high, were spaced eighty feet apart in a rectangular grid pattern. Each tower was crowned with two pairs of crossed dipole antennas. Lower down, fifteen feet above the gravel, an elevated screen of mesh went from tower to tower, forming a reflector and allowing room for maintenance workers and trucks to travel underneath. There were eighty transmitter stations also hidden under the screen, each one linked to a master control room ten miles away on a foothill of the Wrangells, where it could safely overlook the transmission field. In the highly classified books that listed expenditures in the American government's Black Budget, the facility was known simply by the acronym HAARP–High-frequency Active Auroral Research Program.

Snow-covered peaks reached up to gray clouds all around. HAARP was in the center of United States' largest national park, bigger than New Hampshire and Vermont combined. Nine of the sixteen tallest mountains in the United States were in the park. Four of those mountains were over sixteen thousand feet, higher than any peak in the continental United States.

The park comprised over thirteen million acres with another million acres of private land inside its boundaries, yet less than one hundred people lived in the area. They were a tight-lipped group of prospectors and hunters, rugged individualists who valued their privacy and who knew better than to inquire into or stray too close to the strange fenced compound hidden in the midst of their domain.

Inside the two-story concrete building that controlled HAARP, on the top floor, a cluster of scientists and military personnel were gathered around monitors, each doing their assigned duty. Overseeing all of them, in a small room at the back of the control center, a man in civilian clothes sat behind a desk, looking through a one-way mirror at the workers. He was a distinguished looking man with thick white hair combed straight back atop a patrician visage. His eyes were the most striking feature, deep icy blue with flecks in them, that some who had peered into had sworn were silver. He watched as his chief scientist—Dr. Woods—grabbed a piece of paper as soon as it was clear of a laser printer and came into the office.

"What do you have?"

While HAARP was primarily designed to be a transmitter, it could also receive on the same frequencies. Picking up activity on the virtual plane was a passive action, and they had been trying to perfect their ability to pinpoint such activity for over a year now. The problem was that while they could get a direction, determining the distance to such activity was more difficult, as it was not clear what the transmission's power level was. Boreas's initial recommendation had been to build a second HAARP site so they could get two directions, and where the lines crossed would be the location they sought.

However, as with everything associated with the virtual plane, the scientists informed him that it wasn't that

simple. They were like drunks wandering in a forest, trying
to map it by bouncing into trees. Another, more immediate problem was that building another HAARP site would
bring them more attention than they wanted.

The door opened and the lead programmer walked in
with a computer printout.

"Did you find it?" Boreas asked.

In response, Woods put the paper on the desk. "We
have a track line for the new transmission."

Boreas ran his finger along the dark line. It crossed the
location in Colombia where the ambush had been set.
More importantly, it *didn't* cross the transmission track
they'd had for the attack on the Coast Guard cutter.
Which meant that there were two transmitters. Or, Boreas
realized, Souris had developed a portable one. Or both.
Looking out his window at the field of antennas and considering that the Ring might have designed a portable version of what he saw made him accept that the option of
using Psychic Warriors to investigate was much more de-
sirable than it had been. They were too close now to have
a group of drug dealers screw things up.

He was still pondering the problem when the door to
the room opened and two men, one dressed in civilian
clothes, the other in the green uniform of the United
States Army, walked in. Three stars adorned the officer's
shoulders, and rows of medals were stretched across the
left side of his chest. His face was well tanned, a curious
anomaly here in the great white north. The civilian was a
middle-aged, well-built black man with a shaved head. He
wore a pair of dark slacks and a collarless black shirt but-
toned all the way to the neck. A pair of thin metal glasses
framed his eyes.

Boreas dismissed Dr. Woods and greeted the newcom-
ers. "General Eichen, Agent Kirtley, welcome to HAARP."

Eichen took Boreas's hand. "Hell of a trip to get here,

but I enjoyed it. Great country you have. I imagine th
hunting is spectacular."

Kirtley shook hands without comment.

"Depends on what you are hunting." Boreas turned 1
a small cabinet. "Can I get you gentlemen a drink?"

"Hell, yes," Eichen said. "Scotch if you have it."

Kirtley declined. "No, thank you."

Boreas poured the general's drink, then his own. H
sat down behind the desk and slid the glass across the pi
ted surface.

Eichen glanced at the window. "Busy as heck in there

"Yes, they are."

"I've read the documents you sent the expenditur
oversight committee," Eichen said.

Boreas steepled his fingers and considered the genera
An investigator arriving now couldn't be coincidence, no
with the project as close to completion as it was.

Eichen looked out the window. "HAARP. The High
frequency Active Auroral Research Program. Fancy nam
Two billion dollars in research and development mone
over the last two years. And reading between the line
nothing really accomplished."

"Reading between what lines?" Boreas didn't wait fo
an answer. "We've gathered valuable research informatio
and–"

"The ultimate goal of HAARP isn't research, is it
Eichen cut him off. "You briefed the congressional ove
sight committee that this entire complex was designed 1
allow full-time strategic communications and data lin
with submerged ballistic missile submarines." The genera
paused to take a sip of his drink. "You and I know that wa
bullshit, correct?"

"A good cover story, don't you think?" Boreas said.

Eichen downed the rest of the scotch and slapped th
glass back on the desk. "What is it really?"

"It's a weapon, of course," Boreas said.

"A weapon from radio antennas?" the general was skeptical. Kirtley had yet to say a word, his dark eyes going back and forth between Eichen and Boreas like those of a spectator at a tennis match.

"A weapon beyond anything you could imagine," Boreas said. "With it the United States can control the world."

Eichen snorted. "A bold statement. I've been in uniform since I was seventeen as a plebe at the Academy. I've fought in Vietnam, the Gulf, and half a dozen other pissant places our President decided to send us. I heard my colleagues in the Air Force say the Stealth fighter and bomber would totally change air warfare, but they didn't. They said smart bombs would do the job, but they didn't either, contrary to what CNN and the Discovery channel tout on their specials.

"There's always a new weapon that will change everything, but in the end it's always the poor grunt with a rifle in his hand who has to take the ground from the enemy who determines the outcome of war. That's the ultimate weapon. Always has been, always will be."

"This weapon is different than those you mentioned. It targets here—" Boreas tapped the side of his head. "What is a soldier without a mind?"

"A good soldier, according to some," the general replied sarcastically. "One who will follow orders without question. I don't agree with that, of course. How exactly are you going to affect minds with a bunch of antennas?"

Boreas glanced out the window. A dark part of him appreciated the irony of the questions the general was asking. Plus this was information he needed to brief Kirtley on, so it wasn't a waste of time. "A radio sends a wave through the air, the distance determined by the power and line of sight for frequency modulated waves—FM. Certain waves, such

as high-frequency or amplitude modulated–AM–ca
bounce off the atmosphere and even go beyond line c
sight, again limited only by power of the transmitter."

"I have worked with radios," Eichen said patiently.

"This transmitter is on a different frequency tha
those," Boreas said. "We have determined that there is
frequency that affects the human mind."

"Affects it how?" Eichen asked.

"Do you know how your mind functions?" Borea
didn't expect an answer or wait for one. "Most peopl
haven't a clue. Do you know what a thought is? Is
thought real? It is real inside your head, isn't it? But is i
real outside of your head?"

Boreas was frustrated after years of trying to explai
their work to idiots who only believed in things they coul
see and touch. The Priory didn't need the money from th
Black Budget–it needed the access to the land to plac
HAARP on, the satellites that were also to be part of th
system, and the scientists the United States could provide

The Priory had always used existing political struc
tures for its own end. In days of old when a Prior coul
stand behind a king and whisper in his ear, it had bee
easier. It was difficult now but even in a democracy ther
were ways to manipulate power. Out of the paranoia o
the Cold War and the legacy of the Black Budget, th
Priory had found an avenue to operate within the shadow
of the U.S. and Russian governments for decades.

Boreas rapped his knuckles on the edge of his chai
"To you, this is reality. But you will also agree that th
voice you hear over your radio is real too. But you can
see it, can you? What does a radio wave consist of?

"There are levels to reality. And the mind operates o
one of those levels, which we call the psychic plane, or th
virtual one. 'Virtual' means something exists in essence o
effect but not in actual form."

The general, as others Boreas had briefed, focused on one word. "Psychic? You mean like those people who advertise those 1–800 psychic hot lines? Or that fellow who claims he can bend a spoon just by looking at it?"

"All 'psychic' means is something that pertains to the mind." Boreas held his anger in check. "Why do scientists constantly ignore the power of the thing they use the most? The core of our being, that which makes us different from the animals? And why do you military men ignore the vulnerabilities of the mind? Control the mind, you control the man. Destroy the mind, you destroy the man. Target the mind with a weapon, and every man is vulnerable no matter if he is in a highly armored tank or flying at Mach 2 in a plane.

"What we are doing at HAARP is taking warfare to the virtual level. This weapon—the waves that will be broadcast from these antennas—will work in effect but not in form. Once we fine-tune the proper wavelengths for the psychic or virtual plane, there are numerous directions we can pursue research in. There's so much we don't understand about the virtual plane, the physics of it. For example, what is distance in the virtual plane? If I can visualize in my mind a place a thousand miles from here, have I traveled that far in the virtual plane?"

Eichen didn't seem satisfied. "Wasn't there something on the Russian end like this that caused the recent snafu in Moscow? The nuclear weapons going off?"

"Something like it," Boreas acknowledged. He knew the general probably wasn't briefed on Bright Gate or the Russian's SD-8 and the recent battle—there were only a couple of people in the hierarchy of government who knew of the existence of both Bright Gate *and* HAARP. In the Black Budget world, everything was compartmentalized so that the left hand rarely knew what the right was doing. Or did the general know about Bright Gate also? If

Eichen had been recruited by the other side, he migh know much more than he was letting on. Or if he wa Nexus, he also might know about both.

"What exactly is a radio wave?" Kirtley asked, breakin his silence. The question surprised Boreas. Everyone h had briefed had either been too embarrassed to ask such a simple question or assumed they knew the answer, which Boreas knew to be wrong in the vast majority of cases.

"A radio wave is the electromagnetic modulation o particles we call photons. Photons have zero mass but w know they exist because of their effect. The study of then is part of what some call the Many-Worlds Interpretation of quantum mechanics. Photons are all around you, bu you can't see or feel them. At least not consciously.

"When you are in a big city, do you know how many radio frequencies are going through your body? Hundreds if not thousands. And all of them you don't even notice but every so often, while driving your car, do you eve have a certain tune in your mind, and then you turn on th radio and that song is playing? How do you account fo that? It's because parts of your mind, mostly in the subcon scious, are attuned to the virtual plane. Some minds ar better at that than others and can even project som power into the virtual plane, but *all* humans are capable o receiving."

Boreas had been forced to give this spiel several time to those who controlled the purse strings in the Blac Budget—the 160 billion dollars the Pentagon spent on clas sified projects each year.

The general was once more looking at the antenn field. "How far can you transmit?"

"Currently line of sight," Boreas said.

"Why so many antennas?"

"To affect the mind requires much focus and muc

power," Boreas said. "It would be difficult to explain the exact physics to you."

He didn't add that he himself didn't really have an idea of what the physics were. The scientists were like children walking in a dark room, reaching out with hands and feeling things in it, trying to figure out what they were. And they were scavengers, trying to work with what they'd stolen from others who knew the virtual world much better.

"We transmit two sets of signals, both in the high-frequency range. One between two point eight and seven megahertz and the other between seven and ten megahertz, both at very short wavelength. We pulse these rays at increasing levels of power. At the correct power and rate of pulse, it will produce a virtual field around the towers."

"How does this affect the mind?" the general asked. "Make someone think of show tunes?"

"At a certain frequency it is disharmonic to the natural virtual plane of the mind."

"And what will that do?" the general wanted to know.

"It will kill all within range."

There was a moment of silence before Eichen spoke again. "So what do you plan on doing?" the general asked. "Set up a massive field of antennas within line of sight of your target? And what, the enemy is just going to sit there and let you do that? Do you have any idea of the pace of modern warfare?"

"We have some ideas for making it a practical weapon system," Boreas said.

Eichen nodded. "Such as using MILSTAR satellites as retransmitters so the line of sight can cover any place on the planet's surface?"

Boreas stiffened.

"Don't treat me like an idiot," Eichen said. "I just flew from California, where I found out what you've been doing. Now tell me—what is the status of the MILSTAR retransmitters for HAARP? You've had some work done during shuttle missions, haven't you? Four missions to be exact."

Boreas spun the glass in his hand, eyes catching the light reflected through the alcohol. "We had to retrofit the four MILSTAR satellites. That was completed just recently. The entire system, though, won't be operational until SC-MILSTAR is launched." Boreas slid his glass away. "But you knew most of this from MILSATCOM. Why did you come here?"

"To let you know that things are bit more complex than you know," Eichen said. "I contacted Space Command, which will control MILSTAR. They've programmed a lock code into each MILSTAR master computer, which will keep the HAARP retransmitter shut down unless the code is sent. That code has been classified at DefCon Four, accessible only to the National Command Authority."

"We need to test the system," Boreas said. "I assume we'll be given access to the codes for that."

"You assume wrong."

"Why are you doing this?" Boreas asked. "We work for the same government."

"Do we?" Eichen shot back. "It's my job to check on programs like this and make sure they stay within certain parameters. When a weapon system is being developed, especially on such a scale as this, the Black Budget oversight committee requires certain checks and balances." Eichen smiled coldly. "I'm the check. Consider your system in balance."

Boreas said nothing as he considered this development.

"There's one other thing," Eichen added. "What about Professor Souris?"

"She disappeared over two years ago," Boreas said. "Why are you concerned about her now?"

" 'Disappeared'?" Eichen spit the word out. "What the hell does that mean? Is she dead? Kidnapped? Joined a commune?" Once more he didn't wait for an answer. "The woman was the primary developer of HAARP and you simply say she disappeared?"

"I run this program," Boreas said. "The whereabouts of Professor Souris are a matter for the FBI and CIA, I believe. I reported her missing. More than that, I don't know."

General Eichen stood and glanced at his watch. "My helicopter is waiting." He didn't bother to shake hands with Boreas. "Best of luck with your project. I still think we're going to need the infantry though." He looked at Kirtley. "Are you coming?"

"Mr. Kirtley will be staying behind," Boreas said. "He's coordinating HAARP with the NSA."

As soon as the general was out of the office, Boreas hit an autodial number on his secure speakerphone. It was answered immediately.

"Yes?" McFairn's voice echoed out of the speaker.

"Eichen just left my office," Boreas reported. He quickly summarized the meeting, ending with the information about the lock codes and Eichen's inquiry into Souris's location.

"So he could be for real?" McFairn said.

"He could be," Boreas granted. "Have you found out anything about him?" Boreas watched Eichen get into a Humvee outside the building. Kirtley remained in his chair, as still as a predator waiting to strike.

The Humvee was throwing up a spume of snow as it headed for the helipad three miles away, near the edge of the HAARP field. A Blackhawk helicopter squatted there, blades beginning to turn as the crew saw the general coming.

"No," McFairn said. "Do you think he's one of your enemies?"

"I don't know," Boreas said. "Wouldn't you have known of him if he was for real?"

"Not necessarily," McFairn said. "The Select Committee on Intelligence isn't very trusting of the intelligence community. If he is what he says he is, then we shouldn't be able to find out who he is, if you follow the logic, skewed as it may be. And if he is with Nexus, they keep a very compartmentalized organization that I haven't been able to penetrate." There was a pause before McFairn spoke again. "If you would tell me exactly who your enemy really is, I might be able to do a better job."

"We've been over that. You don't have a need to know," Boreas said. "I don't think we can take a chance. We're too close to going on-line worldwide. Even if he is just what he says he is, there's the possibility we could have the plug pulled by the committee. This is bigger than them. We've never been this close, ever."

"Close to what exactly?"

"You know better than to ask that."

"And the location of the last transmission?"

"We're still analyzing the data." Boreas hung up before McFairn could say anything else. He looked over at Kirtley. "What's your take on the general?"

"He takes his job seriously."

"A patriot?"

"Yes."

"And you? Who or what are you loyal to?" Seeing the frown on Kirtley's face, Boreas amplified his question. "Are you loyal to McFairn? The NSA? Your country? Yourself?"

"All of the above."

"It's not possible," Boreas said. "There's inherent conflict." He scanned the black man's face, reading it, something he had long ago learned to do. "I think you put yourself first. Deputy Director McFairn did and look where she ended up with my help. She was a glorified secretary when I first ran into her. My help got her where she is now.

"I know her well. She wouldn't have picked you for this assignment if she didn't think you belonged here." He leaned forward slightly in his seat. "Would you like my help?"

Kirtley didn't blink. "At what cost?"

"You help me when I need it. I help you when you need it."

"And if our goals diverge?"

"They shouldn't," Boreas said. He smiled. "My enemies are your enemies, I can assure you of that." Glancing out the window, Boreas could see the Humvee approaching Eichen's helicopter. "Are you with me?"

Kirtley's head barely moved, but there was no mistaking the assent.

"Good. Come with me."

Boreas walked out of his office, Kirtley behind him, and entered the control room. He gave orders to his staff in a low voice. There were no questions asked everyone here was sworn to secrecy and absolute obedience to the project and more importantly their own self-centered goals, each of which Boreas had uncovered and used as leverage. It was the way the Priory had worked for millennia. Virtually every person had a weak point where leverage could be applied, and the Priory was expert at applying that leverage.

Switches were thrown and power surged to the transmitters. The towers hummed. The dipole antennas were warming, changing the nature of the electric power, pushing it into the air, changing the sky. A red glow suffused the air over the center of the metal farm, antennas making connection with each other through the field.

"Level one," Dr. Woods called out.

Boreas was peering through a large pair of binoculars mounted on a tripod. He could see in the bottom of the view that the general was getting out of the Humvee and into the chopper. He indicated for Kirtley to take a spare pair of glasses.

"Level two." The red glow was now over a hundred meters in diameter, reaching up the same distance into the sky.

The helicopter lifted, banking to the east.

"Level three." There was excitement in Woods's voice.

"Increase," Boreas ordered.

"Level three point five."

The red glow now covered the entire antenna field and was racing after the helicopter, the crew and passengers of which were unaware of what was happening behind them.

"Level four."

Boreas adjusted the focus. He could see into the cockpit as the field reached the aircraft. Both pilots jerked upright in their seats and the chopper skewed about as if on a string. There was blood flowing over the pilot's face, pouring out of his ears.

The pilot slammed forward onto the instrument panel, twitched for a few seconds, then was still. The chopper nosed over and smashed into the ground, exploding in a ball of fire.

"Decrease power," Boreas ordered.

The red field diminished to nothing until the power was completely off.

Boreas turned to Kirtley. "Now come to my office and I'll brief you on what I want from you at Bright Gate."

Chapter Eight

McFairn had four pieces of paper on her desk. One was the intelligence summary from Boreas regarding the activity on the virtual plane HAARP had picked up. The second was an action brief from Southern Command, detailing the disappearance of a Special Forces team assigned to Task Force Six in Colombia. The third was an interception and subsequent decryption of satellite communications between a ground element in Colombia and an unknown location.

She noted the brief introduction to the intercept, which gave information about the way the message had been encrypted—a top-notch program, but not good enough to beat the acres of computers hidden underneath NSA headquarters. The NSA was the largest employer of mathematicians in the world, almost all of them focused on making and breaking codes.

She'd read many such reports in her years, and the dryness of spoken words typed on a page had always struck her as a weak substitute for the real thing, so a DVD disk with the intercept decrypted was attached to the report as per her standing order. Before she read the report, McFairn stuck the DVD in the player built into the face of her desk and thumbed the remote.

There was a hiss of static, then a woman's voice. *"They're surrendering."* Glancing at the report, McFairn noted that her voice analysts had deduced the accent to be Russian, specifically from the Moscow area.

The second voice startled her. Feminine, but with an echo to it. *"Three of them are dead, one is wounded. There are six others. I think Valika is going to kill the surviving Americans even though they are surrendering."*

McFairn hit the Pause button. The report indicated that the speech experts had no fix on the owner of the second voice. The writer of the report summarized that the voice might have been distorted by the transmitting equipment at the source. McFairn thought differently—she couldn't tell herself why, but the edge in the voice went beyond what a machine could do. Besides, they had the machines downstairs to reverse distortion, and they obviously hadn't been able to.

The next voice was male. *"We want them alive."*

The report indicated: male, Colombian, educated. No surprise there, McFairn thought—the Ring. They even had the same voice on other intercepts: Cesar—the leader of the organization. *"I said we want them alive,"* the man repeated. *"Put the gun down, Valika, and send the men in."*

Natasha Valika—McFairn's intelligence officers had a file on the ex-GRU agent. She'd go through that later.

"I don't like being spied on, Señor Cesar. Where is the witch?"

The strange voice again: *"Where I can see you."*

"It worked, Professor. We don't need you any more, Souris. Turn off the Aura generator."

McFairn sat up straight. That confirmed what they had already been almost positive of. It was indeed Professor Souris who was behind Aura.

"This is just the beginning. The world will be ours."

Checking the report, McFairn noted that the voice analyst could not match the voice off this intercept with their file copies of Souris's voice. The two weren't even close. What had happened to Souris? Why had she become a turncoat?

McFairn had read the scientist's FBI file. There was nothing there to indicate treason. Dual Ph.D.s from MIT. The highest clearance possible granted, which meant an extensive background check that she had passed without the slightest blemish. Over a decade of work on various projects before going to the HERTF group when it was founded. From there she went to work at Bright Gate and then to HAARP. And then one day she just didn't show up for work and was gone.

McFairn tapped the end of a pen against her lips. Souris and Professor Jenkins had been the keys to getting HAARP/Bright Gate going. Now Souris was working for the Ring and Jenkins was dead. She wished that Boreas would tell her whom he was fighting.

The other essential piece of information from the report was the fact that the location of Valika and Souris had been pinpointed in Colombia via a KH-14 spy satellite tracking their uplink. Almost exactly where the Special Forces team had been waiting in ambush. That meant that Souris had developed a portable Aura transmitter since the SF team had picked the ambush site. Cesar's uplink had been tracked back to a commercial transmitter in Puerto Rico, which meant he was most likely using a ground line from a distant source to the uplink.

The fourth item on her desk was a copy of an accident report filed to the aviation center at Fort Rucker concerning the crash of a Blackhawk helicopter in Alaska. Four fatalities—two pilots, a crew chief, and General Eichen. Cause of crash was initially being called pilot error pending further investigation. McFairn knew such investigations could take months. And then, they would most likely support the initial conclusion, since the effect of HAARP would not be taken into account because the investigators would have no idea how it worked.

More blood spilled. She took out her Sun Tzu and read for a little while, before going back to her work.

Sweat poured down Dalton's face. His left arm jerked, then lifted up to cover his eyes as his legs kicked the blanket off the bed. He moaned, protesting in his sleep against whatever demon was invading his unconscious mind.

Jackson put a hand on his shoulder and shook gently. "Sergeant Major."

Dalton bolted upright, hand snaking for the automatic pistol under the pillow. Jackson's hand was on top of his, having seen this once before. "Easy, Jimmy, easy."

Dalton's hand stopped, his eyes focusing. He swung his feet over to the side and planted them on the floor, connecting with reality. "What's up?"

"The new boss is here. Kirtley. And he has a half dozen people with him. A new team."

"Military?" Dalton asked as he retrieved the pistol and stuck it in the small of his back, under his fatigue shirt.

"I don't think. Civilian clothes."

"CIA?"

"Maybe," she said. "One of the alphabet soup organizations, for sure."

Dalton scratched his head. "Then why does he want us around?"

"I suppose he'll tell us. After all, we're the old hands—the only experienced people left who have operated as Psychic Warriors."

"Where's Barnes?"

"He was on admin leave, but they called him back. He came in on the same chopper from Denver with the new team."

"Three of twenty-four," Dalton noted. "After PW team one and PW team two, we're going to run out of tubes to keep the bodies."

"I wouldn't mention that in front of Kirtley," Jackson warned.

That startled Dalton. "You think he'll pull the plug on the first two teams?"

"I don't know what he's thinking," Jackson said. "He gives me the creeps. He's one of those no-affect people. I can't get a read on him, which either means he's masking his feelings very well or he doesn't have any."

Dalton looked about. What struck him most were the empty bunks. He'd come here the first time with eleven other men.

Dalton nodded toward the door. "Let's see what our new friend wants."

They left the billets area and walked toward the center of the complex. Jackson swung the door open, revealing the nerve center of Bright Gate. Two rows of ten cylinders—isolation tanks—filled one end. On the other was the control area where a dozen monitors gave access to Sybyl, the mainframe computer.

The first thing Dalton noted was that all the tubes were empty.

Jackson caught the look. "No one's gone over since my last mission. Hammond has been reprogramming and updating Sybyl."

"Hammond have anything on the bug she found?" Dalton asked in a low voice.

"Not yet."

Dalton shifted his attention to the control area. Dr. Hammond was standing next to a black man with a shaved head. He was talking on a cell phone, which he snapped shut as they approached.

He crooked a finger. "Over here."

Dalton led the way, around the row of computer consoles.

"You were supposed to be back yesterday," Kirtley said.

Dalton didn't bother to offer his hand. "I wasn't told that until this morning. I was taking care of my wife's remains."

Kirtley reached into his pocket and pulled out a small pager. He tossed it to Dalton. "From now on you have that with you wherever you go, even if you're taking a shower. You're on my team now, Sergeant Major, until I tell you that you're not."

Dalton took the pager in his callused hands and put it on the desk between him and Kirtley. Then he pulled out the chair and sat down across from the younger man. Dr. Hammond flanked Kirtley on the left. She was middle-aged, her face marked by deep, dark pockets under each eye, her blond hair disheveled and badly in need of a cut. Jackson took a seat next to Dalton. He noted that she had her pager attached to one of the pockets on her flight suit.

"Lieutenant Jackson. Sergeant Major Dalton." Kirtley said the names as if he were reading them off a manifest. "I've been assigned to get a Psychic Warrior team operational as quickly as possible. I expect you to help with whatever I request to get my team up to speed."

"Then we're not part of it?" Dalton asked.

"You're whatever I tell you to be."

Dalton felt old, worn down by his years of hard service, the wounds he had accrued over the years, subtle aches that underlay the most recent wound. Eichen's visit the other night and the hints of treachery echoed in his mind.

He knew the answer but he asked anyway. "Do you have written orders for the lieutenant and me indicating that?"

Kirtley handed him a piece of paper. "Yes."

Dalton read it. They were from the office of the G-1, personnel, at the Pentagon. Such sheets of paper had ruled Dalton's entire life. An order to Vietnam; to Lebanon; all over the world, working for whoever's name was indicated on the orders. He folded and slid it into a pocket to add to the thick sheaf in his personnel records.

A long silence ensued.

Dalton finally broke it. "Why as quickly as possible?" He remembered what had happened last time they were in a rush. He had lost one man in training, even before they became operational, dying inside his isolation tube.

"Because those are my orders. And now they are your orders."

Hammond cut in. "I've updated the program."

Dalton didn't even look at her. He leaned back in his chair and considered Kirtley. A man who controlled his fate because of a piece of paper signed by another man. Finally Dalton turned to Hammond.

"With the update, can you recover the first two teams?"

Kirtley answered. "The first two teams are no longer a factor."

Dalton straightened. " 'No longer a factor'?"

"Don't misunderstand me," Kirtley said. "I'm not pulling the plug on their isolation tanks. I'm saying they are no longer a factor in operational terms. If we can find them or recover them, then we'll do it. However, do understand me that they are not the mission priority."

Dalton reached forward and picked up the pager. He clipped it onto his belt. "What is the priority?"

"I've just been informed that a special ops team from Task Force Six has been lost in Colombia and we've been detailed to find out what happened to it."

"Lost a team? How?" Dalton asked.

"They didn't make extraction and they've missed all scheduled contacts," Kirtley said. "There was no one at primary, alternate, or emergency exfiltration points."

"Why are we getting called on this?" Dalton asked. "Task Force Six can draw from all of Special Operations. Seems like a misuse of a valuable asset."

Dalton was used to that in his career. Special Forces had been designed initially to be teachers, not commandos. Green Berets were to teach the people of other countries to fight as insurgents or to stop insurgencies, acting as a force multiplier and keeping American soldiers from having to do the dirty work. But over the decades from the founding of Special Forces, they had been drawn into every possible type of mission where well-trained, highly dedicated men were needed, from strategic reconnaissance to commando raids.

"We need to operate stealthily and Psychic Warrior is best suited for that. Our relationship with the Colombian government is strained at best, and Task Force is not a sanctioned operation under our agreement with them."

Dalton could see the sense of that, but didn't say anything.

"Also," Kirtley continued, "the team that was lost was from your old unit—10th Special Forces."

"What team number?"

"Zero eight four."

Dalton knew from the number that the team was from Bravo Company, Third Battalion, not his battalion. But he also knew the team sergeant, Mike Garrison. A good man.

"What was their mission?"

"Interdict and destroy a large load of cocaine."

"Task Force Six has no idea what happened to the team?" Dalton asked as he considered the situation.

"It just seems to have disappeared. If the cartel caught them, we'd be seeing it on CNN, so we're not sure what's happened. As I said, the Pentagon wants it handled discreetly, so we've been called in to sneak and peek."

"Well, good luck with it."

"This initial tasking is for you and Lieutenant Jackson and Sergeant Barnes," Kirtley said.

"You've got your men here," Dalton argued, knowing the answer even before he asked the question. "Why us?"

"My men have to be fitted and then trained as Psychic Warriors. That will take a while, according to the schedule Dr. Hammond has given us. You prefer to have this search for your comrades delayed that long?"

"I've never been asked my preferences," Dalton said. "They've never really seemed to matter in the course of things."

Not even the slightest hint of a smile touched Kirtley's face. "True. They don't. I want you, Jackson, and Barnes to prep and depart immediately. My men will observe and learn."

"Who are you people?" Dalton asked. "CIA?"

Kirtley shook his head. "NSA."

"And if we find the team, what are we supposed to do?"

"Report back."

"And leave them there?"

"You can't bring them back via Psychic Warrior, can you?"

"No, we can't."

"Then you leave them there, return, and file a complete report. Then someone else goes in and rescues them."

Valika gripped the arms of the seat while forcing her face to remain expressionless as the Lear dove toward the ocean. From her first time in a plane, the initial jump at the Russian army parachute school at Mukchevo, she had never been fond of flying. She'd enjoyed jumping that first time, simply to be under her own control and out of the plane, where she had to trust the pilot and the mechanic who serviced the plane and even the slugs who built it. She'd seen the mechanics in the hangers, drinking hydraulic fluid they drained out of the airplanes to get drunk. Certainly the pilots of this jet were professionals—Cesar only hired the best—but she still preferred to be in charge of her own destiny.

Valika had received her initial training as a member of the GRU—the intelligence arm of the Soviet army. She served as an assassin, working with elite Spetsnatz teams, killing enemies of her country both inside of Russia and out. When the Wall came down in 1989, she had been one of the first to realize her talent might be better appreciated elsewhere. She'd found work with Cesar as he was taking over the reins of the Ring from his father, and she'd been with him ever since.

Across from her, Souris was engrossed in her laptop computer, her fingers flitting across the keys. They had not exchanged a single word the entire flight from Bogotá.

The blue sea of the Caribbean flashed by below, then suddenly a rocky cliff appeared and the wheels touched down a second later. In her intelligence files she had read this was the shortest airfield in the region, only four hundred meters long, and the first time she landed there had confirmed the data. The screech of brakes and the savage jerk as the pilot went one hundred percent reverse thrust confirmed that. The seat belt dug into her belly and she cursed, as she did every time she landed on Saba, in the Lesser Antilles.

"Still the problem with flying?" Souris broke the long silence. "I could help you with that. A little therapy using Aura."

"No, thank you."

While Valika was almost six feet in height, Souris was less than five feet tall and thin under the robe she wore. But there was a sense of something about the other woman that Valika had never been able to pin down that she picked up every time she looked in Souris's dark eyes. Not a physical threat, but more a piercing gaze that cut through to her core. Of course, the professor's shaved head with the red marks tattooed onto the skin gave her a bizarre appearance.

The plane stuttered to a halt less than thirty meters from the end of the runway, beyond which the ground dropped once more into the ocean. Juancho E. Yrausquin Airport occupied the only level terrain on the tiny island, etched across a small peninsula on the northeast corner.

The door to the Lear swung down and Valika let Souris get off first. The sea battered three sides of the cliffs that surrounded the runway. In the fourth direction, the land rose precipitously to a volcanic peak, and a single-lane road snaked its way upward.

The man who stood on the tarmac next to a shiny Jeep was dressed in very expensive casual clothes. Valika found it amazing that those in the West could spend so much money on a simple pair of pants and shirt. Her own outfit was a nondescript set of khakis that did little justice to her well-conditioned body.

"Welcome, ladies."

Souris walked past him as if she weren't even aware of his presence. Valika knew all she cared about were her computers and where they could take her.

"To what do we owe this honor, Señor Cesar?" Valika tossed her duffel bag over her shoulder as she headed toward the man and the Jeep. Cesar was a young looking sixty. He had well-tanned skin, a startling contrast to the thick silver hair that crowned his head. A nose more like an eagle's beak highlighted his face.

"Ah, my dear Valika." Hector Cesar shook his head. "You must let me take you shopping someday. I can think of many outfits you would look better in." He held out his hand to take the bag, but she ignored him, tossing it into the back of the open Jeep and climbing in after it as Souris took the passenger seat. "You both travel light as usual."

"Just my guns," Valika said. She nodded toward the professor. "And her computer." Behind them a small truck had pulled up to the plane, and the Aura transmitter was unloaded from the Lear's cargo bay.

Cesar got behind the wheel. "You did well with the American commandos. You both did."

"You should kill the survivors and dump the bodies at sea," Valika said. "If the Pentagon discovers we hold them, they will attack the villa in Colombia to rescue them."

"That may be something I want in the future," Cesar said. "And I am here, not in the villa in Colombia, so it is not an immediate concern."

Valika saw no reason why he would want the Americans to attack, but she said nothing further. She was only a piece in the machine, and she didn't know what the big picture was. She hoped this visit would bring some enlightenment. From the results the previous evening, she knew that meant things were developing well after years of work. Where that work was ultimately headed, she had no idea, nor did she deem it her place to ask.

Valika held on to the side as Cesar accelerated down the runway, then spun the wheel, fishtailing onto the thin road. It switchbacked a dozen times as they gained altitude, heading toward the two-thousand-foot-high peak that dominated the terrain. They passed through a small village where the small whitewashed houses pressed in on either side. No one waved a greeting or even looked at them. The few natives who still lived on the island knew their place.

"Did you know this used to be called Lower Hell's Gate?" Cesar asked as they exited the village and took another hairpin turn.

"Excuse me?" Valika asked.

"That was the name of the town. Very imaginative, don't you think? Was that in your intelligence report on the island?"

It had been, but Valika saw no need to mention that. They rounded a corner and a steel pole barred the way, two men with submachine guns standing nearby. They immediately lifted the pole and waved Cesar through.

The gate was probably unnecessary, Valika knew. This was Cesar's island. She'd studied it years ago, before she accompanied Cesar on her first trip here and the decision was made to make this the heart of Aura's development.

Saba was the smallest inhabited island in the Lesser Antilles, about a hundred miles southeast of the Virgin Islands. Saba and the surrounding islands of St. Martin, Curacao, St. Eustatius, and Bonaire were originally claimed by the French in 1625, but that didn't last long, as they were taken by the Dutch in 1636. The larger islands were used as way stations and slave markets, but Saba was pretty much ignored due both to its small size, less than five square miles, and to the lack of any harbor or even a beach for ships to off-load. Over the centuries, a handful of people—mostly ex-slaves—had made the island home.

Cesar's father had first come to Saba just after the Second World War while sailing in the area. Valika had to allow that the old man had had great foresight. While everyone else began using the Caymans to funnel their money offshore, Cesar's father decided to have his own private island. He bought out the people. Those who stayed owed everything to Cesar's family. The islands of the Lesser Antilles had been given self-government after the war, which meant essentially that Cesar's father and now Cesar ruled. It was not a tourist destination, had no industry or business of note, and thus was basically unnoticed among the many islands in the region.

From a security standpoint, Valika believed it was almost the perfect setup. She'd had Cesar position snipers on the flanks of the volcano that dominated the center of the island, able to cover all avenues of sea and air approaches. Two radar dishes were secreted near the top of the volcano, on either side, each covering 180 degrees. Infiltration from the sea had been—and still was—Valika's greatest concern. The two tiny beaches where a very small craft might be able to land with great difficulty were mined. Sensors had been strung along the cliffs that faced the sea for the rest of the shoreline. It was as secure as Valika could make it, although she always came up with a way to improve the defenses each time she came here.

They pulled up to a ten-foot-high concrete wall that blocked the road and extended fifty meters in either direction, following the rise of the land, before doubling back out of sight. The double doors in the center swung open and Cesar drove through. Valika noted the guards on the parapet inside the wall, making sure they were alert, then the mansion directly in front. Souris had not said a word since getting off the plane, nor had she reacted to anything they had discussed.

Cesar stopped the Jeep and shut off the engine. "We have a meeting to attend."

They walked into the mansion, passed through a large foyer and into a centrally located atrium where a half dozen men in expensive suits were seated around a small conference table set to one side. Valika recognized all of them from previous meetings of the group—the leaders of the six major families that made up ninety percent of the Colombian drug cartel. The Ring. Cesar's father had founded it not long after taking over Saba, and it was one of the most closely kept secrets in the world, although Valika knew that Western intelligence agencies were aware it existed. So far Saba still remained a secret, as the West focused its energies on Colombia, the source of the cocaine.

Valika had extensive files on each of the men present and contingency plans to destroy each of their cartels if Cesar gave her the word. Loyalty was never a certain thing when billions of dollars were involved. The Ring controlled an annual take of over ten billion U.S. dollars, and she knew that given the slightest sign of weakness on the part of Cesar, the jackals would be after him.

Cesar went to the remaining seat at the head of the table. Valika took a position to his right and slightly behind. Souris moved to a chair in the shadows beyond the table and sat there.

"Gentlemen," Cesar said, nodding at them. He leaned back and clasped his hands contentedly on his lap. "Last night was a success. We have Señoritas Valika and Souris to thank for that." He turned to the old man seated to his immediate right, the eldest member of the Ring. "And, my comrade, Señor Naldo, you have them to thank for stopping the Americans' attempt to interdict a rather large shipment of your product and kidnap your son."

Valika could see that Naldo was not about to shower thanks on her. The men were never happy with her presence. For the past ten years she had run into the macho Latin attitude of South American men in all her dealings. A woman who killed, who was involved in their business, was a threat to their manhood. And Souris's mere presence was enough to add a level of unease to any meeting. This was the first time they got to see the American scientist, and she could see many curious glances in Souris's direction.

"You have taken a lot of our money." The man who suddenly spoke was the one on the opposite end of the table. Valika recognized him and wasn't surprised at his outburst—Alarico, the youngest of those gathered here, who had been grandfathered into the Ring because his now deceased father had been a founding member. She took half a step forward but Cesar raised the pinkie on his left hand, indicating for her to be still.

Alarico continued to address Cesar, ignoring Valika. "I myself have contributed ten times what the shipment last night would have cost Naldo if lost to the Americans, so I assume he has given a similar amount. That is not a profit. I want to know what exactly has been accomplished with our shared resources. I—and the others here—joined the Ring because of your father, because he promised us a new direction through unity, but years have gone by, your father has passed on, and you have told us little. You tell us of tests, use words one would need a dictionary for, and speak of things that make little practical sense."

"Your father joined the Ring because my father would have crushed him if he didn't," Cesar said in an even tone. "And you, my dear Alarico, stay for the same reason."

Alarico stood, his chair falling back. "I did not come here to be insulted."

"I am not insulting you," Cesar replied calmly. "I am mentioning facts. I called you here to tell you our new direction and what you have been paying for." Cesar leaned back in his seat and gestured for Alarico to sit. Reluctantly, the young man did so. "It began about ten years ago in the United States. They built a facility to work on developing a new type of weapon. Professor Souris was in charge of this research. The place was called the High-Energy Research and Technology Facility. The Americans were planning to develop various weapons that utilized radio waves. One of those programs was called HAARP—which stands for High-frequency Active Auroral Research Program."

Valika could see Alarico roll his eyes, but Cesar either didn't see it or chose to ignore it.

"Two years ago, a good portion of the money that you contributed to our organization was used to lure Professor Souris away from the United States and to our lovely island. Before she left, she took all her research data and the prototype of the HAARP computer which she has developed into what we now call Aura."

Valika was watching the men's faces, noting their reactions. Even though she was Cesar's security chief, the inner workings of the Ring he kept to himself. He had never confided in her what his ultimate plan for Aura was. She could tell some of the men around the table already knew the information he was giving them; to others it was completely new. That gave her an idea of Cesar's confidence in the various men.

"What is this HAARP and Aura?" Naldo asked.

"I will get to that," Cesar promised. "First, though, let me ask you all to think about something. We are very rich from our work, are we not?" He didn't wait for an answer. "But we are always being threatened. The Americans with their Task Force Six have taken their drug war illegally into our own country, and the world turns a blind eye because we are criminals. What are they then when they thumb their nose at international borders and assassinate people? Are they not criminals also, hiding behind a flag?

"Up until now we have dared not fight back, because we did not have the means to do so with any hope of surviving. And then there are others who seek to take our part of the market—the Mafia, the Russians, now even the Chinese Triads with support from Beijing are getting stronger and stretching their muscles overseas into our markets. There is no future in this."

"And?" Alarico asked impatiently. "What future are you crafting here on your private island?"

"The means to keep track of our enemies and when necessary defeat them. To make them fear us."

"How?" Alarico's question earned him hard looks from the other men at the table.

"Professor Souris has developed a computer called Aura that—"

Alarico snorted. "You've used our money to make computers? The Americans are supposed to be scared of a computer?"

Valika could tell that Cesar was controlling himself with great effort. "In a manner of speaking. The computer is just one piece of the entire system."

"I am an old man," Naldo said, interrupting and trying to throw a little water on things. "I am not, how do you say, technically proficient. My grandchild knows more about computers than I do. I do not see the connection between what you are speaking about now and what happened last night, not that I do not appreciate what happened." Naldo nodded slightly toward Valika, the equivalent of a standing ovation in this group.

Cesar nodded in turn. "I will let the expert explain it to you as best she can." He crooked a finger and Valika took a step back as the American came out of the shadows. "Professor Souris has been in charge of developing Aura."

Souris inclined her head briefly in greeting to those gathered around the table. "Gentlemen. You want to know what Aura is." A thin hand fluttered briefly from out of the robe's sleeve. "It is all around you. It is everywhere. And nowhere. It is where we want it to be."

Alarico shifted in his seat impatiently but said nothing as Souris continued.

"Using Aura, I was able to see the Americans last night. But not with my eyes. And I was able to direct Valika and her men to capture them. All without moving from my seat in a Land Rover a half mile away. I traveled through Aura. And I saw them from my place in Aura.

"The best way to think of Aura is that it is a virtual

field like a radio transmission that we can generate that is practically on the same frequency and amplitude as that of our thoughts. Thus we can travel outside of our heads into an Aura field."

"What is she talking about?" Alarico couldn't hold back any longer. "She babbles like a loco woman. And what is with her head? Those marks?"

Cesar spoke up. "Think of having access to a machine that allows you to be able to travel anywhere and see and hear what is happening without ever leaving where you are. Start imagining the potential. And it goes well beyond that. It can also be used as a weapon, as we did three days ago to wipe out the crew of an American Coast Guard cutter, allowing us to land one of the largest shipments we have ever sent."

"A computer that kills?" Naldo was leaning forward.

"Yes," Cesar said.

Naldo ran a finger across his upper lip as he considered that. "Interesting."

"The computer is only one part of it," Souris corrected. "What killed was the Aura field projected by the computer through a specially designed antenna system that I have developed."

Alarico spit once more. "This is nonsense. You bring this loco scientist and your Russian whore here and you waste our time. Just as you have wasted millions of our dollars. I am tired of paying the Ring and getting nothing out. I can protect my own."

Cesar ignored him. "Using Aura, Professor Souris was able to discover who gave up the time and location of Señor Naldo's shipment and thus we were able to ambush the ambushers who sought to kidnap his son."

Valika knew that was partially a lie. Souris had discovered the source of the leak that had initiated the planning for the location of the ambush, but the information about

the timing of the deployment of the Task Force Six team
had been given to her from one of her sources in Bogotá.

"This is ridiculous!" Alarico was on his feet.

Valika had spent thousands of hours on live fire ranges
and negotiating close-quarter combat courses. Alarico's
hand was still reaching under his jacket when she had her
pistol free of the holster. By the time his cleared leather
she was in a classic shooter's stance, a bead drawn directly
between his eyes. Her finger was a millimeter from the
hair trigger as Alarico froze, his gun still pointing down,
his eyes fixed on the muzzle of her weapon, his face
flushed bright red.

"Drop the pistol." Cesar had not even flinched during
the encounter.

It fell to the ground with a clatter.

Valika edged around so she had a better field of fire.
"Move back two steps," she ordered, staying far enough
away from him so he couldn't reach her with a surprise
move. Only amateurs pressed a gun up against a foe,
negating the standoff advantage inherent in a pistol.

"If you do not do as she says," Cesar added, "I will
have her shoot you in your testicles."

Alarico shuffled back, veins in his face bulging from
anger. He was now about two feet from one of the atrium
pillars.

"Turn around." Valika waited until he complied. "Now
grab that pillar without moving your feet. Lean forward
and press your forehead against it. Now, remove your
hands and place them behind your back."

Alarico's weight was now distributed between his feet
and his forehead. He couldn't move without falling unless
he put his hands back on the pillar. She pulled a pair of
cuffs from her belt and quickly snapped them around his
wrists.

"Cesar, why are you doing this to me?" Alarico asked.

his voice slightly muffled as it bounced off the pillar. Unnoticed by everyone but Valika, Souris made her way out of the courtyard, through a dark doorway, and into a descending staircase.

"Don't treat me like I'm stupid," Cesar said. "You made a deal with the Americans. You gave up the route of Naldo's shipment as a sign of good faith on your end. You wanted his son dead or kidnapped. You were planning to give up all of us eventually and be the only one left standing. You should have had more patience. That was your father's problem, which is why I had him killed. He died like the dog he was."

"You bastard." Alarico started to move and his forehead slid.

"Fall to the ground and you die," Cesar said.

"You're going to kill me anyway."

"No, I'm not. If you admit what Professor Souris learned through Aura in front of the others, I will let you go. You are part of one of our tests of the system. I care more about that than I do about you." He turned to the others at the table. "Professor Souris was in Bogotá two weeks ago. I had her follow Señor Alarico using Aura. She 'saw' him meeting with an American intelligence officer. He told them of the shipment and that Naldo's son would be with the shipment."

Valika had seen many face death, whether at her hands or others. Any opening was like placing a meal in front of a starving man. Brave men could resist so long, but eventually they all gave in and grasped for the opening, even if it was an obvious illusion.

"You're old," Alarico said. "Your time is past."

"So it's true," Cesar pressed.

"Yes."

"He's yours," Cesar said to Valika.

"You said you would let me go!" Alarico protested.

"I am," Cesar said. He laughed. "All you have to do is get past my Russian whore and my loco American scientist and you are free to leave."

"In handcuffs and with her having a gun?"

"You whine like a baby," Cesar said. "Are you afraid of a woman?"

Valika stepped forward and uncuffed Alarico and quickly backed away. She put the guns on the table in front of Cesar.

Alarico pushed away from the wall, face flushed. He ripped off his suit jacket, then his shirt. Muscles bulged as he smacked one fist into the other hand. Valika knew he took steroids to supplement his weight lifting.

"I will break her, and then you," he said to Cesar.

"Again, you have no patience," Cesar said. "I suggest you concentrate on the immediate task."

Alarico growled and dashed forward, arms outstretched, but Valika was already moving, dancing lightly to the left and snapping a waist-high turn-kick that caught the man in the midsection. As Alarico doubled over, she backed off and waited.

Alarico straightened up and glared at her. Valika smiled and raised her eyebrows in invitation. He came forward slower this time, like a wrestler looking for an opening. Valika gave ground easily. This wasn't a fight about terrain. She knew men had a basic instinct that they had to move forward, never retreat, but it made no sense in a situation like this.

She stumbled on an uneven tile, right leg appearing to buckle, and Alarico pounced. Right into the toe of her left boot as she snap-kicked, completely airborne. He fell backwards. Blood blossomed out of his broken nose as Valika kept the momentum of her foot swinging, up over her head, and did a somersault, landing to the rear, on her feet, up on her toes, ready.

Like a wounded bull, Alarico shook his head, blood spraying. Valika could see the rage taking over and knew he was now both more dangerous and more vulnerable.

He charged, arms outstretched. Valika snap-kicked toward his groin, but he turned at the last second and the toe of her boot connected with his thigh muscle instead. As she darted back, the tips of his fingers caught her shirt, ripping material, as he scrambled to get hold of her. She jammed her right hand downward, fingers locked straight, right into his inner elbow on the hand that had hold of her shirt. The pain caused him to lose his grip and she moved back several steps. Alarico spit blood, moving his injured arm, regaining control.

Suddenly a look of surprise spread across Alarico's face and he jerked backwards, as if hit in the chest. Valika started to move forward to take advantage, but she caught the gesture from Cesar out of the corner of her eye, indicating for her to halt and back away.

Alarico saw it also. He turned to Cesar, breathing hard, in more pain than what Valika had inflicted. "What are you doing to me?"

"I told you that you must get past *both* my women," Cesar said. "You have not done well against my dear Valika, so I will give you a chance and see how you do against the American."

Alarico suddenly gasped in agony and his hands clutched at his head. "Where is she?"

Cesar pointed at Alarico. "Right there in front of you. Don't you see her? She's in Aura. Using her computer. Her body is below us in the Aura center, but her essence is right here, doing this to you."

More blood was now coming out of Alarico's eyes and ears, turning his head into a grotesque mask of red and white. He shrieked, dropping to his knees in agony, rocking back and forth. The other Ring members were watching in shock, which is exactly what Valika knew Cesar had hoped for with this demonstration.

"If you had had more patience," Cesar continued, "you would have learned more about Aura and its potential as a weapon. But I believe this is a most effective demonstration."

"Please!" The word was torn from Alarico's very soul and all present knew it wasn't asking for release, but for a quick ending. His hands were scrambling at his head as if he could rip out the pain that was resounding inside of it. His fingers came away with clumps of hair, yet still he kept at it, tearing at the skin.

Cesar sat, impassively watching as Alarico collapsed face first onto the tiles, body twitching for several seconds before becoming still.

Cesar stood. "Do I have any more disagreements with my course of action or questions about the effectiveness of Aura?"

Raisor saw the antenna dish on the wall of the atrium pointed at the dead man as the bright ray disappeared. He had homed in on it using a series of jumps in the virtual plane. Willing himself through each leg, drawing closer and closer to the beam.

He felt more substance, or what might be called substance if there was such a thing on the virtual plane. He could also see clearly into the real plane when he wanted.

He had no idea who these people were, but he did know they were working with technology that pierced into the virtual plane. That they were using it as a weapon not only didn't bother him, it intrigued him. He would need a weapon to make those responsible for his sister's death and his betrayal pay.

Like an invisible vulture, he hovered over the atrium and listened and watched.

———

After the fourth buzz, Dalton knew something was wrong. His hand tightened around the SATPhone. After the sixth, there was a clicking noise, then a new buzz, this one somewhat different.

A voice—not Eichen's—answered. "Yes?"

Dalton considered hanging up immediately. But then he would be completely in the dark. "General Eichen, please."

"Who is this?"

"Who am I speaking to?" Dalton asked in turn.

"We can play this game forever," the voice said, "but I have to assume since you have one of these phones and are asking for Eichen that he recruited you. And you have to assume that since your call to him got forwarded to me, I'm legitimate. I know Eichen told you to tell no one other than him anything—even showed you a note from the President, correct?"

Dalton hesitated, then answered. "Yes."

"Let me guess. You're Sergeant Major Jimmy Dalton?"

"I don't think you're guessing," Dalton said. "Where's General Eichen?"

"General Eichen's dead. So I don't think you're going to be able to report to him."

"How?"

"Helicopter crash in Alaska."

"Accident?"

"I doubt it."

Dalton had doubted it too as soon as he'd heard it. "What did he discover about HAARP?"

"You don't need to know that."

"And now?"

"Now you report to me. There are only a few of us. Eichen would have disseminated information you sent him to the rest of the group. Now I'll have to."

"And what do I call you?" Dalton asked.

"Are you familiar with the Greek classics?"

"Not particularly."

"Too bad, Sergeant Major. You can call me Mentor."

"Well, Mentor, do you have anything further for me or who exactly it is I'm supposed to be watching out for?"

"No."

"So this is a one-way conversation?"

"Yes."

Dalton was tempted to just hang up, ditch the special phone, and forget about the entire thing. The only problem was that he knew that wouldn't end it. No, that wasn't the only problem, he admitted to himself. Like Sullivan Balue, he'd sworn an oath to defend his country from all enemies—foreign and domestic.

"So what next?" Dalton asked.

"Keep an eye on Kirtley. Let me know what he has planned."

"Is Dr. Hammond one of General Eichen's contacts?" He knew what Eichen had told him, but it never hurt to ask again.

There was a pause. "Not that I'm aware of. We've been moving people, taking action. Sometimes it means placing a person like Hammond in a position that might have been occupied by someone of questionable background. Of course, with every action, there is a reaction."

"Is Jonathan Raisor one of your people?"

Again the pause, and again the same answer. "Not that I'm aware of. And shouldn't that be phrased in past tense?"

"I'm not sure about that," Dalton said.

"Interesting."

"When you have something to share with me," Dalton said, "perhaps we can talk again." He flipped the phone shut.

"They'll come for us."

Sergeant Lambier stopped tending Granger's wound

to look up at Captain Scott. "Sir, we're in Colombia illegally. If they come for us, they're compounding the problem. As it is, they might have some deniability. Not much but some. We all knew that when we signed on for this."

Scott was seated with his back against a stone wall. The cell they were locked in was lit by a single naked lightbulb that cast a pallor over the survivors. The captain shook his head and repeated for the twentieth time in the past hour: "They'll come for us."

Sergeant Pinello walked across the dirt floor and squatted next to the dazed captain, who had dried blood from Master Sergeant Garrison encrusted on his fatigue shirt. "Sir, no one knows where we are. We have to make a plan to get out of here on our own."

Scott shook his head. "No. We stay in place. They'll come for us. We try to break out, they'll kill us."

"They're going to kill us anyway," Pinello said. He had to fight from grabbing the officer's shirt and shaking him. "I want to go down fighting when it comes to that."

The fifth man in the room, Sergeant Buhler, spoke up. "We never should have surrendered. We could have taken a hell of a lot of them with us. Made them pay. It's what we agreed on."

"I'm the team leader," Scott said. "It was my decision. My command. My responsibility."

"Everybody just calm down," Sergeant Lambier said as he stood, hands covered in Granger's blood. "The captain's right. They'll try to find us and then they will come for us, if they can. But in the meanwhile, we count on only ourselves. So if anyone has a bright idea how to get out of here, you better start talking."

"Sergeant—" Scott's voice cut across the room. "I am the team leader. And I'm ordering you not to do anything. We wait. They'll come for us."

"Sir—" Lambier began, but then he paused. "Yes, sir."

Chapter Nine

Dalton slapped Sergeant Barnes on the back as he entered the bunkroom. "Welcome back."

Barnes had just pulled on the black one-piece suit that they wore when they went into the isolation tanks. "Sergeant Major, how they hanging?"

"Low, real low," Dalton replied as he opened his locker and pulled out his suit. "Ready to go back in?"

"What's the mission? I just got told by one of those agency dinks to get my stuff on and be ready to go."

Dalton quickly briefed him on the current situation. Barnes's next question was a bit unexpected.

"That Feteror dude is really gone, right? We aren't going to run into him on the virtual plane, are we?"

"The Russians shut down SD-8," Dalton assured him.

"And Feteror?"

"The Russians say they turned off the life support to his brain. So Feteror's dead."

"What about Chyort? His avatar?"

"If Feteror's brain is dead, we have to assume his avatar is gone also."

"That means we're the only ones out there, right?"

"Are you worried?"

"Hell, yes," Barnes said. "We got our butts kicked last time. And the other guys—our teammates..." His voice trailed off.

Dalton paused in his dressing. "We're not giving up on

them." He looked toward the door, then leaned toward Barnes. "When we go over, I want you to search for the team. Go back to the site of the battle in Russia. Jackson and I will take care of the recon."

"Won't Hammond know through Sybyl that we're separated?" Barnes asked.

"What are they going to do?" Dalton asked. "Kick us out of here? Besides, Hammond's not as sure of herself as she used to be."

Professor Souris had the complete attention of the surviving members of the Ring. Alarico's body had been removed, and after a short break, Souris had returned to finish her briefing.

"Right now with our current configuration we can generate an Aura field about a mile in distance from the computer/transmitter. We have three working computers. One is fitted on board Señor Cesar's yacht. One is located here in our operations center. And one, the latest generation and the smallest, is transportable.

"Along with making the transmitter smaller, we are working on increasing the distance transmitted and the size of the field. We have also been doing simulations considering the possibility of generating a virtual field by retransmitting from orbital satellites. This was something my comrades at HAARP were working on when I left. I have continued that work here."

"Satellites?" Naldo said. "And how would we launch a satellite?"

"We already have launched one," Cesar said. "From Kouro, in French Guinea. It's the launch site for the European Space Authority and they were willing to launch because we were willing to pay. We've put up a small prototype with an Aura retransmitter and power booster on board."

"We've launched a satellite?" Naldo was shaking his head.

"Last week," Souris confirmed. "We have contact with it, but we haven't attempted to retransmit yet. We're saving that test until other elements are in place."

"So we will be able to use this weapon from space?" Naldo asked.

"Our prototype is rather basic," Souris said. "We can use it once, maybe twice before depleting the onboard power supply."

"I don't understand," Naldo said. "What good is it then?"

"Our satellite is simply there for us to test whether our uplink can generate a tight enough, and powerful enough, beam," Souris said. "Once we have confirmed that, we have a plan for the next stage. The Americans have already done us the courtesy of launching a worldwide network of satellites called MILSTAR that they have been upgrading with appropriate virtual retransmit technology that we can appropriate for our own use if our test works and we can develop a sufficiently powerful transmitter field."

"What are the Americans planning to do with their satellites?" one of the other Ring members asked.

"They are trying to develop a weapon system similar to Aura called HAARP," Cesar said. "This is another reason why we must be successful. If the Americans are successful with their HAARP before we are with Aura, I have no doubt that they will use this weapon against us. They will be able to attack us from space with complete immunity."

"Aura is a better version of what I was working on for the Americans," Souris said. "HAARP is based in Alaska, at a fixed site. They've been experimenting for several years now with it, but they haven't been able to get their transmitter as compact as Aura, and since it's line of sight it's pretty useless unless they can uplink to their MILSTAR satellites, which they haven't attempted yet. However, once the HAARP-MILSTAR system is operational, they can cover the world with their weapon."

"How close are they to achieving that?" Naldo asked.

"We think they are very close to their first test of the system," Souris said.

"We plan to beat them to it," Cesar said. "Once the test using our satellite is successful, we'll know we can transmit Aura on their MILSTAR. The Americans are launching the last piece of their MILSTAR network in two days, which means the satellite system will be in place for us to use and we'll be ahead of them, already having tested our transmitter. Then we have them in a difficult position. If they shut down the satellites, they lose their worldwide secure military net and billions of dollars of equipment becomes useless. If they don't shut them down, anything we do will be tracked back to the Americans and not us."

"You plan on blackmailing the American government?" Naldo asked.

"Yes," Cesar said. "What we have to do next is acquire a more powerful transmitter to make the uplink, and we will be ready."

"And I assume you have a plan for that?" Naldo asked.

"We are in negotiations for a solution to that problem," Cesar said. He opened a file folder and pulled out a photo, which he passed to Naldo. It showed a large ship, the most striking feature of which were the four massive dishes on the deck.

"The *Yuri Gagarin*," Cesar said. "A Russian research vessel. In fact the largest research vessel ever built. Forty-five thousand tons displacement. Seven hundred and seventy-three feet long. Two large dishes amidships and two smaller ones forward. Souris assures me we can readily convert them to transmit Aura. The ship is available for purchase, as the Russians need hard currency more than they need research. The ship's primary purpose had been to maintain contact with their space station, *Mir*, but since that was shut down, they have little use for it. The cost, however, is not insignificant."

Naldo passed the picture on to the next man. "How much?"

"Eight hundred million in U.S. dollars."

There was an exchange of glances around the table.

"We are rich," Naldo began, "but—"

Cesar interrupted him. "Do not concern yourselves about the cost. We have another way to get the money, which we will discuss later. Aura has many uses."

"You just said the Americans are working on HAARP," Naldo said. "What about the Russians?"

Valika knew the answer to that. "The GRU and the KGB both have experimented extensively with psychic weapons and reconnaissance. I don't know what the KGB has done, but the GRU developed a generator similar to Aura which they used against the American embassy in Moscow for many years."

"The GRU's generator is very inferior to Aura," Souris said. "It is more a directional microwave antenna, and its effects are mainly headaches and nausea among those it is targeted against."

Valika spoke up. "Recently the Russians used a different type of psychic weapon but were defeated by the Americans. The details of what happened have been kept very secret, but all the world knows about the nuclear detonation in Moscow that destroyed GRU headquarters."

"That involved this type of weapon?" Naldo asked.

"In some manner," Valika answered. "I have tried to gain more information but have discovered little. The

Americans and Russians are keeping whatever happened very secret."

Naldo raised a finger, pointing toward Souris.

"Yes?"

"How did you kill Alarico?"

"I directed an Aura field at him and then changed the frequency slightly so that it was disruptive to his normal brain patterns," Souris said. "His brain stopped functioning—both the autonomic and parasympathetic nervous systems. So he actually could have died of several things at once. It would be difficult to tell which was fatal first. His heart stopped beating, he also stopped breathing, he lost all motor control; he probably also suffered several aneurysms in the brain."

"It is what we did to the crew of the Coast Guard cutter trying to intercept our shipment," Cesar said. "Think of the power we will have if we have such a weapon orbiting overhead. It is what the Americans are trying to do."

"Aura is more than a weapon," Souris said, her eyes burning in her gaunt face. "It is another world completely. A better world. There are things out there beyond what you can conceive."

Hovering in the virtual plane, Raisor couldn't agree more with the professor. His existence was beyond what this Ring was playing with, he could see that, but they were headed in the right direction. And with some help, they could perhaps rival what had been accomplished at Bright Gate. And if they could do that, then the real world could be his once more and he could wreak his vengeance.

He found the information on HAARP interesting. That there was another program besides Bright Gate working with the virtual world meant he had been kept in the dark by his own agency. And the fact that Souris had yet to say anything about Bright Gate meant either she didn't know about it, which he doubted, or she had a reason for keeping it from the Ring.

The meeting broke up, the leaders following Professor Souris to view the underground lab where the work on the Aura computers and generators was being conducted.

Naldo hung behind to have a private word with Cesar, Valika hovering in the background.

"Very impressive, my old friend," Naldo said.

Cesar had been in business—and in bloody competition until the forming of the Ring—with Naldo for four decades. He knew the old man had something on his mind.

"There are some things that concern me," Naldo continued as they slowly walked across the tile floor.

"And they are?"

"What about the Americans? Will they not attack us first?"

"They already have for years," Cesar said. "With Aura we finally have a weapon that they will fear. The key is that we must get operational before they are."

"There's something else."

Cesar paused and waited.

"The American woman—why did she come to work for you? She does not seem interested in money. I am always suspicious of a turncoat."

It was a question that Cesar had also pondered at length three years ago when he was first contacted by Souris, and he could only relay what he had learned from her. "I give her more freedom to do what she wants here. When she worked for the Americans, she had to do what they told her to. Her research was very restricted. Here, she can do as she wants."

Naldo nodded, but Cesar could tell his old friend was not satisfied.

The President's National Security Adviser was known to both friends and foes alike behind her back as the Pit Bull. To her face she was called Mrs. Callahan. She'd known the President since college, where they had been classmates. She'd served with him since he was a junior senator after her own career in the Marines, rising to the rank of lieutenant colonel and commanding a battalion before answering his call for assistance in the political field and leaving the service that she loved. She'd found Washington to be a much more dangerous place than even the Middle East during the Gulf War.

Her Marine bearing came through in her posture and her gruff manner of dealing with those around her. She was the point person for the President in all national security matters, and in a tradition that had started in the mid-sixties, she had been the first one in his administration to be briefed on Nexus. She in turn had briefed him after he was in office. He had then appointed her to take care of all matters dealing with the group, which in effect made her the head of it, among her many other duties.

Frankly, the President had not been convinced that Nexus's fears were grounded in reality, and Callahan had agreed with him. The Nexus representative had not produced any evidence of his fantastic claims about the organization he called the Priory. Only the fact that the manpower and budget allocated to Nexus were so small—and that Eisenhower's Presidential Directive establishing it was real—had kept him from gutting the group.

Right now Nexus was the furthest thing from Callahan's mind. She had just returned from a trip with the President to the Middle East, and dealing with the egos that had been crammed into one room had left her exhausted. Her limousine was taking her directly from Andrews Air Force Base to her home.

She was leaning back in the deep leather, leisurely skimming through various reports her aides had handed her when she got off *Air Force One*. She knew she should have gone directly to the office, but today was her twenty-fifth wedding anniversary. She'd missed far too many in the past, and the President had been insistent that she go straight home, with no detours.

She was surprised when the smoked glass dividing her from the driver slid down with a whir.

"Mrs. Callahan."

All she could see of the driver were his eyes, dark black, in the rearview mirror. His hair was white, his frame slight.

"Yes?" she replied, her irritation at the interruption clear in her tone.

"General Eichen is dead."

She sat up straighter. "Eichen?" She searched her mind and then remembered. The military officer who had accompanied the head of Nexus to the initial briefing. "What happened?"

"We believe he was killed by the Priory."

"Who are you?" she demanded.

"I was sent to warn you that the Priory is moving."

"Who are you?" she repeated. The limousine had stopped at a light. The driver turned and she could see his face. He had to be in his sixties, judging from all the lines in the leathery skin. But his eyes appeared sharp as they regarded her.

"Is it more important who I am or what I am?" he asked. "I'm from Nexus." The light changed and he turned his attention to driving. "Do you still want to go to your house?"

"What does the Priory have planned?" she asked.

"We don't know exactly. They've been using the Black Budget to develop a system in Alaska called HAARP. A very potent weapon with strategic possibilities. We've managed to deny them access to a critical component of the system by locking it down with an NCA code."

"So the situation is under control?"

"I doubt it."

"Why did they kill Eichen?"

"He went to HAARP. To see what they were doing."

"That wasn't very bright."

"In retrospect, it wasn't. But we weren't sure what they have planned and we still aren't. That was Eichen's job."

"Whose is it now?"

"We need your help in that regard. I can take you to your office."

"Take me home," she barked.

How had they replaced the driver? she wondered. And there was nothing in the material she had been given about Eichen's death. A three-star general getting killed would have surely made her briefing book from the NSA.

"Mrs. Callahan, I think—" the driver began, but she cut him off.

"I want to go home and say hello to my husband and wish him happy anniversary at the very least. Then we can go to the office and find out what the hell is going on." They were only a mile away from her house anyway, and she saw no reason not to finish the trip.

"Yes, ma'am."

She'd met her husband early in her Marine career. He was a lieutenant in a line unit while she was the quarter-master officer assigned to the same headquarters. This was in the early days when women in the Marines were few and far between. She wanted to laugh every time she saw some woman in the papers claiming she'd been sexually harassed by some colleague making a comment. The harassment she had faced had been far beyond the scope of comments.

That was until she met Bill one night in the officer's club. When another officer had committed "rodeo" on her—leaning over, biting her in the ass, and hanging on. She had grabbed a chair and smashed it over the man's head. He'd come up swinging and Bill had stepped between and taken him out with one punch. After that there was no more rodeo in the O'Club—at least not when she and Bill were there.

He'd given up his career for hers, following her from assignment to assignment, and then here to Washington, where he saw her less than before. She felt she owed him at least a brief appearance before dealing with this strange man.

The limousine pulled into the long drive that led to her house. White fences bordered the drive on either side, and she felt a moment of contentment and not for the last time considered that maybe it was time to retire. The driver stopped in front of the double main door.

"Wait for me," Callahan ordered as he opened the door for her.

"Yes, ma'am."

She smiled as she saw the balloons tied to the lights on either side of the door. "Happy Anniversary" on the left and "I Love You" on the right. She felt a stab of guilt for not bringing a gift. There'd been no time on the trip. While others in her position would send aides to do a job like that, she felt it was wrong for two reasons: one professional, the other personal. Professionally, she felt it was abusing an aide to give them such a task. Personally, she doubted if anyone could pick out something that Bill would believe came from her. But as she turned the knob on the front door, she wondered whether perhaps she needed to relax her rules just the slightest bit.

She stepped in and was greeted with the sight of Bill hanging from the chandelier that dominated the large foyer just before the wide staircase. She didn't even have a moment for the sight to impact her senses when a hand snaked over her mouth and a cloth was jammed in, choking off her cry of dismay.

Powerful arms pinned hers behind her back. She reacted instinctively, stomping down with her right heel where the attacker's shin should be. She heard a grunt of pain but the arms didn't lessen their grip. Instead they picked her up and carried her to a large armchair. Padded cuffs were snapped over her wrists, locking her in place.

In that moment when the hands released her and she realized she couldn't get out of the chair, the reality of what she had seen when she stepped in the house hit her, a jagged razor of pain cutting through her stomach up into her heart. Tears poured and her head dropped onto her chest.

But not for long. A hand from behind gripped her chin between its powerful fingers and forced her head up. A man stood in front of her. He was well dressed in an expensive suit. His face was smooth and unblemished, with clear blue eyes under thick, wavy blond hair. His age was hard for her to determine; anywhere from thirty to fifty was her best guess.

"Mrs. Callahan." The man went over to the window and with a finger making a small opening peeked through the blinds toward the drive. Through her grief she noted he was wearing thin leather gloves. "Nexus. Led us right to you. We knew they had a point of contact in the administration; they always do. We just didn't know who." He let the blind fall back in place. "And frankly, we really didn't care who. But–" He shrugged. "Things change."

She turned and looked toward the foyer. She could just see Bill's feet, dangling four feet above the marble floor. It was real. For a moment she thought she'd been having a nightmare. Now she knew she was living one.

"We had to race to beat you home," the man said. "We didn't know who he would be picking up at Andrews."

She shifted her gaze back to him.

"Ah, yes. I know the questions you have. Who am I? Why am I doing this? Why did I do that—" He inclined his head toward the foyer. He left the room and came back with a dining room chair and set it five feet in front of her. He sat down and turned the lapel of his coat. A pin sparkled. Diamonds and other precious stones on a silver background in the form of an elongated cross.

"You didn't think we were real, did you?" he asked as he once more hid the pin. "Strange how that is. After all, you know for certain that Nexus is real. Hell, they must have come to your office and briefed you. Do you think Eisenhower had nothing better to do when he signed that executive order? Do you think there can be resistance without a force to resist against? Not that Nexus has been much resistance. But we can't take any chances."

He glanced at his watch. "Any time now."

The driver checked his watch and looked at the front door once more. He was startled when someone rapped on the glass next to his head. He turned in surprise and saw a child, about twelve, on a bike. He powered down the window. "Yes?"

The child smiled. Then began to ride away.

The driver frowned and the bullet from the silenced sniper rifle hit right in the center of that frown, taking the back half of his head off. Gore splattered the glass divider and front seat. The child had already turned the corner and was gone. A car pulled up behind the limousine and a man got out. He reached in the open window and opened the door. He shoved the body aside, started the engine, and drove off.

The man checked his watch once more. "Well, that's done." He stood, the chair in his hands. "You came home and found that your husband killed himself." He looked down at the chair. "This belongs there."

He carried it to the foyer and lay it on its back below Bill's feet. Then he returned. "The love of your life is dead. There's only one thing for you to do. The question is—how would someone like you kill yourself? I spent the time waiting for you considering that. And the answer was in your closet."

He reached behind him and pulled out a nickel-plated Beretta automatic pistol. The one her battalion had given her at the conclusion of her command. He pulled the slide back, chambering a round. Then he flipped off the safety.

He flipped it expertly in his hand, now holding it by the barrel. The man behind her reached out and took the gun. She began struggling as he unhooked her hands, then recuffed the left one to the chair. The man's left arm went around her throat, applying pressure. She began to feel faint when the cold grip of the gun was placed in her right hand, the man's hand over hers. She had no power to resist as the gun was swung up, the muzzle against her right temple. The man slid her finger through the trigger guard, his on top. Her eyes darted to the side, to see Bill's feet and the chair, and she felt the pain once more.

She *was* content when the man exerted pressure on her finger.

Chapter Ten

The SC-MILSTAR satellite was secured in the cargo bay of *Columbia*. The two cargo doors slowly closed shut on the payload in preparation for the shuttle to be mated with the external tank and solid propellant boosters that waited for it.

A shuttle launch was a highly coordinated operation, and in six hours, when all the parts of the launch vehicle were assembled, the twenty-four-hour countdown would begin.

Dalton felt like a guinea pig as he was rigged up in preparation for entering the isolation tank. Hammond was talking Kirtley's men through the process as her technicians worked on Dalton, Barnes, and Jackson. The three of them had done their premission planning, preparing their jump points to the last known location of the team in Colombia. Dalton was confident that Barnes could make it back to the site where they had confronted Feteror in Russia without the same kind of preparation because he had already been there once.

"The isolation tanks are warm right now," Hammond said, "but once the body is inside, they will be supercooled in order to slow the body processes down to a minimum. This machine here"—she paused next to a bulky machine on the side of Dalton's tank that had a line going from it full of dark blue liquid—"connects to the helmet and provides a cooled, special liquid-oxygen mixture directly to the lungs. By keeping the liquid moving at slow speed over the lung's alveoli, it provides the body with enough oxygen to sustain it while the diaphragm is in stasis along with the other functions of the autonomic nervous system."

Easier said than experienced, Dalton thought as he was placed in the harness that would lower him into the tank. He felt a twinge of pain from his shoulder, but it didn't concern him, since it would not be a factor once he "went over." Kirtley's men were probably very good, but he could see that they were uneasy with what Hammond was telling them. He remembered how the team he had led here had reacted on first being told what they were going to experience, and felt some empathy for the NSA men. Hell, he felt sorry for himself, Barnes, and Jackson, as he had little desire to go through the process another time. Only the thought of the missing A-team made it bearable.

"The isolation tank allows your brain to focus on the virtual plane by removing all distractions and energy drains from the real one," Hammond continued.

She turned to Dalton and picked up his bulky, black helmet. "This is the TACPAD. Actually, this lining on the inside that conforms to the skull is the TACPAD, which stands for thermocouple and cryoprobe projection assistance device. This one has been fitted very specifically for Sergeant Major Dalton's brain. It does two things. One is to give direct electrical stimulation to those parts of the brain that we want to emphasize, while at the same time using cryoprobes to lower the temperature of those parts that are not needed to operate on the virtual plane.

"This hasn't changed since the last time you went over," she added, addressing Dalton, Barnes, and Jackson, "but you will find some changes in the programming which should make the transition easier."

She turned back to the CIA team. "The other critical component that makes Psychic Warrior viable is the cyberlink to Sybyl, our mainframe computer. We have long known that we only use about ten percent of the brain's potential. By linking with Sybyl, our master computer, through the TACPAD, we are accessing some of the brain's untapped areas.

"Sybyl gives you form and power to operate on the virtual plane and then to come out of the virtual plane at a distant point, into the real world in the form of your avatar."

"What's an avatar?" one of the men asked.

"A computer-generated form," Hammond answered. "The power Sybyl sends to you is very important," Hammond continued. "It allows us to make the jump from simply being able to remote view to operating in the virtual and real worlds, to cross the boundary between the two."

Dalton considered that statement. If that was true, then perhaps the lost team members were trapped on the virtual plane, without the forms of their avatars to help them navigate. Of course, Chyort, the Russian avatar, had "killed" their avatars, so perhaps he had killed their psyches. But what about Raisor, he wondered? He had asked Hammond to pull the power going to Raisor's avatar and reroute it to the surviving members of his team so he could transport Jackson and Barnes out of Russia after Raisor went off on his own and abandoned their mission.

That line of thought was interrupted as the techs carefully lowered the TACPAD helmet over his head and locked it down on his shoulders securely. Hammond's voice now sounded far away. His head was fixed in place inside, unable to move at all.

"The cyberlink also gives you complete access to Sybyl's extensive database," Hammond said. "This linkage—well, you will be amazed at the things it will allow you to do."

A hand moved over his chest and he knew a micro-probe was being slid into his heart. He bit down on the mouthpiece, securing it in place. Dalton felt the jerk as his feet were lifted off the ground. He went up, then over the lip of the iso-tank. The embryonic solution was warm as he was lowered into it. The helmet was not airtight, and as he sank lower and lower, embryonic fluid seeped in, press-ing against his face and head in places. He took steady breaths through the mouthpiece, dreading what was coming.

"Ready for TACPAD?" Dr. Hammond's voice came through a small speaker in the helmet.

Dalton gave a reluctant thumbs-up, the only way he could communicate right now. He knew the cryoprobes and thermocouples were so small that he shouldn't feel them going into his brain, but nevertheless, he could swear he felt the pinpricks of needles piercing his skin, sliding through skin and bone.

"We've got green all across the board," Hammond in-formed him. "Just relax; this will be easier than last time. We're making the initial link with Sybyl. Do you see the white dot?"

He concentrated and there it was, floating in front of him against a completely black background. The embry-onic fluid was getting cooler, dropping his body tempera-ture.

Dalton swallowed, a reflex in nervous anticipation. He felt something move in his mouth and he fought against his gag reflex as a smaller, flexible tube slid out of the breathing tube and forced its way to the rear of his mouth. His throat spasmed as the tube slithered down his airway to his lungs.

Then he began to drown as fluid seeped out of the end of the tube, filling his lungs. He used every bit of training he had to try to relax, to accept what was happening, but

Hammond had been wrong—this wasn't any better than last time. His chest spasmed, trying to expel the liquid, but it fought a losing battle. The pain and uncomfortableness faded as the temperature in the tank got lower and parts of his brain were brought to minimum operating status by Sybyl.

"You're completely on the iso-tank system now." Hammond's voice was very distant. "I'm switching you . . ." Her voice faded out and silence and darkness, other than the white dot, prevailed. Dalton felt nothing, no sense of even having a body.

Then a faint feeling throughout his body. He struggled to identify it, then realized it was an itching over every square inch of his flesh. He knew that the feeling was entirely inside his head, since input from his nervous system was shut down, but he had to make sense of it somehow.

The black was changing also, a grayness creeping from the white dot outwards. Dalton "looked" down and saw the beginning of his avatar forming. Two arms and two legs. A smooth trunk in the middle, all featureless white.

He looked about. Another figure was forming to his right—Jackson. Then came a surprise—her featureless form began to shift. Eyes, a nose, a mouth appeared. Even hair, just like hers in real life. Dalton looked down—his avatar had changed also and was a realistic representation of his own body wearing a skintight black jumpsuit. Barnes also appeared and his avatar shifted quickly into an approximation of his normal appearance.

"Do you like the new avatars?" Hammond's eager voice was inside his head as she contacted him directly through Sybyl. "I've been working on this for a while. It doesn't really make a difference when you're in the virtual plane, but when you form on the real, you might be able to pass for a real person. I haven't had a chance to test it yet."

"Looks good," Dalton said. "We can still shift into wings, right?"

"Oh yes," Hammond said.

Dalton willed the change and his arms morphed into wings. He lifted off the virtual ground, keeping his orientation, Jackson and Barnes following. Technically they didn't need the wings to move in the virtual plane, but they had discovered it made movement easier.

"First jump point, now," Dalton said. He pictured the location in his mind—the firing range at Fort Hood where they had conducted their first live fire practice with the team.

Then he was there, two hundred feet above the ground, hidden in the virtual plane. A second later Jackson was next to him, hovering like an angel. Then Barnes.

Dalton indicated for Barnes to break off and go to Russia. Barnes's avatar nodded, and then he was gone in a flash.

Dalton turned to Jackson. "Second jump, now."

He came out above the first lock of the Panama Canal. Even Hammond didn't know how they did the jumps. They probably could have jumped directly from Colorado to Colombia, but Dalton preferred taking it in steps. He also wanted a little time to get reoriented to the virtual plane.

The best explanation Hammond had been able to give them was that since the virtual plane had no substance, there also really wasn't a concept of distance. As long as they could mentally picture where they wanted to go, they could jump there. Dalton and Jackson had discovered, though, that it wasn't that simple. Sometimes the jumps seemed to take time. Other times they didn't arrive exactly where they wanted and had to get oriented and rejump. There had even been occasions in Jackson's longer experience where jumps just didn't happen. There were many bugs yet to be worked in the Psychic Warrior program, and they were learning by doing, which was not the safest way.

"This is our emergency rally point," Dalton reminded Jackson.

"Roger that."

He was surprised to see her lips move, even though the words didn't travel in the nothingness of the virtual realm but were relayed from her mind, through Sybyl, to Dalton's mind.

"Hammond did a lot of work on this," he said.

"This next phase was being prepared when we went on the last mission. She finished it afterwards."

"What's the phase after this?" Dalton wondered.

"You'll have to ask the good doctor," Jackson said.

Dalton knew that Hammond, back in the control room at Bright Gate, could hear everything they were "saying" but there was no reply from her forthcoming.

"Last jump to objective," Dalton said. "Now."

He visualized the road curve in the satellite imagery Kirtley had shown them. The place where the team was to have set up the ambush. And he was there, just above the treetops, looking down.

He floated down as Jackson appeared, until his feet reached the dirt road. This gave him spatial orientation and he switched from wings to a right arm and a firing tube for the left. Using power from Sybyl, the tube could fire a pulse of energy in the real plane that was deadly. Unfortunately, it had not worked at all on Chyort, the Russian avatar, a result that Hammond had been at a loss to explain. Dalton didn't expect any problems, since they planned on staying on the virtual plane, invisible from anybody in the area, but it never hurt to be prepared.

The first thing he noted were the blood trails on the road.

Dalton knew exactly how an ambush would be set up here. He moved to where the machine gun should have been positioned and noted the expended brass. The 7.62-millimeter NATO cartridges confirmed the location. But there weren't many. Perhaps two bursts worth. Since there was no blood trail the firer hadn't been killed here, which meant that either the gunner had moved or surrendered.

"They were in a firefight," Dalton reported back to Hammond and Kirtley.

He moved back to the road and rejoined Jackson, who was looking at something in the far ditch. "Jimmy–" She pointed with a pale arm.

Dalton saw the legs, shreds of jungle fatigue pants still clinging in places, the skin gray and waxy. Looking along the ditch, he could see the trip wires for other claymore mines and knew he was looking at the far side of the kill zone.

"Where's the rest of the body?" Jackson asked.

Dalton doubted a team on the run would haul half a dead body with them.

"They got hit from behind," Dalton said. "At least one of them tried escaping through the kill zone. That means things were really bad."

"And the rest?" The voice was Kirtley's. "We need accountability. Do you have an identity on the body you have?"

"All we've got are a pair of legs," Dalton said. "And we can't exactly bring back a DNA sample through the virtual plane."

"There were ten men on that team," Kirtley said.

Dalton didn't need to be reminded of information he'd received in the mission briefing. He and Jackson circled about, but found no other bodies.

"I'm open to suggestions," he finally announced. "Wherever they are, they aren't here. And someone recovered at least part of one body, probably wanting the head for propaganda purposes."

"I've got an idea," Jackson said. "Mr. Kirtley, do you have the identity of the cartel that was targeted here?"

"Actually, there is a consortium called the Ring led by a man named Hector Cesar. He has many holdings throughout Colombia."

"Find the closest to this location."

"Hold on."

Dalton used the time to move up the road. Tire tracks and footprints in the dirt.

"Do you feel it?" he asked Jackson as she joined him.

There was an essence about the place, like smoke drifting across a battlefield, except this was on the virtual plane. There was also a sense of an intelligent presence, but there was nothing on the virtual plane that Dalton could see.

"Yes."

"Ever felt this before?" Dalton knew Jackson had much more time operating on the v-plane, from her time at Grill Flame, the original remote-viewing unit at Fort Meade, the predecessor to Psychic Warrior.

"Yes."

Dalton turned, facing her image. "What is it?"

He almost didn't hear her as she replied. "The Droza."

"What?"

"A legend. From before the Roma."

"What are you—"

Dalton's question was interrupted by Kirtley. "I've got satellite imagery of a villa he owns nearby, about thirty kilometers away," Kirtley said. "But I don't know how to—"

"Give it to me," Hammond's voice cut in.

Dalton and Jackson patiently waited, then the imagery appeared between them, floating like a hologram as Sybyl relayed it. A villa in the countryside. High walls. Guards all around armed with automatic weapons.

"Where is this?" Dalton asked. "Give us something so we can jump there."

"Wait one," Dr. Hammond said. "I'm having Sybyl spatially orient and expand to include your position."

A new image appeared between Dalton and Jackson.

"You are located at the red arrow. The villa is the green."

"We're moving," Dalton said. He jumped, arriving just short of the villa, then checking his position, jumped once more until he was directly over it. As soon as Jackson was next to him, he went down, into the courtyard.

"Let's split up," he told Jackson.

Dalton didn't wait for an acknowledgment, feeling comfortable working with Jackson. He moved forward, through a wall, still a disconcerting experience, but not much more than everything else on the virtual plane.

Chapter Eleven

Valika had been down in the Aura operations center several times and had witnessed the progression from a rough cavern hewn out of the igneous rock to its present incarnation. The chamber was a quarter mile deep into the side of the volcano and resembled a spacious movie theater for a very elite group of viewers. There were twenty chairs spaced evenly about fifteen feet from each other on a sloping floor. The chairs had high backs and footrests and were made of the finest leather. Behind each chair was a computer with a technician monitoring it.

At the very rear, Souris was seated in her own chair, leads connected to the top of her head in the appropriate places. The members of the Ring were gathered round as she went through the procedures to initiate Aura. A half dozen people in white coats monitored machinery in a balcony above the main floor, controlling the master computer. The dog and pony show was about to begin—Valika had once heard an American officer call a formal presentation that, and she thought it quite appropriate.

"You won't see or feel the field until the computer shows it to you," Souris said. "The frequency it's set on now is perfectly safe."

The lights dimmed, flickered, then came back at a subdued level.

"The power requirement is one issue we need to resolve," Souris said. "The field currently requires tremendous input. We use enough energy in one half-hour session here to light a small city for twenty-four hours. When we use the portable Aura transmitter, we only have about three minutes of transmission time before we completely drain the batteries. We have several promising leads in research that we think will pay dividends shortly in that area."

Valika shifted her feet as Cesar frowned. Souris had no idea how to work people. Valika had known scientists like her before—people who felt their research should be unfettered by such constraints as politics or funding. Valika's skin tingled very briefly.

"Aura is now all around you," Souris said, her eyes closed. A slight smile twisted her lips.

"Will we have to put those things on our head to see it?" Naldo asked Cesar.

"No." Souris's voice was almost a whisper. "The connector that allows you to view Aura is built into the headrest of the chair. All we are doing is giving you a window into the virtual plane. You will not travel there as I do. Go to your chairs and you will see what I am seeing."

Reluctantly the surviving members of the Ring, led by Cesar, each took a chair. Souris indicated a different chair for Valika, one like her own. A technician attached leads to Valika's head. She had done this before and ranked it about the equivalent of flying in terms of fondness. Valika leaned back, feeling her body sink into the leather. The tingling sensation, stronger this time, passed through her. The American's voice came out of small speakers built into the headrest.

"The chair is now beginning to transmit a frequency that will orient your mind to the Aura field. Close your eyes and relax."

Valika was overwhelmed by a sudden weariness as if all energy were being drained from her body. Her eyelids were like sheets of lead, clamped down, darkness encompassing her world. Souris's voice was very distant.

"You are now getting in congruence with Aura. We are going to give you a very simple demonstration of what the virtual plane is like."

Valika blinked as the room grew brighter. But she wasn't in the room. And her eyes—she could swear her eyes were still closed, but it was difficult to tell. The light took on form. Saba. But she was above it. At the very top of the volcano. She'd been here before, marching up with the island security chief to lay out the sniper positions. But how had she—

She turned but there was no sense of movement, just the panorama changing. There was no sense of her body. She looked down and saw a human form, but one without features, with flat white feet on the volcanic rock—no, check that, the feet were floating a couple of inches above the rock.

"I've concentrated on programming it for the members of the Ring as dictated by Cesar." There was a click, then Souris was addressing the members of the Ring. "Now let us show you an example of what Aura can do."

A white plank appeared in front of Valika, extending about twenty feet into space and ending at nothing. Then a square shape came into being at the end of the plank, coalescing into a building, floating in space. The door swung open.

"Go ahead," Souris urged.

Valika tentatively took steps out toward the building. She had no sensation of moving but the door grew closer until she was inside. It looked exactly like the courtyard at Cesar's mansion.

Suddenly other shadowy figures still in their chairs flickered into view.

"You can now see each other in your virtual world," Souris said.

The avatars shifted form until Valika could recognize each. Cesar was to her right. The other members of the Ring appeared. Their faces were expressionless but identifiable.

"This is the safe mode of Aura," Souris continued. "With a little bit of experience we can get to the point where your body receives external feedback, so that your senses other than sight function as if you are really there. Which would make this"—the chamber flickered for a second, then a dozen naked women appeared, some lounging about next to the pool, others strolling provocatively—"more than just a show. It would be real to you."

There was a slight click, then Souris's voice came back. "I am sorry, Valika, about this display. Señor Cesar said I must do something his comrades would appreciate."

"Can I speak to you?" Valika felt herself say the words, but couldn't hear them.

"Yes. We are on a private link. This show is designed to go for another ten minutes. Quite disgusting."

Valika could see that two of the women next to the pool were now kissing. The men's shadows were watching. "Can I leave here?"

"Where would you like to go?" Souris asked.

"What are my options?"

"This Aura field covers a little over a mile in width. You can travel anywhere on Saba inside the field. I can also generate various scenarios from the database—much like this room—for you."

The courtyard flickered, then was gone. Valika stood in a room she immediately recognized. Her mother and father's apartment in Moscow. A dingy, two-room affair overlooking the square, across from the university where he was a guest lecturer.

"I designed it from photos Cesar gave me," Souris said.

Something came into being to Valika's left and she turned. Souris was there.

"Why this?" Valika asked.

"Cesar said it was the last time you were happy," Souris said simply.

Valika remembered talking to Cesar late one night, after she had foiled an attempt on his life by a rival gang. They'd both drunk too much and she'd said too much.

"The others are only able to see the display I put on," Souris said. "They would need the leads on their head, like you have, in order to have an avatar. I did not think them ready for that. The forms you saw in there were just two-dimensional projections."

The door started to swing open. Valika felt a surge of excitement, anticipating her mother, immediately feeling foolish for such a thought.

"Who are you?" There was surprise and shock in Souris's voice as a strange man walked in. "How did you get here?"

The man was tall and thin, his form not quite solid. He looked at both of them and settled into the chair that had been her father's. "My name is Jonathan Raisor."

Valika was surprised to see his mouth move as he spoke. She turned to Souris. "What is this?"

The man looked about. "Not bad, but couldn't you have come up with something a little fancier? Your comrades viewing the women by the pool are enjoying themselves. I did not think it wise to interfere in that presentation. Still, I can't complain. This is the first chance I've had to sit down in quite a while." He laughed, a manic edge to it. "As a matter of fact, this is the first time I've had a body in quite a while."

"Who are you?" Valika asked, seeing that Souris was at a loss for words.

"I told you my name."

"That means nothing to me," Valika said.

"I am—was—part of an American experiment like this." Raisor waved an arm about. "A bit different though." He looked at Souris. "I think you know what I am speaking about. What you're doing here is very interesting. You're opening a window between the virtual and the real worlds. Straddling it, so to speak."

"You're from Bright Gate," Souris whispered.

"Very good. You get the prize."

"They have progressed far in the last two years since I left HAARP. I knew Jenkins, who ran Bright Gate while I was running HAARP. He knew so much."

"He knew much but he was just a pawn," Raisor said. "He is no longer with us."

"What happened to him?" Souris asked.

"I killed him."

Souris did not seem surprised. "Why?"

"He betrayed me."

"What should we do?" Valika's voice echoed inside Souris's mind on the private link.

The man smiled. "I can hear you. I am far more in the virtual plane than you. And you are far more in the real than I am. I saw what you did to that man in the courtyard. And I know who Cesar is. And I've heard of the Ring."

"How?" Valika demanded.

"I worked for the CIA."

"Who do you work for now?" Valika asked, noting the tense. She felt naked, with no weapons, no body even to fight with. This was completely unexpected.

"Me. As I said, I was betrayed. I believe we have common enemies now." Raisor got up and went over to the bureau. He picked up the wedding picture of Valika's parents. "Interesting. You've done a good job. Re-creating—" He paused and closed his eyes.

Valika felt pain in her head and she involuntarily gasped. The man's right hand was at her head, unnaturally extended. The fingers were *in* her skull. She jerked back.

The man opened his eyes and was looking at Valika. "Your parents. This was their apartment. They are both dead now."

"How do you know that?" Valika demanded.

"As I said, I have more power here than you do. I can reach"—he put a hand out toward her once more and she took another step back—"places you know nothing of."

"How did you do that?" Souris asked, indicating the picture in his hand and then Valika. "We're not on a level to interact with the projection or each other on that level. I've been working on getting to that point, but it's eluded me."

"You may not be at that level, but I am."

"Tell me how?" Souris was excited. "How are you being projected? What did Jenkins change in the program?"

" 'Projected'?" Raisor mused. "Interesting choice of words." He tapped his chest. "This *is* me."

The room faded for a second. "It's too soon for the power to be this low," Souris said.

"I'm drawing quite a bit," Raisor said. "I assume you don't mind. What is HAARP?"

"We have to return," Valika told Souris. She considered what he had just said and realized the only control they had over this man was turning off the Aura transmitter. He may have talents on the virtual plane, but he needed their power to exercise them, it appeared.

Raisor put his hand up, indicating they should wait a moment. "What is HAARP?" he repeated. His arm extended, as if it was made of rubber, toward Souris, reaching for her head.

"A projector like this," Souris said quickly, stepping back. "Developed by the Americans. I'm surprised you

ever heard of it. Or saw it, if you were with Bright Gate
nd operated on the virtual plane."

Raisor was nodding as if something finally made sense
o him. "Now I know what she saw that she wasn't sup-
osed to."

"Who are you talking about?" Valika demanded.

Raisor ignored her. "I think we can help each other."
He looked at Valika. "Talk to Cesar. Tell him I can take
Aura to another level that you have not considered."

"In exchange for what?" Valika demanded.

"I will tell you next time we meet. But I assure you that
we can be very useful to each other. You've seen some of
ny powers. I have others you haven't even thought of." He
ooked at Souris. "Or perhaps *you* have thought of but
haven't been able to accomplish yet. I have some things to
heck on. I will be back here in thirty minutes."

The room snapped out of existence. Valika felt her
ody seem to fade, then come back, stronger than before.
She felt the seat, could hear the sound of others stirring,
smell the faint odor of the leather. She blinked, eyes adjust-
ng to the dim lighting in the room. She ripped the leads
off of her skull, not caring about the hair that got torn out
with them.

She swung her legs over the side and stood, feeling
dizzy for a second. She could hear the members of the
Ring exulting over the experience, congratulating Cesar.
She walked to the rear of the room where Souris was peel-
ng one of the leads off her skull.

She kept her voice low so the others wouldn't hear.
"Was that man part of your program?"

Souris shook her head. "No."

"Don't lie to me."

"Why would I invent something like that?"

"I don't know, but you need to understand what we're
doing here is very serious."

"I've spent the last twenty years of my life on this," Souris said. "I know it's serious. Far more than you coul[d] imagine."

"The man said he was drawing power from Aura. How can that be if he didn't come from here?"

"I'll have to check my data," Souris said.

Valika glanced over her shoulder. The men were sti[ll] marveling about the women and what they had seen.

"He said he was American," Valika said. "From thi[s] Bright Gate. You never told us of such a thing."

"It was experimental," Souris said.

"It doesn't look experimental anymore," Valika noted. "If he's still working for the Americans, it means they'v[e] penetrated us."

"He said he wasn't," Souris said.

" 'Said'?" Valika shook her head. "And because he sai[d] this, we should believe him? And even if he has been cu[t] off by the Americans, if they could put him on the virtua[l] plane, couldn't they put others there too? This is a threat!"

"It is also an opportunity," Souris said.

Valika was going to ask her what she meant when sh[e] was distracted.

"Gentlemen!" Cesar's voice cut through the excite[-]ment. "Gentlemen!" When he had everyone's attention, h[e] continued. "What you saw today was only level two. There is much more that Aura can do.

"Please enjoy my hospitality. Although I cannot match what you just saw exactly, I assure you that you will fin[d] the young women I have waiting above much more real."

Valika gave a hand signal to Cesar that she needed t[o] speak to him. After the others left, the leader of the Rin[g] came over to the Russian.

"What is it?"

"We were contacted on the virtual plane," Valika said.

Cesar frowned. "What do you mean?"

"Someone met us on the virtual plane."

"Who?"

"Someone named Raisor," Valika said. "He said he ɔuld help us. I believe he's an American."

Cesar's face tightened. "Come to my office."

aisor jumped from the Aura control center north. Then vice more, until he was above the glass-walled building aat housed the headquarters of the National Security gency. It was shielded on the virtual plane. He knew he ɔuld wait until the bitch got off work—if she ever did, as e had seen her spend the night quite often—but then what ɔuld he do? He was in the virtual plane, without the ower or programming of Sybyl to enter the real. He ɔuld watch, but that was all. And watching was not nough.

He felt rejuvenated, full of energy. Aura had recharged im, but he knew that the effect would not last. He would ave to get back to Aura soon.

Raisor jumped west, to a spot he knew well.

He was above the Mount of the Holy Cross, where •right Gate was headquartered. He could sense the psy-hic shield that surrounded the place and knew he could ot enter. But someone was out. Raisor knew it, from the ne of virtual power that came out of the mountain and rced southward, a connection from Sybyl to wherever the sychic Warriors were.

And HAARP? Wherever it was, the information had •een compartmentalized from him. He had no doubt, nough, that his sister had discovered the existence of IAARP or something about HAARP and because of that he and the rest of her team had been cut off. But why had IcFairn done that if HAARP was just another program ke Bright Gate? Wheels turning within wheels, Raisor nought.

Raisor jumped, following the line south. Until he ar rived above the villa in Colombia.

The bodies were in the walk-in freezer in the basement of the villa. Separated from the meat by a thick plastic sheet hung across the middle of the freezer, the three dead Special Forces men were hung on hooks. Dalton didn't recognize any of them immediately. One's head was half missing; another was lacking the lower half of his body—which Dalton had seen back at the ambush site. The other had taken several rounds, including many which Dalton knew from the lack of blood were inflicted postmortem, especially to his face. What remained of their uniforms had no markings—Dalton knew they had gone in "sterile" with no ID tags or insignia that could be traced back to the States.

"Jackson," he relayed through Sybyl.

"Yes?"

"I've found three bodies."

"Damn."

"You find anything?"

"Not yet."

"Continue searching."

Dalton came out of the virtual plane, into the real, assuming the form of his avatar.

"What are you doing?" Kirtley's voice echoed inside his head.

Dalton ignored him. He went up to the first body and lifted it off the hook, laying it down on the ground. He took a long strip of brown paper and covered the dead man. He did the same with the other two.

Then he knelt next to them silently for a minute. He was startled when Jackson contacted him.

"I've found the others. Alive."

Dalton went back on the virtual plane and moved toward her essence until he arrived in a dark room. Several men lay about in the dark, some of them wounded. Jackson was a glowing form in the corner.

"Should we show ourselves?" Jackson asked.

Dalton considered that. He knew what it was like to be held prisoner. Hope could be a good thing, but disclosing themselves could also compromise the rescue mission. He'd done what he had with the bodies to cause confusion among the ranks of the guards. No, check that, he realized, he had done it out of respect for the men who had died.

"Sergeant Major!" Kirtley's voice was on a power setting unnecessarily loud and brought him out of his thoughts. "You will return immediately. You will not disclose yourself to those men."

"A little hope wouldn't hurt them," Dalton argued, more for the sake of disagreeing with Kirtley than anything else. "To let them know they aren't abandoned."

"You've done what you were tasked to do," Kirtley said. "I'm ordering you to return immediately."

Dalton reached out to Jackson directly, touching her avatar on the shoulder. "Let's go back. We'd have to explain who we are, and then we really couldn't do anything to help them right now."

Jackson turned toward him in surprise. Dalton put a finger over his lip, indicating for her to be silent. He counted—seven men. "Straight jump to the rally point." He let the real world fade from view until he was completely in the virtual and prepared to jump.

Jackson reached out and grabbed his arm. "Jim."

Dalton caught himself just as he was ready to jump. "What?"

"Someone's here—in the virtual plane. Watching us."

Dalton felt foolish as he craned his head and looked about. He saw nothing but featureless gray. "Who? This Droza?"

"I don't know. Maybe."

"Go. Now."

Jackson jumped.

Raisor caught their virtual essence as they snapped by, like a bird looking in the window of a supersonic jet as it flew past, catching just the tiniest of glimpses. He was pretty certain they hadn't seen him, because he had no avatar, just a presence. He headed back to Saba.

He arrived over the island, looking down from the virtual plane. Then he descended, through the building to the underground chamber. Souris was waiting for him. Along with the Russian. And there was someone else with her. They had Aura turned on. Raisor tapped into the power.

Sergeant Lambier started. He rolled to his side, half expecting guards to come through the door firing. But there was only the sound of the others sleeping. His eyes darted about the room, searching for what had awakened him.

Whatever had penetrated his sleeping brain was gone.

Barnes found the site of the battle without much trouble. He hovered over the rail line, noting that it had already been repaired, the derailed cars gone.

There was nothing on the virtual plane that he could pick up. No sign of the men of his team who had been "killed" by the Russian avatar.

Barnes jumped several times, in an ever widening circle, searching, but in vain. It was as if the men had never existed.

Hammond had one eye on the screen that showed the status of the three deployed Psychic Warriors and one eye on the lines of programming code and data files for Sybyl that she was slowly scrolling through. Her right index finger rested on the "up" key, tapping to reveal the lines one by one. She was working her way backward, trying to find the source of the virus and the exact nature of it.

Her finger paused in midair as something caught her attention.

"What happened to your predecessor?"

Dr. Hammond spun about in surprise at the unexpected question. Kirtley was right behind her and she had not heard him enter the control room. She had been alone with the three bodies in the isolation tanks, monitoring the data. She could read the numbers that Sybyl was displaying on the monitor and translate them into information. What they were telling her was that one of the Psychic Warriors—Barnes—was not with the other two. Indeed, he was a long way from them. And she knew that wasn't what the mission called for.

"My what?" Hammond stammered.

"The person who ran Bright Gate before you," Kirtley said. "What happened to him?"

"You mean Dr. Jenkins. He was killed in an accident."

"Really?" Kirtley glanced at the computer monitor that showed Sybyl's data files, then back at her. "Something wrong?"

"No. No. Everything's going fine."

"And the first team? What happened to them?"

"The first team?"

"The CIA team," Kirtley amplified.

"I wasn't here then," Hammond said.

Kirtley sat down, steepling his fingers. "You're not very inquisitive, are you, Doctor?"

"I do my job."

"I've put safeguards in place," Kirtley said, "to guarantee that if you do to my team what happened to the first one, you'll be killed. I'm very serious about this. Do you understand?"

Hammond swallowed, then nodded.

Barnes was back at the battle site, his search fruitless. He was just above a high, craggy peak overlooking the rail line and the site of the battle against Chyort. He was ready to make the first jump to head back to Bright Gate when he picked something up, the slightest of presences on the virtual plane. Not an avatar, nothing he could see. But there was something, someone, nearby. He could feel it. He waited, hoping the presence would get stronger, that it would be one of his teammates, but it was gone, just as quickly as it had appeared. He wondered if what he had felt was real—as real as anything could be on the virtual plane. For all he knew, it could have been a disturbance in Sybyl's programming.

He prepared to jump when he sensed the presence again. He turned, scanning. Out of the east came two forms, pure white, the shapes shifting faster than he could follow, but roughly man-sized.

The only thing he was certain of was that they were not his teammates.

Barnes willed his right arm into the firing tube. He fired at the form to the right. The bolt of power hit. The white glowed red, absorbing the strike, then returned to its original color and continued coming.

Barnes fired once again at the form to the left with the same negligible effect. He didn't wait to try a third shot. He jumped to the point his team had used as the emergency rally point. Arriving, he prepared to jump once more when the forms appeared above him.

He paused, mesmerized as the two merged into one becoming a white parachute that floated down on top of his avatar, enveloping it.

Belatedly, Barnes tried to jump, but nothing happened

Chapter Twelve

Valika spun about, pistol clearing holster as she moved.

"That won't do you any good," Raisor said.

Valika could see through his form, to the other side of the chamber. Slowly she put the gun back.

"Who are you?" Cesar had not moved at the sudden apparition.

They were in the Aura operations center, Cesar in his chair, Valika behind him, and Souris hooked to her computer, projecting the field that allowed Raisor to take his form.

"They told you who I am." Raisor's voice had an echo to it, as if coming through a speaker. He was looking at his hands, as if seeing them for the first time, slowly rotating them in front of his face.

"They told me a name," Cesar said. "Perhaps I should ask *what* are you?"

"First, I want an answer," Raisor said. "Where is HAARP located?"

"I thought you were American," Cesar said. "You told Valika you were CIA. Surely you know about HAARP."

"I am—was—CIA, but I never heard of HAARP."

"Tell him the location," Cesar ordered Souris.

Her voice echoed out of a speaker on top of the computer she was facing. "Alaska. In the middle of the Wrangell Range."

Raisor walked right through a chair until he was opposite Cesar. "How is HAARP different than Aura?"

"It has greater power but is fixed in place," Souris said. "Aura is smaller and transportable but has less power. Aura also is directional."

"Why should we trust you?" Cesar asked, signaling for Souris to be quiet.

Valika wasn't sure what exactly Souris was seeing. Although the American scientist's eyes were open, they had a vacant stare.

"You don't have to trust me," Raisor said. "We just need to work together. I can give you information you need. For example, the Americans know some of the men on their Special Forces team are alive, and they know where they are being held. At your villa. In the basement."

"How are you aware of that?" Cesar demanded.

"Call your villa," Raisor said. "Have them check the bodies in the freezer. You'll discover that they've been removed from the meat hooks and covered. One of the American Psychic Warriors did that."

" 'Psychic Warrior'?" Cesar repeated. He signaled for Valika to make the call. She left the room.

Souris answered. "The program is called Bright Gate and headquartered in Colorado. A program that sends avatars into the virtual plane—like we've done here with Aura—but also allows those avatars to re-form on the real plane at a distant site."

"Why did you not tell me about this?" Cesar demanded of Souris.

"It was only in the first phases when I left the States," Souris answered. "I was not aware that it had gone operational."

"If you could get the master computer from Bright Gate," Raisor said, "and use it in conjunction with what you've developed here, you would have the same capability." He indicated his form and then reached out and put his hand through a chair. "This is just an apparition with no substance. With Bright Gate I would have a real form here that could affect the physical world around me."

Cesar reached into a drawer of the desk and pulled out a cigar. He cut the tip off and lit it as he considered what he had just been told. Valika came back and simply nodded once.

"What do you want out of this?" Cesar finally asked.

"I want my body back," Raisor said. "They cut me off, separating my connection with Bright Gate."

"Who is 'they'?" Cesar asked.

"My government."

"Why did they do that?" Cesar asked.

"I was betrayed."

"Why?" Cesar pressed.

"I wanted to have revenge on the person who betrayed my sister."

Cesar could understand family loyalty coming before all else. "Why was your sister betrayed?"

"She was investigating HAARP. Someone didn't want her to do that."

"What are your capabilities right now?"

"I can travel anywhere in the world on the virtual plane."

"You don't need Aura to support you?"

"No. I only need Aura's power to appear like this—to come into the real plane as an image. And if I was to accomplish something other than watch, I would need its power."

Cesar pointed the tip of the cigar at his scientist. "Souris says that with Aura's power she could enter a computer system. See it from the inside. Can you do that?"

Raisor nodded. "Yes."

"Could you manipulate the computer, change the programs, the data?"

"With Bright Gate I could. I imagine I could with Aura's power."

"Good." Cesar stood. "Then I have a job for you. To test your loyalty. Then I will help you in turn."

Dalton wiped embryonic fluid off his face and tossed the towel into a basket. Jackson and Barnes were doing the same, both of them shivering, the aftereffect of the isolation tube freezing still clinging to their bones.

"Report." Kirtley was standing in front of the control console, arms folded on his chest.

"We found seven of the men still alive," Dalton said. "At the villa. In the basement."

"I want you to come up with a floor plan diagram," Kirtley said. "And a complete report for forwarding."

"Forwarding to who?" Dalton demanded.

"Task Force Six is going to help us mount a rescue mission."

"I don't think that's a good idea," Dalton said.

"It doesn't matter what you think," Kirtley said. "Just do it."

"There's something going on," Dalton said. "We sensed a presence at the villa. On the virtual plane."

"What kind of presence?"

"I don't know," Dalton said.

"The Russian SD-8 program is shut down," Kirtley said.

"It wasn't like Chyort," Dalton said. "Something, or someone, different."

"Write up your report." Kirtley turned and walked away.

Dr. Hammond was behind the console. As soon as

Kirtley was gone, she came around and stepped in front of Barnes. "What are you doing?"

"What?"

"Where did you go? I tracked you splitting off from the others."

Dalton stepped between them. "Does Kirtley know?"

She shook her head. "No. What are you up to?"

"We're looking for our teammates," Dalton said.

Hammond's eyes shifted to the door where Kirtley had gone and then back. "And did you find anything?"

They all turned to Barnes. "No—" He paused. "But just before I jumped to come back, I also picked up a virtual presence, something—I don't know what it was. Something happened—" He shook his head, confused.

"There's more going on than we're being told," Dalton said.

"Or than *anybody* knows," Jackson added.

"Kirtley asked me what happened to my predecessor," Hammond said. "Why would he do that? Dr. Jenkins died in an accident."

"No, he didn't." Dalton had everyone's attention. "Raisor told me he killed Jenkins because he cut off the power to Raisor's sister's team. Do you know why Jenkins did that?" he asked Hammond.

"I never met the man. When I got here to replace him, I was told the cutoff occurred because there was a programming glitch in Sybyl that had been corrected. That it was just a tragic mistake."

"I doubt that." Dalton pulled on his fatigue shirt over the black suit. "I don't like this. I don't like it at all."

"There's something else—" Hammond began.

"What?" Dalton demanded.

"I think there was another Psychic Warrior team. One before the CIA team with Raisor's sister."

That announcement was greeted with a long silence.

"Why do you think that?" Dalton finally asked.

"I'm finding information in Sybyl's data files that doesn't fit the other two teams. Someone obviously tried to clear all records before a certain date, but some of those records are tied to programs that couldn't be deleted without crashing the entire system."

Dalton asked the question that was uppermost in his mind. "What happened to this team?"

"I haven't been able to find that out."

"Your predecessor, Dr. Jenkins, never mentioned a first team?" Dalton asked.

"That's another thing," Hammond said. "I don't think Dr. Jenkins was the original scientist in charge of Bright Gate. I'm finding information from someone before him—this Professor Souris that you asked me about," she said to Dalton.

Dalton turned to Jackson. "You mentioned something while we were out there. The Dropa or something like that?"

"The *Droza,*" Jackson corrected. "It's a story my mother told me."

"And?" Dalton prompted.

"I don't want you laughing at me if I tell it."

"There hasn't been much to laugh at since we've been here," Dalton noted.

"I've been thinking about it a long time," Jackson said. "Ever since I was assigned to Grill Flame years ago." She looked at Dalton and Barnes. "Even when I was just re-mote viewing, I could occasionally sense other presences on the virtual plane. I know now one of those was Chyort, but there were others. Ones I couldn't identify. Then when I came here and was part of Psychic Warrior, I could still sense those presences but I could never see them. Like they were hiding from me."

"Or they were in a place on the virtual plane that you

couldn't see," Hammond said. "We don't know exactly the dimensions or physics of the virtual world."

Dalton couldn't help but wish that Hammond had been more forthright about what she didn't know when he had first arrived at Bright Gate with his team. Things might have turned out differently and some people might still be alive. He pulled a chair out and slid it over to Jackson. She sat down as Barnes and Dalton grabbed other seats and gathered round her. Hammond remained at her place behind the console. Kirtley and his team were in the prep room, running final checks on their fittings.

"There's a legend among my people, among the Roma, the Gypsies, as they're more commonly called," she said. She briefly told Barnes and Hammond the same thing she had told Dalton, about her background and her mother, before continuing her story.

"I tried to get as far as possible from the Roma, but I think I went in a circle." She waved her hand about the room. "My mother would have loved this—Psychic Warriors, remote viewing. Even Chyort. She would have found him fascinating. The devil that she insisted existed." Jackson's eyes darkened as her mind went inward, into her memories. "She wasn't so big on talking about heaven or angels, though—just the dark, scary stuff."

Barnes opened his mouth as if to say something, but the confused look crossed his face once more and he snapped his mouth shut.

Jackson continued. "She told me many stories when I was a child. They were the tales her mother had told her when she was a child. And her mother's mother on down the line through the ages. The Roma are not fond of writing things down. Everything passes by word of mouth. It is an integral part of our culture and one we do not share with the *gadje*.

"The stories were entertaining and interesting but I

thought they were fiction." She glanced over at Dalton. "But now we know the virtual world is real in its own way, right?"

Dalton didn't say anything, not wanting to interrupt the thread her mind was unraveling.

"My mother told me the story of the Roma and of those the Roma came from. I promised her only to tell it to my own children, but I think it is important I tell you this now, given all that has happened. It might mean nothing, but—" She shrugged.

"What you tell us stays with us," Dalton promised. He looked at Hammond and Barnes. "Right?"

Both nodded their agreement.

Jackson rubbed her palms over her eyes for a moment. "Mom—she said that the Roma were special. I told you earlier that the rest of the world calls us Gypsies because a long time ago it was believed we came from Egypt. But we actually came from India. Far northern India on the border with Tibet, in the foothills of the Himalayas. Even that place, though, wasn't where we originated from. My mother told me that much at least, although where we came from before there, she could not—or would not—say. Other than to speak of a people called the Droza. I'll get back to that in a moment, but let me work from what I know to what I'm guessing about.

"We—the Roma—were outsiders there, of different background from the others. Long before Hinduism swept through India and divided all the people into castes, my people were despised and threatened. We learned to survive by making ourselves useful. We made up a large part of the *Kshattriya*—the warrior class. We fought and died for others, so much so that there were those among us who realized something had to be done.

"Some advocated rebellion. We were warriors after all. Others pointed out how terribly outnumbered we were and espoused escape. In the end, that was the decision that was made. The Roma left the lowlands and went into the mountains. They knew they had to find land no one else would want—someplace desolate and remote.

"They found the isolation they sought high in the Himalayas. They did such a good job finding what they were looking for that in just a few generations, there were few Roma left, given the harshness of the land. Then they met the Droza.

"Even my mother could not tell me if they were real. She told me about them as if it were only a story, a legend." Jackson closed her eyes as she remembered. "In the high mountains of Kharta Changri the Droza came down from mountaintops. Our people ran and hid from them for a fortnight, but when it was clear that the strange ones meant no harm, our people came out of their caves.

"The Droza let my people know that they came from a special place they could not mention. And that they could not return from whence they came. They were trapped here. With my people, they built a new place to live. Their homes they hid underground, a great city called Agharti. The Roma were given a fertile valley hidden deep in the mountains near Kharta Changri called Shambhala." Jackson opened her eyes, returning to the present. "I think this is where the modern legend of Shangri-la comes from."

"What do the Droza have to do with the virtual plane?" Dalton asked, disturbed by this talk of creatures from the mountaintops and underground cities. He had traveled all over the world in his military career and seen many strange things, the Psychic Warrior program being foremost among them, but this was stretching the boundaries of reality too far. He immediately corrected that thought—he had no idea what reality was anymore.

Jackson searched her memory for the words her

mother had told her. "The Droza were mostly like us, but different in some key ways. They had a strange power. *Vril* it was called. The power to see things that they could not see with their own eyes; to see places a long distance away. To know things that they should not have known. To see the thoughts of others. To see parts of the future. And they taught the Roma some of this. As much as my people could learn and do.

"The two groups intermarried until there was just one people—the Roma. Even with the help of the Droza, though, it was still a very harsh life in the mountains and food was scarce. The men wanted to launch raids to the south, but many feared this would bring enemies into the mountains to hunt us.

"While all this was happening, the women, who had for centuries stayed at home while the men went off to war, had been focusing their energies inward with the help of the Droza, into their own minds and souls, and they began to develop an ability that we now call being a psychic, working on the *vril*.

"The women saw a path out through the mind. Most of the men would have none of it. They were warriors and believed in the power of the body, of the sword. Except they swore they would never fight for anyone else ever again, but rather, would make others fight for them.

"This time the Roma fragmented and the parting was bitter. Most of the men, with some women, left to go to the west and gain power in the real world. Most of the women, with a few men among them, went even further into the Himalayas to dwell there, to perfect the path of the mind.

"A small segment, eschewing either path, scattered, determined never again to place down roots in land, but to preserve their sense of self in the group, not in the country they happened to be living in. This last group, the ones ny mother drew her lineage from, are what you call the Gypsies."

"And the other two groups?" Dalton asked. "What happened to them?"

"That, Sergeant Major, is a very good question. I think it might be possible that the one group that stayed in the high mountains of the Himalayas might still exist, might still be living in Shambhala, or Shangri-la, and it might be their spirits that we sense on the virtual plane at times. Or—" Jackson paused.

"Go on," Dalton prompted.

"Or maybe we are sensing the Droza. If they ever did exist, then they still might. Maybe not all of them intermingled with the Roma. And the pure *vril* they have is the power to be on the virtual plane."

Dalton checked the faces of the others who had listened to Jackson's story. Barnes was shaking his head, seemingly having none of it. Hammond looked thoughtful, which surprised him.

"If there are others on the virtual plane," Jackson said, "they seem to mean us no harm."

"As far as we know," Dalton said. "And let's remember that what we know is far outweighed by what we don't know. Here's the deal. We've been lied to, and we're being used. I tend to look at those things in a negative light. Regardless of what's out there in the virtual plane, we have a real problem here in the real world, right here in Bright Gate. Add in the fact that someone has planted a bug in Sybyl and has been monitoring the computer and I would say we have to be very careful. I think we need to make a plan to cover our butts in case something goes wrong."

"What kind of plan?" Hammond asked.

"One of the first things we do in Special Forces when we plan a mission is make up an E & E plan," Dalton said.

" 'E & E'?" Jackson asked.

"Escape and evasion," Dalton said. "There's an official one that we turn in to the commander taking our mission briefing just before we go, but we also make up a team member-only plan that we have just in case we get abandoned."

"A little paranoid, don't you think?" Hammond said.

"I think we need to be getting paranoid," Dalton said. "Don't you? Or are you going to go with Kirtley? Do you trust him? You didn't tell him about Barnes breaking off from the mission or what you learned from checking Sybyl, so I have a feeling you don't feel very comfortable with Kirtley."

"I don't think Kirtley feels very safe either." Hammond rubbed her face with her hands. "He told me he has a contingency to take care of me if his team is cut off on the virtual plane. Why would he be worried about me doing that?"

"I don't think it's you he's worried about," Dalton said.

Hammond sighed. "I just wanted to make this work, to do what no one had done before. To make it better."

"You've done that," Dalton said. "But you're not indispensable. Jenkins wasn't, the first team—the first team we know about," he corrected himself, "wasn't, my team wasn't, and we're not."

"But . . ." Hammond was shaking her head. "What can we do? Kirtley runs everything now. He's in charge here."

Dalton had been thinking about that. "Didn't you tell me there was a backup for Sybyl?"

"The computer here is technically Sybyl IV," Hammond said. "Fourth generation. Sybyl I and II were prototypes. Sybyl III was the first one that worked projecting avatars into the real plane."

"Where is it now?" Jackson asked.

"Off-line and in storage. All of the first couple of generations of equipment are here."

"Show us," Dalton said.

Hammond led the three of them to a double-wide door on the side of the control room. "This is the freight elevator that accesses all levels." She entered a code on the keypad. The door silently slid open, revealing a fifteen-by-fifteen-foot elevator with a twelve-foot ceiling. They followed her on board.

"The storeroom is on the lowest level, where the generators are." She punched the button and they descended for fifteen seconds, before coming to a halt. The doors opened, revealing a large open space. The hum of generators producing power echoed through the cavern. A half dozen large tanks supplied fuel to the generators.

"There's Sybyl III." Hammond was pointing at a large crate.

"When is Kirtley's team doing their first orientation mission in the tubes?" Dalton asked Hammond.

"This evening. Eighteen hundred hours. Why?"

"We're going to set up an E & E plan and execute the first preparatory phase then." Dalton turned and got back on the elevator. "I have some calls to make."

Publicly the Pentagon was listed to have five floors, only one of them below ground. In reality, there was a subbasement below that basement which connected with access tunnels leading in various directions, including one that ran to the Capitol and White House. The entire system was designed for emergency use only and had been sealed since construction, with only one access point from the building above. The entrance was occasionally used by maintenance personnel. The floor plan for the subbasement was the exact same as that for the basement, with the five main corridors with rooms branching off on either side. The center, which was a large courtyard on the surface, was made up of strengthened concrete twenty feet thick. Under it, two hundred feet below the subbasement, was the War Room, which was the nerve center of the United States military. One could not access the War Room from the subbasement, only through a single large elevator on the main level of the Pentagon, thus further isolating the subbasement.

Except for a few selected individuals and maintenance personnel, knowledge of and access to the subbasement was forbidden. Roger Killean was one of the select few and he'd been ordered by Mentor to go to the Nexus Pentagon command post to tap into the War Room traffic and begin preparing contingencies for scrapping the shuttle launch with CS-MILSTAR. With the death of Mrs. Callahan and the disappearance of their agent who had picked her up at Andrews Air Force Base, Killean was the sole surviving member of Nexus in Washington.

Killean was a high-level member of the State Department, and the Pentagon was not his assigned province, but with the death of Eichen there was no choice. He had the proper clearance to get into the Pentagon. The elevator entrance to the subbasement was located behind a locked door with a Custodian sign hanging on it. He waited until no one else was nearby and then boarded the designated elevator and put his key in the slot below the buttons.

There was no designation for the sublevel—because it didn't exist for the majority of the people in the building—but the key automatically took the elevator down, below the basement. The doors slid open and he removed the key and walked out.

The corridor before him was bare concrete. The subbasement was unfinished, a relic from the original plans during the hasty construction during World War II. The contract for the Pentagon had been awarded on August 11, 1941, and construction begun a month later. The build-ng was finished in January 1943, a blistering pace for such a large job.

The subbasement had never been designed as office space, but as a buffer between the main building and the wasteland, swamps, and dumps that the land had been before construction began. Over forty thousand concrete piles had been driven to support the subbasement. The ceiling was low, about six and a half feet, and the corridor was crisscrossed with pipes, cables, and phone lines. Widely spaced fluorescent bulbs provided only dim light.

Killean turned right and walked down the long corridor. There were seventeen and a half miles of corridor in the upper five floors of the Pentagon and he estimated another three miles or so down here. He didn't think anybody knew the entire layout. He'd been down here with Eichen on several occasions, and he knew the way to the Nexus Command Post that had been established during the last year of Eisenhower's administration. After several hundred feet, he stopped in front of a steel door. His key it in the slot and the door slowly swung inward. As he stepped in, he turned to the left for the light switch.

He felt the slightest of breezes on the back of his neck and reached up with his left hand, saving his life as the garrote came over his head. It caught on his hand, jamming it against his throat, the wire slicing deep into the skin, but saving his jugular from being severed.

Killean pivoted, feeling the garrote cut deeper into his left hand, while he slammed with his right elbow into the chest of the man behind him. The pressure on the wire lessened and Killean dropped to a knee, freeing himself, pulling his left hand back, feeling skin peel away with the metal wire. He dove into the corridor, got to his feet, and prepared to sprint back the way he had come.

A bullet creased his cheek, a burning line of pain. He spun about and dashed in the opposite direction, into the

labyrinth of the subbasement. As he ran, his mind kept going back to an experiment he'd conducted many years ago
in college as part of a physiological psychology course.
Rats in a maze. Now he knew how the rats had felt. He
could feel wetness on his cheek and he knew it was blood.
The pain from his hand was a steady scream. He could
hear running footsteps behind him and he picked up the
pace.

He came to an angle turn to the corridor and paused,
peeking around to see if anyone was waiting. For a thousand feet the dimly lit corridor was empty. He turned the
corner and began running again, hearing his shoes slap
against the unfinished concrete floor and the sound of his
heavy breathing loud in his ears.

Killean thought of the twenty-three thousand people
who were working in the building above him, yet he knew
that he—and those hunting him—were the only ones on
this floor. He'd started carrying a pistol when he heard
about Eichen, but he'd left it in his car in order to pass
through the metal detectors to get into the Pentagon.
Obviously his hunters had been able to circumvent the security of the building with their weapons.

The bullet hit his left thigh a split second before he
heard the shot. The impact sent him spinning about before
he went down.

He was surprised there was no pain when he looked
down and saw the blood pulsing out of the wound. His
hand actually hurt much worse. But from the squirts of
blood coming out, he knew the artery had been hit.

He could hear someone coming. He held his head up.
Two men, one with a rifle. He pushed with his good leg,
crawling away from them, his good hand scrambling in his
jacket and pulling out his SATPhone. He flipped it open.
Nothing. The signal couldn't get through the floors of con-

crete and metal above him. He kept pushing back until a boot came down on his chest, pinning him to the ground.

Killean knew he had lost a lot of blood. He felt very weary, the pain from his hand more distant now, his wounded leg just a dead weight below his waist. The phone dropped from his hand.

A man leaned close to him, holding something in his hand. In the dim light, Killean could make out jewels and diamonds sparkling. An elongated cross.

The man picked up his SATPhone. "Is there someone left alive to call here in the States?"

Killean spit at the cross.

The man laughed. "That's the most effective thing Nexus has ever done against us." He put the cross away and held the SATPhone in front of Killean. "Who is left?"

Killean heard the voice as if from far away as his head slumped back on the concrete. He knew they'd taken down Eichen. And the agent who had made the contact when they killed Callahan. If the Priory was asking, that meant they didn't know about Mentor.

The man put his foot on the thigh wound and ground the heel, but Killean felt nothing.

"Who is left?"

If Nexus was not much of a threat, why was the Priory so concerned about wiping them out? Killean wondered. It meant the Priory *was* afraid. He felt a slap across his face and he blinked.

"Who is left?"

It was Killean's turn to smile. And that was how he died.

Luis Farruco was thirty-eight years old and had survived sixteen years as a member of Cesar's cartel. He'd risen in the ranks not because of intelligence but rather through ruthlessness and, more importantly, the fact that he had lived so long in such a dangerous occupation.

Since Cesar had begun spending more time at Saba, Farruco had taken over more of the operations in Colombia. Right now, he was pacing back and forth in the master bedroom of Cesar's villa, the naked women on the bed of little interest to him.

The door to the room swung open and two of his men came in, holding a third between them. The man's face was bloodied; his fingers twisted where each had been snapped one by one.

They threw the man onto the floor. The two women made no attempt to cover themselves; indeed they edged closer to the scene, predatory eyes watching, sensing Farruco's blood lust.

Farruco squatted in front of the wounded man. "Alonzo, tell me the truth."

Alonzo lifted his head. "I have!"

Farruco reached forward and grabbed Alonzo's jaw. "You were the one responsible for guarding the bodies. No one can get in that freezer unless they go down the corridor that was your post. So why are you lying to me? Did you leave your post? Tell me."

"I did nothing! I did nothing! I was there. I swear on my mother. I never left."

"Take him to the balcony," he ordered his guards.

He followed as they pushed Alonzo up against the steel railing overlooking the extensive front lawn. The two women were right behind Farruco.

Farruco held a hand out and one of the guards gave him a sawed-off shotgun. He pushed the large barrel under Alonzo's jaw, jerking his head up. The man's eyes bulged and he tried to speak, but the pressure of the steel under his chin only allowed him a garbled plea.

Farruco pulled the shotgun back slightly. "Tell me."

Alonzo was sobbing. "I swear! I was there the entire time. No one passed."

A line furrowed Farruco's brow. He'd seen enough men beg for their lives, and he realized that Alonzo was telling the truth.

He pulled the trigger. Alonzo's head exploded, spraying blood, brain, and bone out over the lawn. The headless body collapsed. Farruco indicated for the guards to toss it over the railing—he didn't want the carpet in the bedroom to get soiled.

Even if Alonzo had been telling the truth, for the other men to see him sobbing and begging meant his effectiveness in the organization was over. Farruco handed the gun back to the guard as his cell phone buzzed. The two women were at his side, running their hands up and down his body.

"Yes?"

He stiffened as he recognized Cesar's voice, and pushed the women away roughly. He listened and then acknowledged the order he had been given.

Flipping the phone shut, he shouted orders to his guards. Then he went to the large gun case on the wall nearest the balcony and opened it. He surveyed the various weapons inside. He could hear shouts now from the lawn as his men brought the Americans out and lined them up.

He chose an American-made M-16, enjoying the not so subtle irony, and walked out to the balcony. Looking down, he could see the prisoners squinting in the bright sunlight, most of them mesmerized by Alonzo's body in front of them, then slowly noticing his presence above.

"Who is in charge?" Farruco yelled.

For several seconds nothing, then one of the men stepped forward. "I am."

"Your name?"

The man said nothing. Farruco shrugged. "It does not matter. Pick one of your men."

"For what?"

"To die."

The man blinked. "What?"

"I am going to kill one of you. You have thirty seconds to pick who it is."

Chapter Thirteen

alika watched the few lights on Saba disappear from sight
s the plane gained altitude. She was armed with only a
ptop computer, a fact that made her quite uncomfort-
ble, especially since she had met the man she was head-
ng toward once before and it had not turned out well. Of
ourse, in that meeting she had been representing herself,
ot Cesar and the Ring.

Cesar, at least, was confident that his backing would
arner her a peaceful reception. Valika wasn't as confident.
he gripped the armrest as the plane banked hard, heading
r Martinique, a neutral place. The flight would be short,
e only good thing about this mission as far as she was
oncerned.

thousand miles to the west, *Aura II* was circling a spot
the ocean two miles off the coast of Grand Cayman, all
ghts blacked out. An Aura transmitter was bolted to the
eck of the ship, cables looping from it to a computer in
e ship's bridge. None of the crew were near the com-
uter. It was linked by SATCOM directly back to Saba.
stead of bunks, the main cabin was full of lithium batter-
s to supply power to Aura.

At the appointed time, the captain of *Aura II* turned
is bow toward the main harbor of Boddentown. He slid
to the small bay and edged as close as possible to the
wn without running the yacht aground.

The SATPhone was answered on the second ring. "Yes?"

"I need some help," Dalton said.

"Are you still at Bright Gate?" Mentor asked.

"Yes."

"Something is happening," Mentor said. "We've los two others besides General Eichen."

" 'Lost'?" Dalton repeated.

"Killed."

"By the Priory?"

"Most likely."

"Then I really need your help." Dalton quickly tol Mentor about his plan to establish an alternate Brigh Gate. "I've got transportation lined up," Dalton said. "I ca get the stuff out of here, but I don't have a place to tak it to."

"What are your requirements for a location?" Mento asked.

"Someplace secure. Hidden. And access to power."

There was no static in the SATPhone, just a dead si lence for several seconds, which made him wonder Mentor was still on the other end.

"I think I might have a place that fills those require ments," Mentor finally replied.

Deep inside the extinct volcano in the center of Sab Cesar rolled an unlit cigar between his hands. Souris wa hooked to Aura I, the main transmitter located in the con trol center. Cesar knew there was no need for her to be i the virtual world, as there was nothing on the island tha needed watching, but she spent all her spare time like tha

Cesar's fortune was built on addiction, so he knew th signs. Whatever she was in the virtual world, wherever sh went on the other side, Cesar had no clue. But there wa no doubt Souris definitely preferred the virtual world t

he real to the point where she had little control over the
decision about which to be in.

Using Raisor to do what had originally been slotted for
Souris to accomplish was a bonus. He had not been very
comfortable sending Souris on *Aura II* to help get the
shipment ashore in Florida. If Raisor truly wished to be an
ally, he would do as ordered, but if he was a spy, that
would come out very shortly and then Cesar would have
Souris do it as originally planned. He was having his
doubts about the American scientist, though, and having
someone waiting in the wings to replace her if she began
to break down from her addiction was something he had
long considered, but had only been able to be serious
about with the appearance of Raisor.

He glanced at the digital clock. Each second that
clicked by meant another stage in the plan was closer to
fulfillment.

At Fort Carson, two Special Operations MH-60K
Blackhawk helicopters, assigned to the elite Task Force
160, the Nightstalkers, and on temporary duty with 10th
Special Forces Group, lifted off. The pilot in charge was
Chief Warrant Officer Roby, a twenty-two-year veteran,
with sixteen of those in the Nightstalkers. He was a veteran of numerous operations, including behind-the-lines
flights during Desert Storm. It was on one of those flights
that his craft had been shot down.

With his copilot injured, Roby elected to stay with the
chopper even though they could see the lights from Iraqi
vehicles closing on their location. The crew chief elected
to try to escape and take his survival radio into the desert,
where he would have more of a chance.

Roby had called in his position, then grabbed the
MP-5 submachine gun they carried on board for personal
defense. When the first Iraqi troops approached, he let

them come within fifty meters, then fired a burst, killing three. The rest went to ground.

Then the air support came. Every Allied craft in the vicinity with ordnance to expend came by, surrounding his location with a wall of explosive and cannon fire. But as night fell, Roby could tell that the Iraqis were creeping closer and would soon be so near his position the air support wouldn't help.

That's when the rescue chopper came in. Another Nightstalker craft with four Special Forces men on board. The bird came in fast and blacked out. It touched down and the SF guys had his copilot on board in less than fifteen seconds, Roby jumping on board right behind.

Then he told them about the crew chief. The man in charge of the rescue team, Sergeant Major Jimmy Dalton, ordered the crew to search for him. They found him five miles away, wandering in the desert. So Roby returned with all his crew. And thus he owed Dalton and now he was paying back in response to the phone call he had received from the sergeant major that afternoon.

The Task Force MH-60K Blackhawk was a vast improvement over the standard UH-60 model the rest of the army used. It had an air-to-air refueling probe that poked from underneath the front of the cockpit, two M134 7.62-millimeter miniguns, one mounted on each side, and an external hoist. Most important, though, were the advanced avionics to help Roby fly the ship. He had interactive multifunction displays, forward-looking infrared, a terrain-avoidance/terrain-following radar, and a digital map generator that followed the flight of the helicopter, constantly updating the pilot with the helicopter's exact location.

Making sure his equipment was working properly, Roby turned the nose of the chopper toward the high peaks.

inding Grand Cayman via the virtual plane hadn't been
oo difficult for Raisor. Cesar had ordered the ship's cap-
ain to turn on the Aura transmitter intermittently and
Raisor had located it on the virtual plane. Then it was a se-
ies of short jumps to the island itself. The yacht was less
han two hundred yards from shore, and his target was
nly two blocks away from the ocean.

Now he waited.

stretch limousine was waiting for Valika as she got off
Cesar's jet at Martinique. Two men, guards, stood on the
ide, one opening the door. As she started to get in, he
eached for the laptop case. She gave it to him and got in-
ide. There was no one else in the spacious interior. The
nen got in the front.

It was a short drive to the four-star hotel where the
neeting was to be held, and Valika did not use the time to
artake of the car's bar. One of the guards opened the
loor, handing the searched case back to her.

"Room 114," he informed her.

Valika slung the carrying case for the laptop over her
houlder and entered the hotel. Room 114 had a small
laque on the door informing her that it was the
resident's Suite, which she found ironic given she was
neeting a former high-ranking Communist.

The door swung open immediately at her first knock.
'wo more goons flanked the door on the inside. One
ointed at an entrance to another room. Conversation had
ever been Kraskov's strong point, Valika reflected as she
valked through, and that must have seeped down to his
ecurity element.

The man who was sitting on the couch had once been
escribed to Valika as a troll, but she thought that was a
isservice to the mythical creature. He was short, fat,

hairy, and ugly. And he had bad teeth, which Valika found unforgivable in a man with access to money. That at least could be corrected.

"My dear Valika, you are beautiful as ever." His greeting was effusive, but he made no attempt to get his rotund form off the couch.

Valika went to the chair on the other side of the coffee table. "And you, Kraskov, look the same as I remember."

"Ah, such wit. I missed that. If I remember rightly, the last time we saw each other, you were shooting at me."

"Unfortunately I missed." Valika unzipped the bag and took out the laptop.

"But if you hadn't, we wouldn't be able to conduct our business this evening," Kraskov said.

"There would be someone else in your chair."

"But it is me here, Valika."

The tone caused her to look up from turning the computer on. Kraskov had a gun pointed at her—a nine-millimeter Browning High Power, she noted, before she shifted her gaze back to his eyes.

"We are here to do business," she said. "You know who I work for."

"I know who you whore for." The gun didn't waver. "I am supposed to be afraid of some pimp drug dealer from a third-rate country?"

"Eight hundred million will be yours, as you asked."

The gun moved slightly, Kraskov's thick eyebrows bunching. "You joke. I gave you that number simply to not have to bother with you. I was amazed when you asked to meet."

"Then what is the ship really worth?"

"Eight hundred million, of course."

Valika smiled wryly. "I assume you have an account where you want the money transferred to."

"You're serious?" Kraskov put the gun away. "Of course
ere is an account. Swiss, naturally."

alton walked past the tubes holding Kirtley's team.
Keep them in until I give you the all clear," he told
ammond.

"Orientation training will take about four hours any-
ay," she said and turned back to her control console.

Jackson and Barnes were waiting for him just inside
e vault door. As he approached, Jackson punched in the
ode and the door rolled open. She then hit the command
 open the hangar door. The opening in the side of the
ountain appeared as the metal grate slid out.

Dalton checked his watch. Five minutes.

"Let's get the computer up here."

he cell phone rang. Cesar flipped it open. "Yes?"

"We're ready," Valika informed him.

He shut the phone. "Souris." Cesar waited but there
as no response from the woman in the deep chair.
Souris!" he yelled.

Reluctantly he got up and went over to her. He hit the
SC key on her keyboard.

Her eyes flashed open. "You bastard!"

Cesar reached forward and grabbed her chin.
Remember who pays for all of this."

"You're ignorant," Souris hissed.

Cesar pointed at the computer. "Activate Aura II and
ll Raisor it's time for him to earn our assistance."

aisor "saw" the field race over the harbor toward him. It
ruck like the wind hitting a glider's wings. He felt the
ower, his virtual avatar gaining form and strength.

The data was also there in the wave, formed by the

Aura computer. He accessed it. It wasn't as good as Brigh
Gate, but enough for the task at hand.

He glided into the Bank of Grand Cayman, passing
through the thick outer walls. He found what he was
searching for with ease—the glow of a screensaver on the
computer screen drawing him in.

It might be night on Grand Cayman, but the bank's
main computer never slept, as accounts were constantly
being accessed from the entire world via secure Internet.

Raisor slid into the computer, a feat he had done before as a Psychic Warrior. He found the first of the names
he'd been given and accessed the account, already having
bypassed the need for a password, as he was part of the
computer itself.

One hundred and thirty million was in the account.

Raisor sent the account on its way, using the information he had been given. Then he searched for the next
name.

The numbers appeared on Valika's screen. "The first deposit has been made. One hundred and thirty million. The
rest will be there shortly."

That was enough to get Kraskov off the couch. He
came around and looked over her shoulder, standing
much too close, his fetid breath on her neck.

"Let me check." He waddled to a briefcase and took
out a satellite Internet phone and began punching in numbers.

"The first transfer has been made," Souris reported in
distracted, distant voice.

Cesar cut the tip off his cigar.

Raisor had been given six names. He reached eight hundred million by the third account. For the excess he

switched the destination account, sending the money to Cesar's own Swiss account. Until there was one hundred million left in the last account. That he sent to a different destination.

In all, he had cleared out 1.2 billion dollars. He had no idea who he had just stolen from, but he assumed they were people who would not go running to the authorities; not that there were any authorities to run to in Grand Cayman, which was why the accounts were there in the first place.

"I am impressed," Kraskov said, closing the phone.

"Where is the ship?" Valika said.

"Not far. Off of the European Space Port at Kouro, monitoring launches."

"Excellent."

He handed her a sheet of paper. "The ship's call sign. The command code word. The captain will do whatever you ask once you give him that code word."

"Good."

"What will you do with the crew?" Kraskov asked as he went back to the couch and sank down into the cushions.

"They're like you, aren't they? Several suitcases full of cash and they'll work for us, won't they?"

Kraskov nodded. "True."

"Everything in Russia is for sale, isn't it?"

"Just about." He smiled, revealing misshapen and discolored teeth. "We are embracing capitalism wholeheartedly."

"I left just in time. What about the other items?" Valika asked.

"I don't understand why you asked—" Kraskov began but Valika cut him off.

"Don't do any thinking. Where are they?"

Kraskov grunted something to one of the guards. The man left the room and was back in a minute with a large metal briefcase in each hand. He put them on the table. Valika flipped the lids open.

"This was difficult to come by," Kraskov said. "My GRU contact raised his eyebrows at the request."

"And you lowered them with cash." Valika closed the lids, having confirmed the contents.

"I've reserved a room for you," Kraskov said. "Right next door as a matter of fact. I could order from room service. They have some excellent wines, or I can order vodka if you still drink the swill."

"I'm leaving." Valika stood. She slung the laptop case over her shoulder and picked up the two cases.

"You don't know what you'll be missing," Kraskov said as she headed for the door.

"I don't even want to consider thinking about that," Valika threw over her shoulder as she left.

The first Blackhawk landed, blowing snow into Dalton's face. The side door slid open and the crew chief jumped out. Dalton waved at him to help. With Barnes's and Jackson's assistance they manhandled Sybyl III's mainframe to the helicopter and inside. It filled most of the cargo bay.

That helicopter lifted and the second one came in. As Jackson, Barnes, and the new crew chief loaded the other gear needed for Sybyl III to work, Dalton got in the cargo bay and leaned between the seats. He shook Roby's hand.

"Thanks for making it, Chief."

"Long time no see, Sergeant Major. We needed some blade time for training anyway. Where do you want me to take this stuff?"

Dalton handed him a map. He tapped a location. "Right there."

Roby squinted, making out the markings. Then he looked up, eyes widening. "Oh, man."

"There will be someone there waiting to off-load this gear."

"All right."

Raisor's essence was drained of power as Aura II was turned off. He was once more a formless being on the psychic plane. He headed toward the United States.

Cesar picked up the phone and dialed the direct number for his villa in Colombia where the Special Forces team was being held. His instructions to his man in charge there were brief and to the point. It was time to get things moving and the Americans weren't playing along as he would like.

Farruco took the photo of the American he had killed and slid it into the slot on the top of the fax machine. He punched in the number he had been given and waited until he heard the confirming squeal, then punched the Send button.

Once the picture came out, he put it back in the top slot and dialed a new number.

McFairn stared at the photo that had just been faxed to her office. She almost jumped as her secure phone rang.

"McFairn."

"General Carlson here. I just got a faxed picture from Colombia."

"I also just received it," McFairn told the chairman of the Joint Chiefs of Staff.

"My office. Now. Bring everything you have on these sons-a-bitches."

Dalton watched the lights of the second Blackhawk disappear into the night sky and listened as the sound of the blades faded until there was silence. He stood on the landing grate, looking out over the starlit mountains.

"Marie?" he whispered.

A cool breeze blew by and he thought of the poem.

He reached out, above his head, ignoring the pain in his shoulder, spreading his fingers wide, the breeze touching his skin. "I feel you."

Chapter Fourteen

Deputy Director McFairn rarely traveled away from her office for meetings. It was a sign of power in Washington to have people come to her, but in the case of General Carlson, chairman of the Joint Chiefs of Staff, she had to make an exception.

The sun was barely tingeing the eastern sky with light as her limousine pulled into the Pentagon lot. She was quickly escorted to Carlson's office, her briefcase tucked tightly under her arm.

"Director," Carlson stood and indicated for her to sit in the chair directly in front of his massive desk.

"General, good to see you again."

Carlson wasted no time in pleasantries. He threw the faxed photograph in front of McFairn. A dead man in unmarked jungle fatigues, splayed out on a neatly maintained lawn, a bullet hole in the left side of his chest. "That's Captain Scott. The team leader."

"I know," McFairn acknowledged.

"What do you have on the Special Forces team?" Carlson demanded.

She put Dalton's report on his desk and waited as he leafed through it.

"How did you get such detailed information?" he asked when done.

"Bright Gate."

"I thought the Psychic Warrior team was inoperative."

A fancy term for lost, McFairn thought. "We still have some operators and I'm currently reconstituting another team."

"How did the Task Force Six team get compromised? You don't have that in the report."

"We think there's a possibility the Ring is using remote viewers and they spotted the team."

"Oh Christ." Carlson slammed the report down on the desk. "You people and your weird psychic crap."

"You know Bright Gate works and you know it works well, given what happened in Russia not long ago," McFairn pointed out.

"If your people went down there, why didn't they free our men? They might have saved Scott's life."

"They could only do a recon. There was no way they could have gotten the men out without all of them getting killed."

Carlson grumbled something.

McFairn leaned forward. "I have an idea how we can kill two birds with one stone."

"What do you mean?"

"Rescue the captured soldiers and destroy the Ring's RV capability."

"I'm listening."

As McFairn laid out her plan to use the Psychic Warriors to spearhead a rescue mission, Raisor listened in, floating in the virtual plane in Carlson's office. The Pentagon wasn't psychically shielded, which Raisor found interesting, but not surprising. It was simply too large and had too many people coming and going to be shielded. He also knew there was the fact that the conventional military distrusted something as radical as Psychic Warrior.

He had followed McFairn's limousine from Fort

Meade to the Pentagon, seething with the inability to do anything, but now he saw an opportunity to strike back.

When she was done presenting her plan, Raisor made his first jump south, heading back toward Saba.

Captain Mikhal Lonsky had been in command of the research ship *Kosmonaut Yuri Gagarin* for almost ten years, and he had watched their operating budget shrink with each new appropriation out of Moscow. Named after the first man to go into space, the ship had maintained communications with *Mir* as long as that station had been operational. With the space station's demise the previous year, this year's appropriation had been appallingly low. The crew was at forty percent, the rest laid off by the new capitalistic Russian society to save money, which was spent first on necessary repairs.

The most recent mission given the ship was to monitor launches from the European Space Consortium's base at Kouro, in French Guiana. It was a boring job, but one the new KGB, called the SRU, wanted done, more for industrial espionage purposes than military necessity.

When all four radar dishes were oriented forward as they were now, the *Gagarin* lost two knots in speed due to wind resistance, but that was of little importance to Lonsky as they were stationary, thrusters fore and aft holding them in place against the wind and current.

Lonsky turned as his senior communications and computer officer, Tanya Zenata, entered the bridge. There was supposed to be separate officers for each specialty, but the combining of the jobs was another cost-cutting measure forced on Lonsky.

"Sir, we have a radio communiqué from Moscow."

Lonsky took the paper and read it. His eyebrows arched as the import struck home. Lonsky started laughing, causing the scant bridge crew to turn and look at him. He couldn't help it. He fell backwards into his command chair, still laughing, tears now flowing down his cheeks.

"We've been sold," he finally managed to get out.

Boreas paced back and forth in his office, staring out the large bullet-proof window at the field of antennas that was his province. When HAARP was off, the entire facility was guarded by an electromagnetic wall, impenetrable to remote viewers, Psychic Warriors, or any living thing. Numerous local animals had died when they crossed the buried cables that transmitted the field. A brain, whether in the real world or a virtual essence, could not cross the electromagnetic barrier that was on a frequency inimical to the mind's own electromagnetic operation.

Beyond the field, the Wrangell Mountains loomed over the site. Boreas often looked to them. Not to enjoy the beauty of their white peaks against the blue sky, but because of the threat he felt lurked there.

The phone rang, cutting through his dark mood. It was McFairn, confirming the plan they had come up with the previous night.

After hanging up with her, Boreas made a call on his secure satellite phone to Kirtley, giving the necessary order. Then he made a final call. The other end was answered immediately.

"Yes?" The voice was deep, one used to authority, the overseas connection perfect despite the scrambling and encryption. The equipment was cutting edge, not penetrable even by the NSA.

"We are taking action against the Ring."

"Good. Nexus has been dealt with in the United States."

"Are you sure you got all of them?"

There was the shortest of pauses. "We're not certain.

But we've taken care of the important ones. They have no immediate access to the President, and by the time any survivors make contact and are verified, it will be much too late."

"What about Souris and the Ring?"

"Try to track down their Aura transmitter using your new Psychic Warrior team. Then destroy it and the Ring. What is the status of HAARP?"

"CS-MILSTAR goes up soon. We'll be on-line world-wide in less than two days. We still have to get the unlock codes for the MILSTAR satellites, but I anticipate being able to do that without too much trouble. And then it will finally be over. After all these years."

"Don't underestimate them."

Boreas looked at the mountains. "I won't."

"We're going operational in eight hours." Kirtley had satellite imagery of Colombia spread over the conference table, his team gathered round. Dalton, Jackson, and Barnes stood in the background.

"You've only been 'over' once," Dalton pointed out. "I don't think you're ready to be operational."

"It's not debatable, Sergeant Major." Kirtley slapped the tabletop. "We're leading the effort to rescue your fellow green beanies. I would expect even you to be happy about that."

"The team got ambushed," Dalton said. "What makes you think the team going in to save them isn't going to be ambushed also?"

"Because *we'll* be going in first, clearing the way," Kirtley said. "The conventional team that follows us is coming just to recover the hostages."

Dalton rubbed his forehead, trying to keep the growing headache at bay.

"And we will have one practice session this afternoon

before the actual mission," Kirtley added. "A live fire run-through at the urban combat range at Fort Campbell, Kentucky."

"What do you want us to do?" Dalton asked, indicating Jackson and Barnes along with himself.

"We're done with you. You'll be released to go back to your units once my team is operational."

"That's it?" Dalton was surprised, even though he had known this was coming eventually. "What about the rest of my team?"

"They've been officially classified as missing in action," Kirtley said. He turned back to his imagery and his own team.

"They're not missing," Dalton argued. "They're in the other room."

"Then wake them up," Kirtley said sharply. "Bring them back, have them walk out here, and you can take them with you."

"You told me they wouldn't be abandoned." Dalton took a step forward, several members of Kirtley's team getting between them.

"And they won't," Kirtley said, "but they also won't be going home with you, will they? And they have to be classified as something, don't they? Some sort of explanation given?"

Dalton knew what Kirtley was saying made sense, but he viewed it as the first step to eventually pulling the plug on the bodies in the other room. And once he was gone from Bright Gate, there was nothing he could do about it.

"I have a suggestion," Dalton said.

"What?" Kirtley's response was less than enthusiastic.

"Let Jackson, Barnes, and I participate in your test this afternoon. We'll be part of the opposing force. The big problem my team had on our training exercise at Fort Hood was that we had no one shooting back." He turned to Dr.

Hammond. "Couldn't our avatar weapons be set on a low power, enough to indicate a hit but not hurt each other?"

Hammond nodded. "Yes. I'm sure I can get Sybyl to program that."

"Our opponents won't be avatars," Kirtley said. "They'll be real flesh-and-blood people."

"I wouldn't count on that," Dalton said. "We sensed a presence when we were at the villa. Besides, we can act like flesh and blood—keep our avatars on the real plane and not use the virtual to do any jumps once we're at the training site."

He could tell Kirtley wasn't thrilled with the idea, so he pushed. "You need all the help you can get. Trust me on that. You don't want to end up like the other two teams."

He could see the flicker that passed over Kirtley's face as the last point hit home. "All right. You go over with us and to the first jump point. Then you'll go on ahead to be part of the opposing force."

"Now it's your time to prove your loyalty to me." Raisor's avatar floated an inch off the floor, a disconcerting image when combined with the translucent aspect of his appearance.

"How exactly?" Cesar asked. Valika stood behind him, off his right shoulder, Souris was working, preparing for the next test of Aura, the final one before they were ready to be fully working in combination with the *Gagarin*.

"Not only will you help me," Raisor added, "but you'll also be helping yourself."

Cesar waited for more explanation.

Raisor had searched through the computer's files for what he was looking for. Now he used Aura's capabilities to project an image of the Mount of the Holy Cross in the air between him and Cesar and Valika.

"That's where Bright Gate is located. Inside that

mountain in the middle of Colorado. You're going to help me get in there, and out with what I need."

"And how am I going to do that?" Cesar asked.

"You're going to lend me your associate"—he pointed at Valika—"and her laptop. I transferred more than the eight hundred million you needed. You can spare, say, ten million—a drop in the bucket—to hire the men and equipment we need in the United States to accomplish my task. If you need contacts, I have some that I met while working for the Agency. And they will have my assistance." He turned to Souris. "You have your original prototype of Aura, don't you?"

"Souris!" Cesar snapped, drawing her attention away from the computer screen. "The original Aura prototype—you still have it, correct?"

Souris nodded. "But it is weak. The field is small, less than half a mile."

Raisor smiled. "That's all I'll need in order to be with Valika on the mission."

"You said this would also be helping me," Cesar noted.

"The Americans are planning to raid your compound in Colombia where you are keeping their soldiers prisoner."

"I expected that," Cesar said.

"Did you expect their Psychic Warriors to be leading the assault?" Raisor asked. "Are you prepared for that?"

Cesar turned to Souris to answer.

"We are, actually," she said.

Raisor was surprised. "How?"

"Do not concern yourself with that," Cesar said. "I think you have a good point though. Attacking Bright Gate while the Psychic Warriors are out on the virtual plane is a good idea." Cesar lifted his right hand to Valika. "Go with him."

———

The U.S. aircraft carrier *Roosevelt* had just traversed the Panama Canal into the Pacific on its way to rejoining the Seventh Fleet after a refit at Norfolk Naval Station. On the massive flight deck dozens of planes were crowded wingtip to wingtip. Among them were two MH-60 Special Operations Blackhawk helicopters. A new Department of Defense policy, designed to be more in line with the threats of terrorism rather than World War III, had designated that a Special Operations task force be on board each fleet carrier. The Spec Ops task force consisted of a Special Forces A-team and a Navy SEAL element, along with Task Force 160 helicopters to transport them.

The order for the raid to help rescue the Special Forces soldiers in Colombia was greeted by the Special Ops men with enthusiasm and professionalism. The original team had come from this ship and they had friends among the missing men.

As the *Roosevelt* turned its bow to the south, they began making their plans, even though the supporting role they were to play puzzled them. If they were to be second fiddle, who was to do the actual assault?

"Eat it," Sergeant Lambier told Granger. The wounded man was staring at the tin plate of unrecognizable slop a guard had just shoved in the cell.

"Why?" Granger asked. "So I can puke just before they shoot me?"

"Because we don't know how long we're going to be here," Lambier said.

The other two men made no move to grab their plates either. Lambier picked up his and began shoveling the food into his mouth, swallowing as quickly as he could to avoid tasting it. When he was halfway through, the others began doing the same.

Chapter Fifteen

Captain Lonsky was actually not overly surprised the *Gagarin* had been sold. The previous year, Moscow had rented it out to an American movie company making a science fiction film, and before and after that they had done monitoring missions for other countries and corporations when the price was right. Lonsky had been a crew member aboard the ship during the Cold War and remembered how they had always been shadowed by American submarines, planes, and ships doing counterintelligence missions against them. Things were very different now. For all he knew, the Americans were the buyers.

"A message from our new owners," Zenata said, holding several sheets of paper in her hand.

Captain Lonsky took the message and read through. He turned to the bridge crew and barked out orders. "Shut down the thrusters. Orient dishes horizontal for minimum wind resistance. Our new heading will be three zero zero degrees, at flank speed."

As the crew did as commanded, he reread the next to last sheet. "Do you think this is serious?"

Zenata shrugged. "Whoever sent this bought the ship, which even Moscow would not sell cheaply. I would assume they are serious about the money. It is probably cheaper than training their own crew."

Lonsky picked up the mike. He switched the intercom so that he could broadcast to the entire crew. "Ladies and

entlemen, as you are now aware, the ship has been sold to
omeone, whose name we do not know. However, we have
eceived a communiqué from them with a job offer for each
f us to stay on for another month of work, remaining in
ur assigned jobs on board ship. The terms of the deal
re simple. A bonus of one hundred thousand dollars
American for each member of the crew for that one month.
Paid in cash. If anyone does not want to stay on board,
lease notify me immediately." He clicked off the mike and
vaited. As expected, the message board remained unlit.

Zenata had a last sheet, which she gave to him.

Lonsky read it. It detailed specific instructions. "Can
ou do this?" he asked Zenata.

"It is simply preparing our master computer for inter-
ace with another computer," she said. "It is not very diffi-
ult. But I wonder why someone would want us to do
hat."

"Any clue who bought us?"

Zenata shook her head. "This message came from a
ommercial satellite. It could have originated anywhere. It
oes have the proper authorization code word," she added
nnecessarily.

"Do what they want," Lonsky ordered.

"Where are we headed?" Zenata asked.

"The Lesser Antilles. Saba, to be specific."

"Saba?"

"A small island with no harbor."

Zenata hadn't left yet. "And what do you think they
vant us to do when we get there?"

"That is a very interesting question to which I do not
ave a clue."

Dalton watched the team appear on the virtual plane above
he Mount of the Holy Cross. Jackson was above him,
ormed in her eagle avatar, Barnes to his right. Kirtley had

seven men with him, lined up like a row of ghostly images behind him. Dalton noted that Kirtley's avatar was larger and stronger looking than the man appeared in real life.

"First jump point," Kirtley ordered.

Jackson was gone before he even finished the sentence. Dalton visualized the spot, and then he was there. Barnes appeared. Then one, two of Kirtley's men. The rest straggled in, one by one.

"You need to appear on target at the same time," Dalton pointed out.

"That's why we're practicing," Kirtley responded shortly. "Dr. Hammond, project an image of our target."

In the center of the group, a scaled version of a special range at Fort Campbell, Kentucky, appeared. Dalton had been there before, in the real world, when his team had gone for urban operations training. The range was an example of a village in Germany, complete with buildings, town square, sewer system, and roads. Kirtley had had the range personnel put automatic targets in, then clear the area.

"Our objective is here." Kirtley pointed at a large building facing the small square. "It's as close as we can come to simulating the villa." He looked at Dalton. "Time for you to go there. I don't think it would be quite fair if you heard our assault plans."

"Roger that," Dalton said. "Dr. Hammond, I want a private link that only Jackson and Barnes can hear."

"You've got it," Hammond informed him. "I'm also blocking the team's communications from you."

"Let's go," Dalton said. He jumped and was above the building Kirtley had indicated as the main objective.

"What's the plan?" Barnes asked.

"Let's see what's set up first," Dalton said. He flowed through the roof of the building and descended to the basement. There were targets set up to indicate guards and sev

eral dummies placed on the floor to simulate the prisoners.
It was the best that could be done on such short notice.

"Barnes, you've got this building. Shoot the hostages
the minute the first avatar comes in here."

"Roger that, Sergeant Major."

"Jackson, I want you to be our eye in the sky. Relay
what you see to us."

"I thought we were supposed to pretend to be people,"
Jackson said.

"Rules are made to be broken," Dalton said.

"And where will you be?" Barnes asked.

In reply, Dalton simply pointed down, then he vanished from site as he jumped.

Sailors watched as the Green Berets and SEALs test-fired
their weapons off the deck of the *Roosevelt*, spewing lines
of tracers into the ocean. Satisfied their weapons worked,
the men began smearing camouflage paint on their faces,
loading magazines, and sharpening knives. The air crews
walked around their helicopters, making sure they were
ready for flight. They all knew the members of ODA 054
who had launched from this very ship, and they had been
shown the photograph of Captain Scott's body. Rescue
was the primary mission, but silently accepted among all
the men was the desire for revenge.

The coast of Colombia was directly ahead of the bow
of the carrier, a hundred miles over the horizon.

Valika had spent the entire flight on her cell phone and
laptop, coordinating what she would need. She had operated in the United States many times before for Cesar, so
she had had no trouble lining up the men and equipment
to do the task—in a capitalistic society, money could indeed buy anything. She had already transferred over
sixteen million dollars into various accounts and upon

completion of the mission would transfer another fifteen million.

The small Aura projector sat across from her, hooked to the plane's power. At this low level it generated a large enough field for Raisor to appear, floating across from her, listening in on her conversations. She had not needed his help or contacts. The rest of the passenger compartment of the Lear jet was empty.

"Make sure they have explosives," Raisor advised her for the third time.

"I've already insured we will have adequate means to get inside the complex," Valika said. "I have a question for you, though."

"Yes?"

"What if we are confronted with Psychic Warriors? What if not all of them are in Colombia?"

"The most critical time will be when you land," Raisor said. "You must get inside the complex quickly—it's the one place where the Psychic Warriors can't operate, since it's shielded. It's the same way Dalton destroyed the Russian facility."

"Dalton?"

"One of the army people at Bright Gate," Raisor said. "He betrayed me also. They all did."

"You still did not answer me what we should do if we are confronted," Valika noted.

Raisor smiled and pointed at the two cases that Valika had bought from Kraskov. "I know what you have there."

"Will they work on Psychic Warriors?"

"I don't know for certain," Raisor said, "but I imagine they will have some effect. That's if you see them first."

"They can't stay invisible from you, can they?"

"No."

"Good. Then you will warn us if you see them on the virtual plane, correct?"

"Correct."

The rest of the trip was made in silence.

The Lear touched down at a small airfield outside of Granby, in north-central Colorado. It had been chosen because one of her contacts knew that there were four Army National Guard Huey helicopters parked there—exactly what they would need.

The mercenaries she had hired had already taken over the small field, capturing the two full-time employees. As the Lear rolled to a stop, a Ford Explorer came racing out of a hangar and up to the plane. The man who stepped out was short and wiry, wearing khaki with a combat vest strapped on his chest. He carried an MP-5 submachine gun casually in his right hand.

"Good-bye, Mr. Raisor," Valika said as she crossed the aisle and flipped off the switch for the Aura generator. Raisor's form popped out of existence. She then unhooked the generator and went to the now open door of the plane. She hopped down the steps and met the man.

"Mr. Gregory," Valika said, nodding in greeting.

"Ms. Valika. It's a pleasure to do business once again." Gregory led her toward the truck. "You do know, of course, that due to the mission to be accomplished, the location here inside my own country, and the amount you are paying, this will be the last time I will be working. My men and I will be retiring to a remote location after this."

"That would make sense," Valika agreed.

"I could use some more specifics on what actually we are looking for and what is to be recovered."

"Get us in first," Valika said. "Then you'll be shown what is to be taken." She paused at the door. "There's something in the airplane—a computer—that you need to off-load and place inside the helicopter I am to ride in. There are also several cases of high-power lithium batteries. Those are to be placed near the computer."

She waited while Gregory's men hauled out the small Aura transmitter and the batteries. Then she got in the truck and they drove to the hangar.

"They're here," Jackson's voice, modified through Sybyl, sounded inside of Dalton's head. Or actually, he realized, his avatar's head. He still wasn't comfortable operating on the virtual plane. She relayed what she was seeing, through the computer, to both Barnes and Dalton.

Kirtley's team appeared, popping into existence, almost simultaneously. Four men on the roof of the main building, one in each cardinal direction. Targets began popping up and the avatars fired, small balls of power exploding the wooden silhouettes.

Dalton moved down the sewer tunnel he was in, forcing himself to not "jump" but move totally in the real plane. He shoved open a manhole cover and fired as he came out, hitting one of the team in the back with a low-power shot. Dr. Hammond froze the avatar.

"You're dead," Dalton said as he ducked back down into the tunnel. He raced back toward the building, keeping track of Kirtley's forces via Jackson. The four men that had appeared on the roof were working their way down through the building, a classic clearing technique. Dalton had expected Kirtley's men to jump from the roof to the hostage room in one move.

Dalton popped his head up in the hostage room, Barnes's avatar not even turning. "Hey, Sergeant Major," Barnes said.

"I'm taking a couple of the hostages," Dalton said.

Barnes nodded. "They're too slow."

Dalton grabbed two of the dummies and ducked back down in the tunnel. He "saw"—via Barnes—the first avatar appear in the basement.

Barnes fired, spinning, hitting the remaining dummies

even as Kirtley's men shot at him. Barnes hit all of the "hostages" before being shut down by Dr. Hammond. Dalton lost his "eye" in the room.

Dalton made it across the street and up into the next building. Through Jackson he could "see" that Kirtley had called in his other three men from their guard positions. And then all went black.

No form, no input. Nothing. Just self.

Dalton knew immediately that Kirtley had had Hammond shut him down. He felt a moment's panic, but then used the techniques he had used in the Trojan Warrior program to regain control of his psyche. He was completely isolated on the virtual plane, unable to move, unable to even sense the grayness of the plane itself.

Panic overwhelmed him, his mind screaming without a voice. The memories of the prison cell in Vietnam came rushing back, led by the feeling of helplessness.

"Jimmy."

He didn't hear at first, so lost was he in his primal fears.

"Jimmy."

Like a lifeline in a vast, dark ocean, the voice got through. Dalton seized on it, focusing.

"Jimmy. It's me."

"Marie."

"Be careful, Jimmy. There are others here."

"Who?"

He felt power course into him, the black giving way to gray. He was moving, being jumped back to Bright Gate by Sybyl automatically, retracing the route he had taken to Fort Campbell.

And then he was back in the tank, the program bringing him back from the virtual world into his body.

"Marie?" Dalton queried into the gray, but there was no response.

Chapter Sixteen

The shuttle was mated with the external tanks and boosters, nose pointing toward the roof of the vehicle assembly building. The entire system rested on a crawler transporter forty meters long by thirty wide. Propelled by eight sets of huge tracked propulsion units, the entire thing began moving, starting the trip to the launch pad. At a speed of less than one mile an hour, it would take four hours to reach the launch pad overlooking the Pacific Ocean.

Inside the cargo bay, the SC-MILSTAR satellite was secured.

It wasn't long into the Cold War before the United States realized that housing its command and control facilities in surface buildings, easily susceptible to attack, was not a good idea. Once the decision was made to build a "hardened" facility, politics and practicality chose Cheyenne Mountain, overlooking Colorado Springs, which already had a large military presence in the form of Fort Carson, the Air Force Academy, and Peterson Air Force Base.

Work was begun on the one-hundred-million-year-old mountain in May 1961. A four-and-a-half-acre grid was hollowed out deep inside the mountain. Then over thirteen hundred metal springs were placed on the floor. Each spring was four feet long and twenty inches in diameter and could withstand a pressure of sixty-five thousand pounds. The theory was that the springs would allow the facility to withstand the shock wave of a thermonuclear blast on the surface of the mountain. On top of the springs, fifteen steel, windowless buildings were built to house NORAD, the North American Aerospace Defense Command, a joint U.S.-Canadian facility.

There were only two tunnels into the underground base, allowing security to be very tight. The main entrance tunnel was over a third of a mile long and ended at a set of massive steel and concrete blast doors. Over eleven hundred people worked in the center, and it had operated 365 days a year, round the clock, since inception.

The facility had opened for business on the sixth of February, 1964. Through the sixties and seventies, the major mission of the center was to provide missile warning, primarily through the Defense Early Warning line established across Canada and Alaska. In 1979 the Air Force established the Space Defense Operations Center there to counter the perceived growing threat by the Soviet Union toward satellites. In the 1980s the Air Force Space Command was established, and it absorbed all the subordinate units working in Cheyenne Mountain.

In 1981, Space Command supported the first shuttle launch, as it has done ever since. It was also tasked to coordinate the deployment of the MILSTAR constellation. In preparation for the coming deployment of the last satellite in that system, a group of Space Command men and women deep inside Cheyenne Mountain were running through a practice exercise insuring that once the SC-MILSTAR was put in orbit by *Columbia*, they would be ready to begin worldwide operations.

"Don't ever do that to me again!" Dalton was inside Kirtley's personal space, causing the agent to take an involuntary step backward.

"Don't worry," Kirtley said. "It won't ever happen again, because you're never going over again."

Dalton didn't back off. "Were you embarrassed because we killed most of the hostages and stole the others? Because you screwed up?"

"It was time to come back." Kirtley slipped out from between Dalton and the wall and walked to the control console, stepping up on the higher platform, looking down on the sergeant major.

"You should have jumped right into the room where the hostages were held," Dalton said.

"That's not proper technique," Kirtley argued.

" 'Proper technique'?" Dalton pointed at the isolation tubes where the rest of the team were being removed. "There's no book on this. There is no proper technique. You have to use the advantages Psychic Warrior gives you to the max. Why clear a building in the normal way, when you're not normal? I guarantee you that those cartel guards will put a bullet in the hostages' heads the second they realize something's wrong."

"I'll take your advice under consideration," Kirtley said. He turned to Hammond. "We'll be ready to go in three hours." He left the control room.

Dalton went over to Jackson's tube, waiting as she was lifted out and her TACPAD helmet removed.

"Son of a bitch," she said, then spit some fluid out of her mouth. "That jerk cut us off. Goddamn," she cursed once more as Dalton draped a thick towel over her shoulders.

"I've already talked to him, for whatever good it did," Dalton said.

Jackson shivered. "Geez—if that's what those people in the other room are experiencing since they were cut off—" She shook her head. "That was bad, real bad."

"We've got to do all we can to help them," Dalton said. "Before Kirtley turns off their iso-tubes."

Jackson nodded. "Hell, yeah. Sign me up."

"I've got a call to make," Dalton said. "Get Barnes when he comes out and meet me in our bunkroom."

"Do you have contact with the satellite?" Cesar asked.

Souris's eyes were closed, the leads from Aura covering her head. "Yes."

"Is it working?"

"I wouldn't have contact with it if it wasn't," Souris said. "Everything is developing exactly according to plan. Exactly."

"The coordinates are programmed?"

"Yes."

Cesar nodded. He didn't like waiting. He left the operations center and went upstairs to the atrium, his favorite place. All the other Ring members except Naldo had gone back to Colombia, satisfied that their money was being well spent and that their future in Cesar's hands looked bright. Or to plot to overthrow him, perhaps, but Cesar thought that unlikely given the display he had presented and Alarico's fate.

Naldo was seated in a chair by the pool, a tall glass by his side.

"Old friend," Cesar said as he sat next to him, a bodyguard quickly bringing his own drink.

Naldo laughed. "Old enemy is more like it. We were at each other's throats many more years than we have spent sitting by the side of a pool drinking together."

Cesar raised his glass in toast. "To old enemies then."

Naldo acknowledged the toast. "Things are different now. It's a new world. I miss the old days, though, when things were simpler."

"They were never simple," Cesar said. "Just differen
The deals and double-deals and triple-deals you and m
father used to do to each other—there was nothing simpl
about those."

"True. But it was between us. Two men. This—" Nald
fell silent.

"Go ahead."

"This doesn't feel right, Cesar. Even you, you're differ
ent. Why do we need to fight the Americans?"

"Because we finally can," Cesar said. "Don't tell m
you are not angry that the Americans tried to kidnap, c
even kill, your son."

"Angry? Yes. Stupid? No."

A vein popped up on Cesar's forehead, blood throt
bing. "You saw what we can do with Aura. And we will b
more powerful after tonight."

Naldo leaned forward so that listening ears beyond th
immediate vicinity could not hear. "I have to admit, yes,
was very impressed with the demonstrations of this Aur
But I have had time to think about it since. And I have t
tell you that I do not understand what you are doing. Yo
act as if this Aura is the final answer. The Americans hav
other weapons. They have not hesitated to even invade
country when it was in their interests. Noriega learned tha
and now he rots in an American prison."

Naldo could see the stiffness in the younger man. '
know you are angry that I speak these words, but I feel a
if ever since you moved from Colombia, you've been di
ferent. The others asked me to talk to you; that is why
stayed behind. They think this Aura thing is fine—as a d
vice to spy on people. But your plan to take over th
American satellites, that makes them fearful. They see it a
inviting unnecessary trouble."

"Yes, you are right," Cesar said. "They are fearful. The
are whipped curs who want to keep their few bones an

ide. Why should we hide? Why should we bow down to
ome group just because it has a flag?" Cesar's arm swept
ut, flinging the glass across the tiles, where it shattered.
He stood. "You have said what you needed to. I have work
o do."

Naldo watched Cesar walk away into a dark doorway.
lowly he shook his head. He got up. It was time to leave
his place and go back to Colombia.

alika opened the case holding the Barrett .50 caliber
niper rifle. She lifted it out and checked the bolt. Across
om her, Gregory whistled. "Big gun."

Valika checked her watch. "Are your men ready?"

Gregory nodded. "We're ready. I would assume that
nce this base is so isolated, it's a military facility?"

"It's affiliated with the military," she acknowledged.

"Many guards?"

"Actually, none, as far as we know. Not, at least, in the
ay you envision guards."

"What does that mean?"

"I'll tell you on the way." She rested the barrel over her
houlder and headed for the hangar doors. "Let's go."

lades began turning on the two MH-60K Blackhawk hel-
copters parked on the runway at Fort Carson Army
irfield. Crammed in the cargo bay was red webbing that
ey used for sling loads.

"Wheels up," Chief Warrant Office Roby ordered.

Both choppers lifted off the tarmac and headed into
e night sky, noses pointed northwest.

oreas stared at the computer screen. He was seeing what
ammond had on her control console two thousand
iles away at Bright Gate. Kirtley's team was beginning to
o into their isolation tubes.

He picked up a headset and put it on. Then he typed in commands, covertly accessing Sybyl.

He spoke into the boom mike. "Kirtley."

The voice that came back was muffled. "Yes?"

"This is our private link through Sybyl. Neither Hammond nor your teammates can access it. You know your job, right? The real objective of this mission?"

There was a long pause. "Yes."

"Good." Boreas keyed off the connection. He spun about in his chair and looked out at the mountains. Even at night the white peaks were clearly visible. Soon he and his people would have nothing to fear from the high country.

On board the *Roosevelt*, blades also began turning on both Blackhawks and Apache gunships. Rangers, Green Berets, and Navy SEALs piled into the transport choppers while the gunships took off to lead the way.

Low over the ocean, the air flotilla headed for the shoreline of Colombia.

Linda McFairn stared out her office window, but she wasn't really seeing the Maryland countryside. Her mind was on events happening far to the south. The photo of the executed Special Forces captain was the only item on her desk. She knew the Colombians had done that to spur action, and she'd told Boreas that, warned him that she saw an ambush coming, but he had not seemed concerned.

Whenever she was faced with a problem, she tried to see it as Sun Tzu would have. She had no doubt that the Ring was preparing a trap for the rescue mission. On the other hand, her forces held the advantage of surprise with the Psychic Warriors leading the assault.

Things were accelerating, something she had experi-

ced before during times of national crisis, yet no one in
e government other than her knew there was a crisis.
ie had read the report on Mrs. Callahan's death. She had
iown the National Security Adviser and her husband
asonably well, and she had no doubt they would never
ive committed suicide, but the FBI had labeled it that.

McFairn had never liked Callahan, a relative new-
•mer to Washington, coming in on the President's coat-
ils. The Adviser job should have been hers, so the death
dn't bother her as much as the implication if she added
the death of Eichen: There was no doubt the Priory was
oving against Nexus.

Since she had supplied Boreas, thus the Priory, with
ost of the intelligence about Nexus, she knew she was
sponsible for more deaths. Whatever guilt she had over
at was assuaged by her anger that she had never been
•proached to be a member of Nexus. Who better to
ep an eye on the Priory than the Deputy Director of
e NSA?

All her thinking brought her full circle to the funda-
ental problem with her position—what did the Priory
ive planned and who was its enemy? The Priory had re-
·atedly shown that it cared little who or what it had to
·stroy in accomplishing its goals, and she had little trust
Boreas's word that the plans were beneficial to the
nited States.

She turned back to the desk, looked once more at the
cusing photo, then picked up the phone linking her to
e NSA operations center. At the very least she could
ive her agency monitor what was going to happen and
: prepared to react whichever way was needed. She
ade sure the ops center was operating at full staffing and
. the lines of communications with other government
encies were open.

Then she waited.

Dalton watched from behind Hammond's shoulder as the last member of Kirtley's team was lowered into his isolation tube. "Let me know when they're all on the other side," he told Hammond.

Barnes and Jackson were already in the other room where the extra tubes holding Dalton's team were stored preparing them for movement.

"Who are we working for?" Hammond suddenly asked.

Dalton was startled. "What do you mean?"

Hammond shrugged. "I'm just a scientist, but even can see things here are anything but straightforward. Why did Jenkins cut off that team? He worked for the government, right? Then why did Raisor kill him? He worked for the government too. And I'm supposed to be working for the government—as are you—yet we're getting ready to hide from our own government."

"The government—" Dalton began, but he realized she was asking questions that didn't have simple answers. "The government is supposed to serve the people," he finally said. "But things have changed over the years. I've seen the same thing in the Army. We exist to defend our country; it's what we swear a binding oath to. But most officers, and a heck of a lot of NCOs, are only interested in their own careers, their own interests."

He looked at the isolation tubes and the NSA team as he searched for words. "You're just a scientist and I'm just a soldier. Just." He laughed shortly. "You know, people want to believe there is a 'they.' A bunch of other people who run things. Maybe there is a 'they,' but even if there is, it's our fault for giving up responsibility. And if there isn't a 'they,' then we're at fault for not taking responsibility."

He thought of some of the places he'd been ordered to go and what he had done. "Sometimes good people do bad things with a good motive. Sometimes bad people do bad things for a bad motive—does it matter?"

Hammond smiled, a most unusual event on her worn face. "I wouldn't have pegged you for a philosopher." The smile was gone so quickly, Dalton wondered if he had really seen it as she continued. "I think I became a scientist to avoid asking all those questions. I wanted things in black or white. It either worked or it didn't. You either proved a hypothesis or you didn't. Then they sent me here, and if there's one thing Bright Gate isn't, that's black or white. Even when we go over to the other side, it's all gray." She leaned forward and typed instructions into Sybyl. "They're all on the virtual plane now."

Dalton turned to give Barnes and Jackson help, when Hammond placed a hand on his arm, halting him. "Can I ask you something?"

Dalton was afraid she was going to ask him who *he* was working for now, but the question was different.

"Why did you go into the Army?"

Dalton laughed. "I'm an old soldier. We had a thing called the draft way back then."

"Then why did you stay?"

There was no hesitation in his answer. "The people." It occurred to him that at parties he would joke if someone asked him that question and answer that by the time he was released from the POW camp, he was a quarter of his way toward retirement, but the fact he had well over thirty years in now had proved that to be a lie.

Hammond was nodding. "A good reason." She looked about the control center. "I wish I had one as good for doing what I'm doing."

"Tell me," Dalton said.

She shrugged. "Why am I here?"

"No," Dalton said. "Why did you decide to become a scientist?"

"Knowledge. To learn new things. To discover."

"All good reasons," Dalton said. "Hang in there, I have a feeling we have a lot more to learn," he added as he headed for the freight elevator.

Chapter Seventeen

The *Aura IV* satellite had been launched from Kouro the previous week using a French-designed Ariana 4 rocket. The basic design of the satellite was the same that the HAARP team was using to renovate the MILSTAR satellites. The retransmit plans were part of the wealth of information Souris had taken with her when she defected.

To implement the plan and build the satellite, Cesar had been able to hire Russian scientists. Getting the European Space Agency to launch it had simply required putting the appropriate amount of money in the specified bank account. With the establishment of Kouro as an international launch center, space was truly becoming open to all, as long as they had enough money.

Given that there were over eight thousand objects in space, one more small satellite had excited little interest among the world's intelligence agencies. ESA had announced the launch as a communications satellite for a private company. It was now in a geosynchronous orbit, centered over the Caribbean Sea, halfway between Saba and Colombia.

Once the satellite was released from the rocket, it had unfolded and spread the retransmit antennas, forty feet wide on either side, mirror images of the towers at HAARP. The bulk of the rest of the satellite was a very powerful battery, capable of adding strength to the signal when it came. The uplink was a specially designed antenna on top of the volcano on Saba. Souris had estimated they would get only one burst out of the battery, maybe two. But all they needed was one to confirm they could do what they needed.

Farruco had to climb over one of the women to get to his cell phone, which was on the nightstand. He ignored her yelp of pain as his knee pressed into her stomach.

"Yes?"

"The Americans are coming," Cesar informed him.

Farruco jumped out of the bed, one hand on the phone, the other reaching for his pants. "I will—"

"Shut up and listen," Cesar cut him off. "I want you to do exactly as I say."

"Careful," Jackson warned Dalton as he and Barnes finished unhooking the dolly under the last tube in line. They wore heavy work gloves, as the eight-foot-high tubes were still supercooled. Cables looped all around, providing power from portable generators and life support for the bodies inside the tubes. The job had been made considerably easier given that the iso-tubes were designed to be moved if needed.

Dalton wiped the sweat off his forehead and surveyed what they had accomplished so far: All ten cylinders that held his team were free and ready to move; ancillary equipment had also been loaded on the movable platforms.

"What about Raisor?" Barnes asked. "And the other team?"

Dalton shook his head. "We'll be lucky to get all these in the sling loads. Hammond says they'll last like this on generator power for about two hours, then we've got to hook everything back up."

"Where are we taking them?" Barnes asked.

"We'll see it when we get there," Dalton said.

"Enough yacking," Jackson said. She had her padded shoulder against the first tube in line. "Let's get these to the landing pad."

"Yes, ma'am." Dalton snapped a half salute and turned her.

lika had secured the Barrett to the floor of the helicopter. She doubted whether she would need the long gun, but she had always thought it best to be prepared. She checked the function of the MP-5 submachine gun Gregory had brought for her.

She leaned close to Gregory, who was seated next to her. "How long?"

"Thirty minutes."

She looked at the Aura generator, debating whether to turn it on yet. She decided to wait until they were just about to land. She opened one of the metal cases. A dozen canisters were secured in the foam padding. She pulled one out and handed it to Gregory.

"What's this?" he yelled.

"A special type of grenade. Russian. We called it a beer can. When it detonates, it sends out an intense electromagnetic pulse. It is designed to be used inside headquarters and communications centers to destroy electronic equipment while not injuring personnel."

Gregory frowned. "Why do we need it?"

Now that they were in the air, Valika was pretty certain that Gregory and his men would follow through on the mission. It was time to tell him the nature of the objective and how she envisioned the grenade being used against Psychic Warriors if they appeared.

Two avatars materialized on the roof of Cesar's villa, the lead element of Kirtley's team. Kirtley himself was two miles away with the rest of the team, still on the virtual plane at the objective rally point.

"No guards that we can see," one of the men reported. "The roof is clear."

"Jump," Kirtley ordered the rest of his team. He, however, remained where he was. "Hook me into the command net of the Special Ops team," he directed Hammond through Sybyl.

The Special Operations task force from the *Roosevelt* was less than ten minutes out from the villa, flying low-level just above the treetops. The soldiers on board the Blackhawks prepared their weapons, putting rounds in the chamber. Forty men, the elite of the American military, they were as prepared as they could be.

The team leader listened as a radio call came in from the satellite receiver. "Hammer Six, this is Eyes Six. Over."

The team leader keyed his radio. "This is Hammer Six. Go ahead. Over."

Kirtley's voice came back. "Hold at final line for my command. Over."

"Roger."

"Also, be prepared to go to the location I give you. Over."

The team leader frowned. "We have the location of the villa. Over."

"The villa is not your priority objective. The priority objective will be where I tell you to go. Out."

The team leader turned to his executive officer, eyebrows raised in question. The XO could only shrug his ignorance of this change.

Sergeant Lambier started as two forms materialized in front of him. "What the hell?"

"We're friendly," one of the forms spoke, the voice

choing. As Lambier watched, the smooth white surface of the forms transformed into clothes, skin, hair. A man in a black jumpsuit with no identifying badges or insignia.

"Who are you?" Lambier demanded.

"NSA," the first form answered. "Helicopters are less than ten minutes from here. Where are the guards?"

Lambier shook his head as the other members of his team gathered round. "I don't know. We haven't heard anything in a while." He reached out to touch the form. "Unbelievable. *What* are you?"

On a hillside a half mile away, Farruco could see the strange forms appear on the roof of the building. Just as Cesar had told him would happen. He flipped open his SATPhone. "They're here."

Cesar put his hand on Souris's shoulder. "Now!"

She pressed the Enter key.

From the antenna on top of Saba's volcano, a tight-wave beam darted up into the sky toward *Aura IV.* It hit the retransmit panels, triggering a surge of power from the main battery, and was redirected down to Earth.

Kirtley's avatar staggered, the screams of his team members' dying psyches hitting him like a wave of pain.

The last thing Sergeant Lambier saw was the two forms getting wiped away, like pencil images under a powerful and extremely fast eraser. Then his brain exploded in agony, blood poured from his eyes, mouth, ears, and nose, and he collapsed to the floor dead.

They just disappeared," Farruco reported.

Cesar slapped Souris on the back. "It worked!"

"Of course it worked," Souris said.

"Go in and see what happened to the prisoners," Cesar ordered Farruco.

"Did you track it?" Kirtley demanded. "Did you track the transmitter? Is it close by?"

Boreas was staring at the data HAARP had picked up. It made no sense.

"Where is it?" Kirtley's voice had risen to a panicked pitch. "They wiped out my team, goddamn it! I've got the choppers on hold at the final line. Give me a location."

"You knew that was going to happen," Boreas said calmly, still trying to figure out what the information he was looking at meant, as it wasn't like the previous Aura transmissions they'd intercepted. "Stand by."

In the air next to Mount of the Holy Cross, Roby was watching his radar screens, and he didn't like what they were telling him. Four helicopters were coming in from the north. He tried contacting them on the guard frequency, but there was no reply.

"This ain't good," he muttered.

"I've lost them!" Hammond said as she came running into the loading bay.

"What?" Dalton spun around, his attention diverted from the sky outside. He could hear the inbound Blackhawks but he hadn't seen them yet.

"The team. They're gone. Except for Kirtley. The rest of them flat-lined. All at once. No mental activity at all."

"Damn it," Dalton muttered.

With a blast of cold air, the first Blackhawk came to a hover, the side door opening. The crew chief shoved out the cargo netting and Jackson and Barnes began spreading it out on the grate.

He ran over to Jackson, grabbing her shoulder to get her attention. "Get this first load out, then get on board the second chopper."

"Where are you going?"

"Hammond's lost the team. Something happened to them."

"There's nothing you can do," Jackson said.

"Kirtley isn't gone—he must be in a different place. I'm going to have Hammond extract him and find out what the hell is going on. The pilots know where to take you if it comes to that."

He could see that Jackson was going to protest further, but they were both interrupted by the crew chief throwing an expended aluminum flare tube at them. It clattered on the grate and Dalton picked it up. He pulled the top off and took out the note crammed inside.

Four helicopters inbound. Not responding to hails. You have six minutes.

He shoved the note into Jackson's hand. "Get them loaded and get out of here."

"What about you?"

"We'll get out," Dalton said. He reached over and pulled the emergency radio off her flight vest. "Come back for us." Then he turned and ran to Hammond, leading her back into the complex.

'It came from a satellite," McFairn's voice echoed out of the speaker.

Boreas slapped his palm on the desktop. That fit the data but was unexpected.

"My people tracked the downlink," McFairn continued, "but we didn't catch the uplink."

"Do you have a lock on the satellite?" Boreas asked.

"Space command is tracking it. I've got an F-15 out of Eglin Air Force Base scrambling. It's armed with ALMV."

"A what?"

"ALMV stands for air-launched miniature vehicle. It's an ASAT—antisatellite—missile."

"We need the uplink," Boreas said.

"First things first," McFairn said. "We take out the satellite before someone else gets killed."

Boreas leaned back in his seat. Souris was one step ahead of them again. What the hell were she and the Ring doing? He spoke into his headset, directly to Kirtley. "Order the helicopters in."

"Where's the transmitter?" Kirtley demanded.

"In space. Order the helicopters in and clean up the mess at the villa."

Farruco kicked one of the American bodies with the tip of his boot. The amount of blood surprised him. How had Cesar done this? And who were the strange beings who had just appeared on the roof, then disappeared?

He cocked his head at the sound of helicopters approaching. Barking orders, he ran upstairs. Reaching the main level, he flipped open the cell phone as the first American helicopter came racing in over the treetops.

"Can you do another burst?" Cesar asked Souris.

"I'm checking on the status of the satellite's power right now," she replied. Reading the screen, she nodded. "I think we can get one more."

"Stand by," Cesar told her. He spoke into the phone, ordering Farruco to pull his men back.

Afterburners kicked in as the F-15 roared into the sky, nose pointed almost vertical. Slung beneath the left wing was a long rocket. The F-15 passed through the sound barrier less than two minutes after wheels-up and continued to accelerate.

"Pull Kirtley back using Sybyl," Dalton ordered Hammond.

"What about the rest of the team?"

"You've got no contact with them?"

"No."

"Then there's nothing you can do. Leave them alone. I want to know what's going on. These inbound choppers are probably Kirtley's people."

The first load of commandos off-loaded on the roof, blowing holes in the ceiling, working their way down.

Farruco and his men were beating a hasty retreat across the back lawn, firing as they went. An Apache gunship raced by, thirty-millimeter cannon spitting bullets, killing half of Farruco's gunslingers before they reached the relative safety of the jungle.

Two more lifts of commandos off-loaded on the roof. Thirty men were in or on the villa.

From his vantage point, Kirtley could see the action, but he made no move. The plan had been for him to redirect the commandos to capture the Aura transmitter, which Boreas had expected to be located nearby. Given that it was in space, he was at a loss what to do.

He started in surprise as he sensed a shift in his link to Sybyl. Against his will, he was being drawn back. The villa disappeared and he was in total blackness.

The first Blackhawk carefully gained altitude, lifting the cargo net full of isolation tubes off the grate. Jackson and Barnes had managed to put six in that net. The second bird dropped its net and they quickly spread it out. The unknown helicopters were three minutes out.

Valika turned on the Aura generator. Despite her warning, the men inside the helicopter bay were startled when Raisor's image appeared, floating half in and half out of the left side door, just in front of Valika.

"We're three minutes out," Valika informed him.

"I know."

The F-15 was shuddering as it passed through fifty thousand feet altitude. The pilot was linked to Space Command in Colorado Springs, which had a lock on the target satellite and was relaying the data to his targeting computer. In turn, the computer was automatically downloading updates to the ALMV every second.

The second sling load was attached to the bottom of the Blackhawk, then Roby carefully maneuvered the chopper away from the platform and down, until his cargo door was level with the metal grate. The crew chief waved for Jackson and Barnes to get on board.

"What about the sergeant major?" Roby asked as soon as Jackson put on a headset.

"He said to come back for him after we deliver this load," Jackson said.

Roby shook his head, but he added power, moving up and away from the mountainside. He cursed as something flashed by, coming around the side of the mountain, narrowly missing. Another helicopter. The equally surprised crew of that chopper swerved away, then continued down the platform, disgorging a swarm of armed men.

"What the hell?" Roby muttered, but he didn't have time to contemplate the scene below any longer as a second Huey came around the mountain and someone leaned out the side and fired an MP-5 on full automatic at his Blackhawk.

Roby banked hard, trying to keep from losing the slingload, and headed to the south. One of the Hueys tried to follow but it was no match for the speed of the more modern Blackhawk, even one carrying a sling load.

After five minutes of chase, the Huey gave up and turned back.

"Are you clear yet?" Cesar demanded of Farruco over the SATPhone.

"Yes. We're in the jungle."

Cesar turned to Souris. "Do it."

The F-15 peaked out at seventy thousand feet, the air no longer thick enough to keep the engine firing. Just before stalling, the pilot hit the release for the ALMV. The eight-foot-long rocket separated; the first stage ignited and it soared toward the darkness of space as the F-15 rolled over and headed back toward Earth, the pilot nursing his engine to keep it from flaming out.

"It's going to take several minutes for his body to warm up enough to bring him back in completely," Hammond said.

They both turned as a thunderous explosion echoed down the entrance tunnel into the control room. Alarms began stridently ringing. Dalton pulled his pistol out of its holster and chambered a round.

Souris hit the Enter key and the signal left the antenna.

The heat seeker on the nose of the ALMV had picked up the energy in the *Aura IV* satellite. It closed at over five thousand miles an hour.

The uplink hit the satellite and the battery surged, adding power to the downlink just as the ALMV slammed into the satellite. The kinetic energy of mass times the extreme velocity resulted in complete disintegration of the satellite.

Space Command recorded the hit.

"You've got to go back for Dalton," Barnes insisted.

Roby was concentrating on flying. "Hauling a sling load reduces options greatly. We'd be sitting ducks. Even a pig Huey could fly circles around me right now. I can only outrun them going straight."

"We've got to get the isolation tubes hooked back up," Jackson said. "The sergeant major told me to do this."

"Hell, *you're* the officer," Barnes said.

Jackson looked at Barnes. "You Green Berets are always the one saying the most experienced person should be in charge."

"Where are we going?" Barnes changed the subject.

"Cheyenne Mountain," Roby said. He could see the first helicopter ahead of them, the red cargo netting holding the iso-tubes and other equipment hanging below. It was hard to believe there were living people inside of the dark tubes.

"Space Command?" Jackson was surprised Dalton would have picked that as the place to bring the iso-tubes.

"Not Space Command," Roby answered. "The west side of the mountain. We'll drop the load and go back for the sergeant major."

"Who the hell were those people?" Barnes wanted to know, but no one could answer that.

Jackson wanted to know what was on the west side of Cheyenne Mountain, but she figured she would see soon enough for herself.

Dalton checked the security monitor. A half dozen men dressed in black were slipping through the hole ripped in the vault door. He had no clue who they were, but their method of entry left no doubt that they would not be friendly when they reached the control center.

"How long before you can pull Kirtley?"

"Three minutes."

"Set the controls to refreeze. We have to leave him," Dalton said. "We don't have three minutes."

"We can't—"

"Do it," Dalton cut Hammond off. "It's his only chance."

Hammond quickly entered the commands, having Sybyl reverse the process.

"Where are your technicians?" Dalton asked.

"In their billets along the main corridor. I always clear the control room once people go over. Standard procedure, since I can run everything through Sybyl."

"How many?"

"Eight people."

Dalton saw it was too late for Hammond's support team. The main corridor was already half overrun. As he watched on the monitor, one of Hammond's white-coated techs stepped out of a door to be instantly cut down with a burst of automatic weapon fire.

Dalton turned to Hammond. "There has to be a main air shaft for this place. Something that comes out on the mountain other than the main entrance."

"I don't know," Hammond said.

Dalton knew they didn't have time to stand around and think. One of the tenets he'd learned early in his military career was that action, even the wrong one, was better than standing around in the kill zone, which is what he figured the control room was going to become in about a minute.

"Come on." He ran toward the service elevator. Hammond pulled a CD-ROM disk out of the mainframe before following.

The door slowly slid open when he hit the button.

"Sergeant Major and Dr. Hammond."

Dalton spun about in surprise at the familiar voice. Raisor's image was floating in the air behind them. Dalton didn't hesitate, pressing the Down button. The doors slid shut.

Raisor appeared inside. "Can't get rid of me that easily. You both should know that." He considered Hammond. "You cut me off."

"I ordered her to," Dalton cut in. "You disregarded the mission." He was watching the numbers click as the elevator descended.

"No, I was doing *my* mission. You have no idea what's going on here, do you?"

"I don't think you do either," Dalton answered. The elevator came to a halt. The doors opened. The cavern that had housed Sybyl III was in front of them. The generators still hummed, providing power to Sybyl IV. "You know who betrayed your sister, don't you?"

"McFairn," Raisor said.

Dalton laughed at the image floating in front of him, while his eyes darted about, searching. "Who's McFairn?"

"Deputy Director of the NSA."

The generators were diesel. There had to be an air duct bringing in fresh air for them and removing the exhaust. "McFairn is just a puppet. Your sister discovered something about HAARP. About the Priory. That's your real enemy. And my enemy too. Do you trust these people you are with? Do you know who *they* are? Who they work for?" Dalton asked as he walked toward the generators, Hammond close by his side.

"I don't have to trust them. They're giving me back my body. I know for sure I don't trust you," he added.

"Fine. I recommend you go back then and make sure everything's all right, because I left charges on all the tubes." He checked his watch. "Set to go off in two minutes. That will guarantee you never get back to your body, because it will be in a thousand pieces."

Raisor's image disappeared.

"Come on," Dalton was ripping off a panel on a large tube that ran behind the rows of generators, connected to each by several rubber hoses. He was greeted with the stench of diesel exhaust. The tube was three feet in diameter. A tight fit.

"Cut off the generators," he told Hammond.

She threw the master switch and a sudden silence filled the cavern. Then there was a hum as the rows of backup batteries kicked in power. Dalton stuck his head in. Utter darkness. "Let's go."

Raisor appeared in the room holding his sister's team and his own tube. Valika and her mercenaries were searching the operations center. He heard another burst of automatic weapons firing as he searched for the charges. Nothing.

The Russian poked her head through the door and saw him. "What do we need to take with us?"

Dalton had lied about the charges, he knew that now. Raisor would have laughed if he were capable of it. He had what he had come for. He pointed. "My sister's tube. And mine. And the master computer. I'll show you. And there are two people trying to escape in the generator room. You might want to go down there and stop them."

Valika ran toward the freight elevator, calling for several of the mercenaries to come with her. She ordered others to work with Raisor, who was now behind the command console.

"The power's been cut off," Raisor said. "We're running on backup batteries. You need to restart the generators."

Valika acknowledged that as the elevator doors shut.

She rode down to the lowest level. As soon as the door began opening, she jumped through, weapon at the ready. "Search," she ordered as she slowly made her way to the generators, weapon sweeping back and forth. She saw that the master switch was off. She flipped it back up and the room filled with the roar of the diesel engines.

"Here!" one of the merks yelled from behind the generators.

Valika ran around to where he was pointing. She coughed at the foul fumes that were pouring out of the removed panel. She knew exactly where the two Raisor had mentioned had gone. "Put the panel back on."

Dalton heard the sound of the generators starting. "Go!" he shoved Hammond not too gently on her derriere. He had no idea how far it was to the outlet. They were scrambling as quickly as they could, but it was difficult in the narrow tube.

He bumped into Hammond's rear as she suddenly halted.

"What's wrong?"

"Do you hear it?"

"Hear what?"

"There's something just ahead of us. Something running."

Dalton tried to hear over the roar of the generators reverberating up the tube. He caught the first whiff of exhaust fumes. She was right. A rhythmic sound ahead.

"A fan," Hammond said. "There's got to be a fan pulling the exhaust out. Jesus, I could have run right into it."

"We can't stay here."

"I don't know where the fan is," Hammond said. "I can't see a damn thing."

"We need to go forward." Dalton squeezed up against Hammond, trying to get by. Their bodies pressed tight together and he inched past her. Once past, he began moving. "Come on." He focused all his senses forward, keying on the sound of the fan, hearing it get closer, feeling the air moving on his cheeks getting stronger. As was the smell of the diesel exhaust.

Soon he knew they were close to the fan. The sound of it turning was louder than the generators, filling the tube. He could feel the backwash from it. A dozen feet away. Maybe more. He edged forward.

Stop.

For a second Dalton thought it was Hammond who had spoken.

Now.

He knew that voice better than any other, but it was inside his head. Marie. Dalton stopped.

A drop.

He reached forward with his hand. The floor of the tube abruptly ended less than a foot in front of him. Feeling about, Dalton realized the tube made a ninety-degree turn down. If he had continued, he'd have fallen in, to meet the fan, which he could now hear clearly just below.

Dalton pulled his pistol out and pointed it downward, hoping he was aiming for the center. He fired, shifting aim slightly each time he pulled the trigger. He heard several of the rounds hit metal. The seventh one did the trick, hitting the motor in the center of the fan. It stuttered to a halt.

Dalton could hear Hammond coughing. He felt lightheaded and very calm. He knew both were a bad sign. The lack of anxiety meant his mind was starting to shut down from the exhaust poisoning.

Reholstering his pistol, Dalton edged his feet over and

lowered himself until he came in contact with one of the blades of the fan. He tested his weight–it held. Of course, he had no idea how the drop was below the fan.

Slide.

"Come on," Dalton called to Hammond. He reached up. "Give me your hand."

He searched in the darkness and then finally felt her flesh. He gripped it and pulled her toward him, despite her screech of protest. He held her weight in his arms. "We have to slide between the blades."

" 'Slide'?" Hammond coughed. "Are you crazy? It's a straight drop, God knows how far."

"We'll be safe. I know."

There was no answer. Dalton shook Hammond and she stirred, muttering something. He lowered her between the blades and let go. Then he followed.

He dropped straight for about ten feet, then hit the side of the tube. As he slid he realized it was curving back to the horizontal. He put his arms and legs out, trying to slow down, afraid of slamming into Hammond whenever the tube reached the end.

Despite his efforts, he hit her hard, slamming her up against a grate. He felt fresh, cold air on his face.

Raisor had wanted to go back to his body before they left Bright Gate, but Valika denied him that option. She had seen the two Blackhawks leaving as they arrived and was sure some sort of alert had already been broadcast and reinforcements were most likely on their way. She had her mercenaries racing about, unhooking Sybyl and moving the two designated isolation tubes to the landing grate.

"What about the others?" she asked Raisor, indicating the tubes containing the rest of the other three teams.

"According to the computer, the only one who is still technically alive is him." Raisor pointed at Kirtley's tube.

"Do we need him?" Valika asked.

"No. And he'll be lost as soon as you finish unhooking ｅe computer."

She tucked the stock of the MP-5 in her shoulder and ｍed at the tube. She fired a sustained burst, shattering ｅe tube and freeing the freezing liquid. An alarm went off ｉd a yellow warning light began flashing. One of the anｌlary computer monitors flickered and came on. A man's ｃe appeared.

"Dr. Hammond." Kirtley's voice came out of the comｕter's speakers, his face appearing on the screen.

Raisor and Valika went to the screen.

"If you are seeing this," the man on the screen continｊd, "something has gone wrong and I am dead. I warned ｊｕ not to do anything. You should have taken me more ｒiously."

Valika looked from the screen to the body halfｊnging out of the tube she had just shot. "It's him," she ｊd, pointing. She had a very bad feeling about this, which ｊas immediately confirmed as the man on the screen conｊued talking.

"If this program is activated, it means that life signs ｊm my isolation tube have flat-lined—that you've killed ｅe. So in keeping with my warning, I will now kill you ｊd everyone else in the facility." The face on the screen ｊiled and his right hand appeared, holding a watch. ｊixty seconds. How does it feel to know you only have a ｊinute of life left?"

Valika didn't wait to see any more. "Bomb! Evacuate!" ｅe screamed at the mercenaries as she raced toward the ｊit. They dropped what they were doing and followed her.

Raisor didn't run. The tube containing his body was ｊ a cart near the door to the corridor abandoned. Along ｊth the Aura generator that was giving him what little ｊwer he had. He looked at the screen.

"Fifty seconds," Kirtley said. "I have to assume, though that is more time than you gave me when you did what ever it is you did to me."

Raisor reached out and flowed into the computer Perhaps whatever Kirtley had planned was being run by the computer and he could stop it. He raced along elec tronic pathways, searching.

"Forty seconds. I was recruited by the Priory. Do you know that?" Kirtley's voice echoed in the now empty con trol room, but inside the computer Raisor could still hea the words. He found the location of the recording, the followed the thread of data to a link with Sybyl's monitor ing program. Wrong way, Raisor realized with alarm—thi was the direction the alert had come to start the destruc program. He reversed direction.

"Thirty seconds."

On the grate, Valika jumped on board the Huey, grabbing a headset. "Lift," she ordered the pilot. "Now!" she added with emphasis.

The helicopter shuddered as the pilot increased power. The blades began turning faster, but they were sti on the grate. Valika knew it took time to gain enough blade speed to take off. She smacked the firewall in frustra tion at the blades turning overhead, willing them to go faster.

Raisor was back through the computer that Kirtley ha used to display his message, passing along a data line to the computer that ran Bright Gate's environmenta system.

"Twenty seconds."

Then Raisor "saw" it. Plastic explosive wired to each o the tanks holding the fuel for the generators. The detona

or switch on each wasn't electric—which he could have
manipulated—but rather an acid drip over which he had no
control.

"Ten seconds."

The Huey's skids lifted.

"Get us away from here as quickly as possible," Valika
told the pilot.

He responded by nosing over and dropping altitude
along the slope of the mountain to gain speed. Valika
turned and looked back, waiting.

The acid ate through, activating the detonators.

Raisor's essence was right next to the first of the fuel
tanks. He would have laughed if he had had a mouth to issue the sound.

All four tanks exploded, ripping through the levels of
Bright Gate.

Dalton staggered.

"What the hell was that?" Hammond cried out as she
fell to her knees.

The entire mountain trembled. Dalton could see the
night sky on the other side of the grate. His fingers scrambled around, trying to find a latch. He could hear something coming from behind them, like a freight train out of
control.

He gave up looking for a latch and threw his shoulder
into it, feeling the pain of his recent wound reopening. The
grate didn't give. He yelled and threw himself against it
once more, holding nothing back, feeling the shock of hitting the metal through every cell of his being, but it gave
way and he tumbled out, half expecting to go sliding down
the mountain out of control, but instead landing on a

ledge. He scrambled to his feet. The sound was getting closer. He grabbed Hammond, pulled her to his chest, then pressed against the side of the mountain, to the right of the opening.

A tongue of flame exploded out of the opening and into the night sky.

Chapter Eighteen

Searchlights highlighted the shuttle *Columbia* against the night sky at Vandenburg Air Force Base. The countdown was proceeding on schedule for a dawn launch. The shuttle was mated with the two solid rocket boosters and external fuel tank, putting the tip of the external tank 184.2 feet above the ground, while the base of the two external rockets reached the ground. The entire system weighed over four and a half million pounds.

"*T minus six hours zero zero minutes. Next planned hold is at T minus three hours. Tower crew perform ET and TPS ice, frost and debris evaluation. ET is ready for LOX and LH2 loading. Verify orbiter ready for LOX and LH2 loading.*"

The reason Vandenburg was the launch site instead of the more traditional Cape was the need to put the last MILSTAR satellite in a polar orbit. The Cape was used when a shuttle was to be put in an equatorial orbit, Vandenburg for polar insertions. The trajectory for *Columbia* was planned to be within twelve degrees of due north. The first mission once reaching orbit was to deploy the CS-MILSTAR satellite, thus making the system—and HAARP—operational worldwide.

The Blackhawks descended on the west side of Cheyenne Mountain, the opposite side from the well-known entrance to the underground complex that used to be called NORAD and now housed Space Command. Lieutenant

Jackson watched as sheer rock walls—spurs from the mountain's side—slid by on either side of the helicopter.

An infrared strobe light flickered below, the intermittent glow visible in the pilot's night vision goggles. A thirty-meter-wide expanse of smooth rock was nestled between the two spurs. Gently they touched down the sling load, punched the release, and then moved over and landed the chopper. Jackson slid the door open and hopped out. The landing zone was just big enough to handle the load and the helicopter, surrounded on two sides with rock. The open side led to a precipitous drop, as they were about a third of the way up the slope of Cheyenne Mountain. On the fourth, mountain, side, a pair of large doors were swung wide open.

"We need to go back for the sergeant major." Barnes had hold of Jackson's elbow and was pointing back toward the chopper.

Jackson had thought about it on the forty-minute ride here. "We have to get the iso-tubes stabilized first."

The first Blackhawk was lifting, leaving room for the second one to deposit its load. Jackson waited until the man with the strobe light succeeded in guiding the helicopter to the correct spot and it lifted off, before going over to him.

The stranger was dressed in jeans and a leather jacket over a T-shirt. He clicked off the strobe and stuck it in his pocket before extending his hand in greeting. "You must be Lieutenant Jackson."

"Yes. And you are?"

The man appeared to be in his mid-forties, with thinning dark hair. His face was thin and he looked tired. "You can call me Mentor."

He looked past her at the two sling loads. "We need to get those inside. One of the Blackhawks is going back to Fort Carson. The other will land here as soon as we clear

e LZ." He turned toward a flatbed electric truck. "You
n load that and we'll take it in."

They quickly loaded four of the iso-tubes and gear on
e bed, working in silence and as quickly as safety al-
wed.

"Get on," Mentor told them. With just a slight hum
e truck headed for the dark opening. "Welcome to the
anch."

" 'The Ranch'?" Jackson asked.

"No time for explanations now. All in due time."

They entered the tunnel and he stopped. The doors
vung shut on large hydraulic arms. Only then did red
ghts come, illuminating the interior without destroying
eir night vision. Mentor drove them down the tunnel.

cFairn's desk was covered with paper. Reports from the
entagon, intercepted messages, analysis summaries—all
e result of what had happened so far.

There was good news and there was bad news, which
emed to be the way it always was. The hostages were all
ead, but the rescue team from the *Roosevelt* had not suf-
red the same fate and had wiped out the cartel members
uarding the villa. Communication with Bright Gate had
en lost. The Ring was capable of retransmitting an Aura
irst via satellite, but the satellite had been destroyed.

She reached for *The Art of War*, to search for a passage
give her soul peace, when her secure private line rang.

"Yes?"

"I need the unlock code for the MILSTAR retransmit-
rs."

McFairn rubbed her hand across her eyes as she lis-
ned to Boreas's words. Nothing about the death of the
ostages, the loss of the Bright Gate team, or the loss of
byl and the isolation tubes. Or the Nexus murders.

"I can't do that."

"Can't or won't?"

"Both."

" 'Won't' is simply an unwise decision," Boreas said. " 'Can't' indicates a lack of effort."

"Eichen had Space Command place that code in the Defcon Four package," McFairn explained. "That means the only way it can be accessed is if the President alerts the military to Defcon Four, which is our highest alert standing. That has only happened twice before in the entire history of our country."

"I'm not asking you to get the President to go to Defcon Four," Boreas said. "I just want the code. You're in charge of the most powerful intelligence-gathering machine in the world. Surely you can get a code tucked away in a computer somewhere."

"You don't understand," McFairn said. "Space Command's computers are the most secure in the world, because they control both the communications nodes and authorizations for the use of nuclear weapons. It's an entirely separate system that the NSA helped establish."

"Then you can get into it."

"No, I can't. When we set it up, we made it tamperproof, even from us. After all," she added, "we never saw that there would be a need for the NSA to break into Space Command's computer."

"I'm very disappointed in your attitude," Boreas said. "I recommend you spend this evening thinking of a way to get the code. You don't have much time. I don't think I need to tell you that the results will be most dire if you don't comply."

Dalton had never been so grateful to see the stars. Hammond and he were on a small ledge, about two thirds of the way up the side of the Mount of the Holy Cross. He was missing his eyebrows, which had been singed off by

he explosion, but he was otherwise unhurt. He pulled the
ATPhone out and flipped it open, punching in one.

After the third buzz, it was answered.

"Yes?"

"Mentor?"

"Of course. Where are you? I have some people here
vho are most concerned about your welfare."

"Aren't you?"

"Of course."

"Right. I can feel it."

"There's no time for this. Where are you?"

Dalton gave Mentor his location.

"We'll be wheels up in five minutes," Mentor said, clos-
ng out the conversation.

Hammond, meanwhile, was sitting with her back to
he mountain. Her eyes had the "thousand-yard stare"
Dalton had seen before, a precursor to going into shock.
The diesel fumes combined with the surprise of the sudden assault and the subsequent explosion had taken its toll.
He knelt down next to her and took her hands. They were
ce-cold.

"You've got to hang in there," Dalton said. "The heli-
opter will be on its way soon."

"They just killed my people," Hammond said.
"Gunned them down like animals. Then they destroyed it."

"I know," Dalton said.

"Why?"

"I don't know." He took off his fatigue shirt and draped
t over her shoulders. He started talking, telling her about
ome of the places he'd been, trying to draw her mind
away from what she had just experienced.

Chapter Nineteen

Captain Lonsky turned on the light above his bunk and squinted, trying to make sense of the message Zenata had just woken him to read. He could feel the vibration of the *Gagarin*'s engines through the floor plates.

"Your glasses," Zenata reminded him.

He groped on the small shelf next to his bunk and retrieved his reading glasses, slipping them on.

"I have received a set of instructions," Zenata said.

"Reference?"

"Changing the antenna dish arrays. Modifying them I've already got my people working on it."

"What kind of modifications?"

"Rather interesting," Zenata said. "Adapting the two main dishes to transmit on different bandwidths at very high power."

"Why would someone want to do that?" Lonsky yawned. "There is no one listening on those bandwidths."

"I don't know. It's most strange."

Lonsky turned the light off. "I am going to get some sleep. Wake me when our owner contacts us again."

"Who were they?" Dalton demanded as soon as he put the headset on. "The Priory? It doesn't make sense that they would attack Bright Gate. And why destroy it?"

Mentor reached up and flicked the controls for the in-

ercom, insuring that only Dalton could hear him. "The
'riory has an enemy."

"Besides Nexus?"

"Yes."

Hammond was collapsed next to Dalton, no headset,
ier eyes closed. The Blackhawk was racing away from the
idge where it had picked the two of them up. Dalton
vaited, then finally tapped Mentor on the arm. "Some
nore information would be helpful."

Mentor leaned back against the web seating. "We don't
eally have a current name for this enemy. If the Priory op-
rates in the shadows, then this group operates in the
•itch black."

"The Droza," Dalton said.

That caught Mentor's attention. "Where did you hear
•f them?"

"Never mind where I heard of them. Are they the
'riory's enemy?"

"Not exactly. That's where the Priory came from. And
his enemy."

"And Gypsies—the Roma?" Dalton added.

"Yes."

"Who is the enemy?"

"Because we've never met one, or even talked to any-
•ne who has met one of this group, we had to take the
'riory's name for their enemy. Mithrans."

"Mithrans," Dalton repeated.

"Most people associate the name Mithras with the pa-
an Roman sun god, but it actually predates Rome. The
Romans picked up Mithraism in the second century A.D. via
heir army's conquests of areas where it still thrived. Mithras
vas originally an Indo-European god way back around the
fteenth century B.C. And we've learned that Mithra actually
ven goes back before then. Have you ever heard of Kali?"

The words stirred some vague memories in Dalton. "A statue with a lot of arms? India?"

"Kali is most commonly known as the primordia Mother Goddess of Hinduism. But the same name, or der ivation of it, goes far beyond India. In prehistoric Ireland people worshipped a goddess known as Kelle. Ancien Finland has an all-powerful goddess named Kal-ma. I Greece there was Kalli. In the Sinai there was a goddes named Kalu. I think the similar names in very dissimila languages makes it more than just a coincidence."

"So the Priory's enemy is a goddess?"

"The Mithrans are undoubtedly matriarchal," Mento said. "While the Priory is patriarchal."

"Lieutenant Jackson thinks the Mithrans exist on th virtual plane," Dalton said. He could see the glow o Colorado Springs behind Cheyenne Mountain, a large dar bulk directly ahead of them. Pikes Peak was off to the left.

"That may well be," Mentor said. "It would explai why we've never met one."

"Maybe you have met one and you just don't know it, Dalton said.

"That is also possible," he allowed.

"This Ring is just a front for the Mithrans then, cor rect?"

"Yes. But we don't think the members of the Rin know that they are being used."

"How can that be?"

"We don't even know exactly what a Mithran is, Mentor said, "so I can't tell you how they operate. Bu while the Priory pulls strings through their various agents I think the Mithrans are less direct in getting others t work for them. I think they subtly affect people's mind and make their victims think the goals they are after ar their own, when in reality, they are the Mithrans' goals."

Dalton considered that as they flew over the moun

ains: two ancient enemies going at each in a very modern
ay. And he and his people were caught in the middle.

"What is this place?" Dalton asked as the Blackhawk
escended down the western side of mountain.

"Remember Eichen told you about what happened to
K?"

What Dalton remembered was that Eichen had hinted
ut not explicitly said the Priory was behind the assassina-
on, but he simply nodded.

Mentor continued. "President Johnson, upon being
riefed about Nexus and the fate of his predecessor being
ost likely at the instigation of the Priory, decided he
eeded a secure location for Nexus to headquarter itself
nd for him to retreat to if the proverbial manure hit the
n. He had to assume, as our Nexus advisers did, that Blue
Mountain in West Virginia, the alternate White House,
as compromised by the Priory. There is a Nexus com-
and and control center hidden under the Pentagon, but
was felt that was also probably known to the Priory"–
Mentor gave a bitter grimace–"which was borne out not
ong ago. The only way to insure he had a place not
nown to the Priory was to build something under the su-
ervision of Nexus.

"He authorized the extra millions to build an adjunct,
ighly classified, smaller facility next to the NORAD base.
was the logical place for such a facility, as we could eas-
y tap into one of the underground, secure communica-
ons tunnels that connected the larger base with the
utside world, and thus be able to communicate and be
ooked into NORAD."

The chopper was just about to touch down on the
mall landing pad. Dalton could see Jackson waiting for
nem, hand raised to protect her eyes against the blade
ownwash. She was seated in what appeared to be a golf
art.

"The Ranch, which is what Johnson christened it, over two miles away from the main NORAD and Spac Command complex. Besides communications, we tap int them for power, water, and sewage. There's enough foo stocked in the Ranch to keep a group of a dozen going fo a year. It's been running since NORAD was establishe and no one has ever noticed the power or water drain be cause it's never changed since the first day NORAI began."

The wheels touched down.

"Have you told Barnes and Jackson about Nexus yet Dalton asked.

"No. They've been busy setting up the isolation tubes

As Mentor reached for the handle to slide the doc open, Dalton halted him. "Are you going to tell them?"

"That's not my decision." Mentor opened the door an Dalton and Hammond followed him out. As soon as the were clear, the Blackhawk lifted. Within a minute, silenc reigned.

Jackson greeted Dalton with a smile. "Good to see yc again."

Dalton smiled. "I think we've broken you for the mil tary." He took Hammond's arm and helped her into th front passenger seat, before hopping in the back wit Mentor. Jackson drove them through the tunnel door which swung shut behind them. Red lights came on ove head.

"The Ranch is a quarter mile ahead," Mentor said. "I the old days, that was thought deep enough to survive direct nuke hit on the mountain. Nowadays, we know pr cision strategic nuclear weapons could take out Spac Command and in the process probably destroy the Ranc also."

"Do you live here?" Dalton asked as they came to second set of large steel doors.

"The Ranch was left unoccupied since 1966. It was thought that was the best way to keep it safe."

"Why open it now?" Dalton asked. "Because we needed to relocate Bright Gate?"

"I was here when you called," Mentor said. "As soon as I realized we had been compromised in Washington, I moved here and opened the facility up."

They were in a cavern about two hundred meters in circumference with a ceiling forty feet high. Four steel buildings were directly in front of them. The walls of the cavern were lined with thousands of crates, which Dalton had to assume held supplies.

Mentor pointed at the buildings one by one. "Billets and galley. Communications and science center. President's quarters, which we've stripped out and placed the isolation tubes in. War room with direct links to the operations center in Space Command. Everything they see on their displays we can see in there."

Dalton helped Hammond out of the cart. "Why were you here when I called?" he asked Mentor.

"Because I'm all that's left of Nexus in the United States. Everyone else is dead."

"Who's doing the killing?" Dalton asked.

"The Priory."

"What about the Ring?" Dalton asked.

"I'm not sure what they're up to."

"How did the Ring destroy the last Psychic Warrior team that went to Colombia?"

"The woman who basically started Bright Gate and HAARP now works for the Ring. They've developed a virtual plane projector called Aura. We're not sure where it's located."

"So both sides are working on the same type of weapon?"

"We're not sure the Mithrans are designing Aura

specifically to be a weapon," Mentor said. "They might be developing it to do the opposite of Bright Gate—if they exist on the virtual plane, they might be developing Aura so that they can come into the real plane. Using it as a weapon is just a by-product."

Dalton considered that. "So both sides are doing the same thing so they can go to the other side's plane and fight them?"

Mentor nodded. "As near as I can tell, that's what appears to be happening. If the Priory can uplink to MILSTAR and transmit on the virtual plane, they can target the Mithrans. And they can target the entire human race. If the Mithrans can use Aura to come out of the virtual and have real form, they can directly attack the Priory. And, in turn, the entire human race. So the war might be between the two groups, but the collateral damage will most likely be the destruction of life as we know it."

Chapter Twenty

Valika bid farewell to Gregory, knowing that she would never see him again. She expected he would be on some South Seas island within a couple of days with a new identity, along with the rest of his mercenaries.

As the Lear lifted off the runway at Granby, she was considering whether the mission had really been a failure. She was glad that they hadn't recovered the Bright Gate equipment and that Raisor was gone. She wasn't certain he liked the direction things were moving in. Psychic Warriors, being able to appear anywhere out of the virtual plane and take action—she had a feeling that might make her and her unique skills obsolete. It was best to be done with it all.

On a more professional level, she also hadn't trusted Raisor. She wondered if he was really gone, or if he was able to survive on the virtual plane without his body. It was a question she would have to ask Souris. From her own experience she knew that once someone betrayed what they had sworn obedience and fealty to, the second betrayal would be much easier.

A helicopter. Now? At night?" Lonsky rubbed the sleep out of his eyes.

"I've got the crew clearing the pad," Zenata said. "It's due in five minutes."

Lonsky stood, his uniform wrinkled. "Do you have i
on radar?"

"Not yet. It might be flying low, near the waves."

Lonsky's cabin was just behind the bridge, so it onl·
took them a few seconds to make it there. He went lefi
out onto the wing, which gave him a view toward the rea
of the ship. He couldn't see the landing pad, but he coul·
see the glow, which meant the landing lights were on.

"I wonder what the proper etiquette is," he said t·
Zenata. "Should a captain go greet his new owner, o·
should the new owner come to the captain on his bridge
How does it work?"

"I would say it would depend on what kind of impres
sion you want to make," Zenata said.

"We have an inbound helicopter on radar," one of th·
crew announced. "ETA two minutes."

Lonsky looked toward the bow. They could see th·
red and green running lights of the aircraft as it ap
proached. It flew by quickly on the port side, then swun
around and disappeared as it landed on the aft deck.

"I think I will meet halfway," Lonsky said.

"A smart choice," said Zenata.

"You have the bridge." Lonsky grabbed the handrail
for the ladder that led down to the main deck and swun
onto it. He headed along the side of the ship, the massiv
radar dishes looming above him, blocking out the star·
He saw one of his crewmen approaching leading anothe·
figure. Lonsky stopped and waited.

He was surprised to see that the stranger was ·
woman. He was further disconcerted when she steppe·
into the light of one of the portholes. Her head was shave·
and there were strange marks on it.

"Captain Lonsky, at your service," he said in English, ·
that was the language the messages had been transmitted i·

The woman paused and looked at him as if he were i·

her way. "Captain," she said. "My name is Souris, Professor Souris. I was sent here to make sure you are ready to receive our equipment. Who is your senior scientist?"

"Tanya Zenata is my—"

"Take me to her. Now."

Dalton forced Hammond to check everything, making sure the isolation tubes were stable and that Sybyl was properly hooked up. She was slowly coming out of her funk, and these definitive actions were helping. While she, Jackson, and Barnes were doing the checks in the presidential building, Dalton was with Mentor in the operations center building.

"Whose decision is it to bring them in on it?" Dalton asked Mentor, getting back to what he had asked him at the landing zone. "If you're all that's left of Nexus, isn't it your decision?"

"I'm all that's left of Nexus in the United States," Mentor said. "There are other cells overseas."

"But right now, this is an American problem," Dalton noted.

"It's a worldwide problem," Mentor disagreed.

"Originating here in the States."

The conversation was interrupted by the entrance of Hammond, who had just finished running a diagnostic on Sybyl. She was holding up the CD-ROM she had taken from the computer at Bright Gate. Barnes and Jackson entered behind her.

"Before we were forced to leave Bright Gate, I found something in Sybyl," Hammond announced. "About the first Psychic Warrior team."

That drew the attention of Mentor, as well as Dalton, Jackson, and Barnes. She put the CD into one of the computers in the ops center.

"What about it?" Dalton asked.

"There were ten people on it," Hammond said, looking at the monitor. "They spent time remote viewing first, then gradually ran tests with their avatars. All this happened close to Bright Gate. Then they conducted a mission. Professor Souris was the one running the operation back at Bright Gate."

Dalton glanced across at Jackson, then back to Hammond. "What kind of mission?"

"That it doesn't say. I only have what Sybyl tracked. The team went over to the virtual plane and then made several jumps. And then nothing. Everyone flat-lined."

"Where did they jump to?" Jackson asked.

"It doesn't say exactly yet. They were all together. Somewhere..." Hammond scrolled down. "Somewhere in Asia. China maybe. Or India. Wait a second. Okay. I've got their planned jump points. The last one they checked in at was Mount Everest. Right on top."

"Mount Everest?" Dalton considered that. "And then?"

"Then they made one more jump close by and they all disappeared."

"What happened to the bodies?" Jackson asked.

"Souris had them removed from the isolation tubes. As soon as she took them off of Sybyl's support, they all died. All signs of the team members were removed. She attempted to remove all material from Sybyl about the team. Did a pretty good job of it actually. It's taken me all this time just to learn this. And then she left the project and they brought Jenkins in, telling him the new team he was given was the first team."

"So what was that team looking for?" Barnes asked. "Any ideas?"

"Mount Everest." Jackson was thoughtful. "That's where the Droza were."

"And maybe still are," Dalton said. He faced Mentor. "Tell them."

Mentor hesitated.

"We are now Nexus," Dalton told him.

" 'Nexus'?" Jackson repeated.

"If you don't tell them, I will," Dalton said. "I'm not lying anymore."

"You're under orders," Mentor said. "You don't—"

"A piece of paper shown to me in the dark by a man who's dead now," Dalton cut him off. "I know for sure I swore an oath to defend this country, and right now I'm seeing a threat and I think my fellow soldiers here need to know what's going on in order to fight that threat."

"All right," Mentor snapped, his first display of emotion since Dalton had met him.

As he briefed Jackson, Barnes, and Hammond on what he had already told Dalton, the sergeant major tried to put the pieces together. When Mentor was done, Jackson was the first to speak.

"It all fits. The Priory and the Mithrans have been fighting for ages, but since each is on a different plane, it hasn't amounted to much."

"And now we've managed," Dalton said, "to break the barrier between the virtual and real with our technology. No wonder they're fighting over HAARP and Bright Gate and Aura."

Hammond was shaking her head. "My God. Do you realize what you just said? *Our* technology. It isn't our technology. It's technology we're making for them. For the Priory. They were behind Souris from the very beginning, weren't they?"

Mentor shrugged. "We don't know. We were late catching on to the significance of the work she was doing, and Bright Gate and HAARP were already established before she defected."

" 'Defected'?" Dalton snorted. "Don't you think the Mithrans recruited her? So they could have access to the same technology the Priory was using? The Priory invented Bright Gate and sent that first Psychic Warrior team to try to attack the Mithrans. They must still be located somewhere in the Himalayas. In Shangri-la, or Shambhala, whatever you want to call it," he added, glancing at Jackson.

"And the Priory lost," he continued. "The first Psychic Warrior team was wiped out. So the Priory cut its losses and its interest in Bright Gate, realizing Psychic Warriors couldn't defeat the Mithrans on their own plane, much like we couldn't stop Chyort on the psychic plane. So they shifted their emphasis to HAARP."

"But what good is HAARP?" Barnes asked.

Hammond answered. "If HAARP can uplink through MILSTAR and then transmit down worldwide, they can destroy everything—and everyone—on the psychic plane. And, most likely, everyone in the real plane who isn't shielded."

Barnes held up his hand, like a schoolchild. "I've got a question."

They all turned to him.

"Who's *our* enemy? The Priory? The Mithrans?"

That brought a moment of silence as they all considered the question.

"Maybe that's the wrong question," Dalton said. "I think we should consider *both* groups our enemy simply from the fact they ain't us and both sides seem to have no problem killing people when it suits their goals. It appears that both Aura and HAARP kill people when activated. If either goes worldwide through MILSTAR, the results will be devastating.

"I think right now we need to figure out who the most immediate threat is and focus on that."

"Let's deal with the Ring first," Jackson said. "They

killed those Special Forces men and our people at Bright
Gate. We can deal with HAARP and the Priory after that."

"The shuttle–" Mentor began but stopped.

"What about the shuttle?" Dalton asked.

"The *Columbia* is launching tonight with the last MIL-
STAR satellite on board. Once it deploys, MILSTAR will
be operational worldwide."

"And?" Dalton prompted.

"Eichen had a code built into the last satellite so that it
couldn't be used by HAARP."

"Then HAARP's not an immediate problem?" Dalton
asked.

"As long as they don't have the code."

"And where is it?"

Mentor pointed to the wall. "Next door in Space
Command. Secure inside the DefCon Four targeting and
launch authorization computer. No one can get into that
computer from the outside."

"Then it's safe for the time being," Dalton noted.
"Unless there's someone on the inside of Space Command
who has been corrupted by the Priory. I think we need to
destroy the code to insure that HAARP is never used."

"Unless," Jackson said, "you really believe the Mithrans
are our enemy also. In which case destroying the code de-
stroys our best weapon against them. If we fine-tune
HAARP, we might be able to target just the virtual plane."

Barnes sat down, exhausted. "Great. We're back to
square one. We don't have a clue who we're really fighting."

"We know where HAARP is located, right?" Dalton
asked.

Mentor nodded. "I have the location."

"And it's not going anywhere anytime soon, so I would
say it's not a priority target since they can't access

MILSTAR," Dalton continued. "But we don't know where the Ring is or where the Aura generator is located. I'd say Dr. Souris and the Ring are our priority right now. What do you have on the Ring?" he asked Mentor.

"They're led by a man called Cesar. The other main leaders of the drug cartels are members. Cesar's been very hard to locate. He hasn't been seen in public in almost ten years, which led us to speculate he is no longer in Colombia, but has relocated."

"But one of the other drug cartel leaders might well know where that is, right?" Dalton said.

"Right," Mentor confirmed.

Dalton looked at Hammond. "How long before you can send us over?"

"Everything's running," Hammond said. "As soon as you are ready."

"All right," Dalton said. "We're going to Colombia. It's time for some payback for the Special Forces team and for the people at Bright Gate." He turned to Mentor. "What do you have on this Ring organization?"

In reply, Mentor sat down at one of the computers. "We can access the Department of Defense secure Internet via that, tapping through Space Command." He logged on and quickly searched while the others gathered round.

"Not much," he finally said. He brought up a picture. "That's Hector Cesar, but as I said, no one knows where he is." He accessed another page. "That's Naldo, one of the inner circle. The DEA does have a location on him."

"I have an idea," Dalton said.

Souris was back on Saba after her initial visit to the ship and had immediately hooked into the computer, disappearing into her other world after telling Cesar it would take about six hours for the necessary modifications to be completed on the *Yuri Gagarin*. Cesar was supervising the movement of other equipment out of the command post and on the treacherous trip down the volcano to the airfield. He paused when Souris started and opened her eyes, returning to reality without having to be called.

"There is a problem," she announced.

"And that is?" Cesar asked.

"The retransmitters on the MILSTAR satellites have to be unlocked with a special code."

"Do you have the code?"

"No."

Cesar waited but when she said nothing, he asked the inevitable question: "Where is the code stored?"

"The American Space Command in Cheyenne Mountain. It's shielded on the virtual plane."

"How do you know this?"

Souris smiled. "There is a spy among the Americans."

"A spy? Who? Where?"

Souris didn't answer, closing her eyes to retreat back into her alternate world.

Cesar walked up to her and lightly slapped her on the cheek. Her eyes flashed open. "Can you get the code?"

"There might be a way."

Dawn was less than an hour off and the launch two hours past that. Spotlights illuminated *Columbia* on the launch pad, allowing the thousands of people who were gathering to watch to see it. A gantry stretched from the launch tower to the shuttle waiting for the crew to board shortly. Four bolts in the bottom of each of the solid rocket boosters secured the entire flight system to the launch platform.

The astronaut with the code name Eagle Six was already on board. He had checked the payload, insuring that the satellite was secure. After NASA's unbelievable mistakes with the various Mars probes, he left nothing to chance. Now he lay back in his launch seat, a set of headphones relaying to him the various communications come out of launch control:

"*T minus three hours. The count has resumed. Perform T-three-hours snapshot on flight critical and payload items. Initiate LOX transfer line chilldown. Verify SRB nozzle flex bearing and SRB nozzle temperature requirements. Activate LCC monitoring software. The next planned hold is at T minus two hours. Go for flight crew final prep and briefing.*"

Chapter Twenty-one

Cesar was waiting once more as the Lear set down on the airstrip, the sun just over the ocean to the east. Valika was tired. Not just physically but emotionally. Gunning down unarmed scientists wasn't what she had envisioned during her combat training years ago. Shooting a body suspended in solution didn't add to her positive feelings. On top of that was the failure to bring anything back from Colorado because she had acted in haste.

"Where is Raisor?" Cesar asked.

"I believe he is dead. His body is at least." Valika quickly summarized the action.

Cesar seemed satisfied. "So Psychic Warrior is no longer a potential threat, correct?"

"Yes, sir." Valika noted the helicopters waiting on the edge of the airfield. "What is happening?"

"We're getting ready to move."

"Where is Souris?"

"She just returned from the ship. I'm sending her on the jet to the United States."

"Why?"

"To get the unlock code for MILSTAR." He quickly explained.

"How did she find this out?" Valika asked.

"She said there was a spy among the Americans. When I asked her for more about this spy, she wouldn't say anything."

"I don't trust her," Valika said.

"We need her. Especially since we don't have Raisor."

"How long before we load the ship?"

"It arrives this evening. I want everything prepared by then."

"Do you have the code?" Boreas asked. He was seated at his desk, leaning back in his seat.

McFairn's voice echoed out of the speaker phone as she replied. "Bright Gate was destroyed. We believe by the Ring."

"Do you have the code?" Boreas got up and walked over to the outside window.

"No."

"Time is running out for you."

"I think time is running out for *you*," McFairn said. "The Ring must be very confident to take the battle to the United States. I lost all my people there, including Kirtley. People here in Washington are asking questions."

Boreas stood at the window staring out at the Wrangell Mountains, his hands clasped behind his back. "I know about Kirtley. I saw his transmission go off-line. But it's not important since we don't need Bright Gate anymore. What I do need is the unlock code."

"What exactly do you have planned?" McFairn asked. "You've assured me that our goals would be in common, but I don't see how getting you the unlock code for HAARP-MILSTAR is in my or my country's interest."

"Are you becoming patriotic now?"

"No, practical as always. What are we going to do about the Ring destroying Bright Gate?"

"The Ring won't be a problem," Boreas said. A vein throbbed in his temple and his hands twisted in fists behind his back.

"Why not?"

Boreas turned and stalked back to his desk. He leaned ver the speakerphone. "I don't have to explain myself to ou. You're nothing but a tool, do you understand? You're o concerned about your country—your country? That's een around for what? Two hundred and some years? A link of an eye in the time my people have existed.

"We have been at war for millennia. Can you conceive f that? And soon, very soon, the war will be over. So on't whine to me about your country. Get me the code!"

He slapped his hand down on the phone, cutting the onnection.

IcFairn stared at the now silent phone. There was only ne possible way she could get the code, and that was to o to Cheyenne Mountain. She picked up the phone and rdered a jet to be ready at Andrews Air Force Base.

She tucked her dog-eared copy of Sun Tzu in her vernight bag and walked out of her office.

'hey'd done the best they could setting up Sybyl III and ne rest of the equipment, but there were some things cking. One was the crane they had used to lift and lower eople into the tanks. Dalton, Jackson, and Barnes had to tack cartons of supplies next to their tanks and clamber p the makeshift platform. Then, making sure their lines reren't tangled, Hammond sealed their TACPAD helmets n each, one by one. Then they blindly eased themselves own into the ooze.

Dalton resigned himself to the discomfort as the tube lithered down his throat and filled his lungs with liquid. Iis diaphragm fought and lost the battle as his body was lowly chilled. The white dot appeared and he focused on . Soon he had assumed his basic avatar and was standing n the virtual world as Barnes and Jackson appeared.

Dalton was ready for action. "Jump," he ordered and he

visualized their next point. They were at the ambush site i
Colombia. Their target was a compound twenty mile
down the road. They proceeded there by the process c
jumping along the road, staying in the virtual plane hig
above it, using it for guidance. The intelligence that Mento
had given them indicated the villa was home to one of th
inner members of the Ring, a man named Naldo.

Dalton halted directly above the house in the center c
the walled compound. Jackson and Barnes flanked him.

"Dr. Hammond?" Dalton projected the message back t
the Ranch.

"I'm here."

"Were you able to do what I asked?"

"Yes. Sybyl's programmed. You should be able to access it."

Dalton checked the data stream. *"All right, I see it."*

He heard Jackson's voice. *"We'll find him. You wait her*

Before Dalton had a chance to agree, both Barnes an
Jackson were gone, jumping down inside the building
While they were gone, he accessed the new program h
had asked Hammond to construct.

Jackson popped into the virtual plane next to him
"Geez. If you weren't floating here, I wouldn't know it was you

"Looks good?" Dalton asked.

"Spitting image."

"Did you find Naldo?"

*"This way. Barnes is waiting for us, keeping an eye on hin
He's in his office. Alone."*

Dalton followed as Jackson swooped down on th
building. He passed through the roof right behind he
They dropped through a room, through the floor, and int
a room paneled with expensive wood. An old man sat be
hind a large desk—Naldo. Dalton saw Barnes's avatar i
the corner of the room.

"I'll come through the door," Dalton said.

"All right. I'll wait here," Jackson replied.

Dalton passed through the door to the office, then stopped on the other side. He was in an empty corridor. He began forming on the real plane, his avatar gaining substance, using the power from Sybyl.

When he was completely in the real plane, he turned around and opened the door and stepped through.

Naldo looked up and surprise raced across his face as he jumped to his feet. "Cesar! What are you doing here? When did you arrive? Why didn't my guards let me know?"

The only thing Dalton wasn't sure about was the voice, but they had accessed an NSA interception of Cesar on the radio and Hammond had programmed that into the avatar as well as the appearance.

"I wanted to talk to you alone," Dalton said, impressed with the accent and flawless Spanish. He walked across the room and sat down on the other side of the desk. Through the link with Sybyl, he knew that Barnes and Jackson were still in the room, although now that he was completely on the real plane he could not see into the virtual.

Naldo slowly sat. "It has been a long time since you have honored me with a visit."

"The situation is becoming critical," Dalton said.

Naldo nodded. "Have you been thinking about what we talked about last?"

"I have," Dalton said, having no clue what the old man was referring to.

"I do not think we should anger the Americans further," Naldo said. "I have talked to the others and they agree."

"Why did they not come to me themselves?" Dalton asked.

Naldo frowned. "They just left the island two days ago. I told you that is what they were thinking. Are you all right? You do not look well."

"I have to get back to the island soon," Dalton said, picking up the cue. "Why don't you come with me?"

"I just left there," Naldo said. He cocked his head. "Is everything all right? Has that American gone loco on you?"

"Souris is all right," Dalton said. "I left her on the island."

"And the ship?"

Ship? Dalton thought. "As planned."

"That was a lot of money."

"It was worth it."

"It wasn't our money anyway." Naldo leaned back in his chair and steepled his fingers. "So what did you want to see me about?"

"I've been thinking about the island," Dalton said.

"Saba?"

Jackson's voice was immediately inside Dalton's. *"Saba Island. In the Lesser Antilles."* An image relayed from Sybyl also appeared. A small volcanic island resting in a deep blue sea.

Dalton stood. "I am sorry. Things are uncertain. I should not have come."

Naldo also stood, confused. "What is wrong?"

Dalton couldn't have Naldo checking on things or perhaps giving Cesar a call and finding out he'd been duped. He also remembered the bodies of the Special Forces men hung in the meat locker at the other villa.

He accessed his original avatar program. Naldo's eyes widened as the figure in front of him changed from Cesar to that of a featureless, white-skinned form. Dalton's left arm flowed into a power tube and he aimed.

"Who are you?" Naldo was fumbling for a gun.

"What ship?" Dalton demanded.

Naldo fired but Dalton was a step ahead, re-forming behind the old man. "What ship?"

Naldo's face was red, his breathing labored as he
turned, trying to bring the gun to bear. Dalton grabbed it,
ripping it out of the old man's hand. Naldo staggered back,
hit his desk, then fell to his knees, hands grabbing his
chest. He fell over on his side.

"Damn," Dalton muttered as he knelt next to the old
man. He checked the pulse. Nothing. Dalton stood.

"Let's go," he ordered as he slipped from the real to the
virtual.

"Where to?" Jackson asked.

"Saba."

"I thought we were going to adjust the frequencies to affect only the virtual plane," Dr. Woods, the man in charge
of the HAARP machinery, said. He had the latest data
from HAARP in his hands and he spread it out on the
desk in front of his supervisor. "This is the same frequency
we used to kill those people on the helicopter. We can't
transmit that via MILSTAR."

"There isn't time to tinker with it," Boreas lied.

"But this will kill people unless they're shielded,"
Woods argued. "And you want it broadcast from all four
satellites at once through CS-MILSTAR. I thought we
were going to localize the transmission."

Boreas considered the man in front of him. The members of the HAARP team had been recruited with suitcases full of cash. Some of them thought they were
working for the CIA, others had different ideas, but none
knew the truth. The objective of the project was clearly a
weapon, but like most people who worked on such projects, they had not really considered the ultimate aim of
such a weapon.

"The broadcast will indeed go worldwide," Boreas
said.

"But this frequency." Woods shook his head. "I can't—"

He paused, looking down on the small hole in his ches
just to the left of his sternum.

A small puff of smoke was wafting out of the silence
of the .22 High Standard pistol in Boreas's hand.

"You—" Woods fell forward and hit the floor with
solid thump.

Two jets were headed toward Colorado Springs, one fly
ing west from Andrews Air Force Base, the other nortl
west from the Caribbean.

On board each, a woman plotted how she would ge
access to a code locked in the most secure place in th
country. One had an Aura transmitter with her, the other
copy of *The Art of War.*

Eagle Six, the only name by which he was known to th
NASA people, watched the crew walk toward the gantry
waving at the TV cameras. Even though shuttle launche
were pretty much routine, there was always media o
hand. After all, they might get lucky and have anothe
Challenger. Eagle Six's predecessor had been on that fligl
and his name withheld from the public in the ensuing ir
quiry into the disaster.

This was his eighth shuttle launch and he knew th
math. No system was foolproof and there were so man
subsystems in the shuttle that failure was bound to occu
again. He could also get run over by a bus when crossin
the street, and that didn't pay as well as this gig. Eac
flight he took earned him half a million dollars, and he fig
ured this one to be his last. He could retire and easily liv
off the interest, plus he would be taken care of by th
Priory.

The crew came on board, pointedly ignoring him. H
was used to it. They thought he was a spook, from th

CIA or the military, and had been briefed to only interact with him on mission requirements.

He checked the readout on one of the monitors. Two hours to shuttle launch and all systems were go.

From the virtual plane, Dalton was able to safely detect the island's defenses. The guards all about, the hidden snipers, the mines along the shore, all were essentially worthless against a Psychic Warrior. He, Jackson, and Barnes bypassed these defenses and jumped to a spot directly above the large house that dominated the eastern slope of the volcano.

Valika was walking through the operations center, making sure nothing was left that they needed, when the hair on the back of her neck tingled. She paused, looking about for the cause of her alarm. She could almost hear a voice in her head whispering *Danger.* She drew her pistol and keyed the transmit button on the radio clipped to her belt.

"Anyone see anything?"

The reports from the various guard posts came back negative, but that didn't make her feel any better. She went to her small room and unlatched one of the suitcases she'd bought from Kraskov. Clipping a half dozen of the "beer cans" to her belt, she began searching the villa.

Dalton found Cesar in the atrium seated at a table near the pool.

"I've got him," he informed Jackson and Barnes through Sybyl. *"Any sign of Souris?"*

"Negative," Jackson replied.

"I'm in some sort of control center," Barnes reported, *"but no sign of her."*

"Home in on my position," Dalton ordered.

In a second both were next to him on the virtual plane, hovering over the atrium, looking down on the man who had killed their comrades.

"Cover me on the real plane," Dalton ordered. He shifted, passing the thin line that separated the real from the virtual, taking form on the other side of the table from the cartel leader.

Cesar was startled but quickly regained his composure as Dalton began to appear. Dalton continued to take shape until he approximated his normal appearance.

"Who are you?" Cesar demanded.

Dalton could see Jackson and Barnes appear, one on either flank, their right arms ending in firing tubes. Cesar noted them too and for the first time seemed concerned.

"Who are you?" he repeated.

"Why did you destroy Bright Gate?" Dalton asked, using Cesar's own voice.

"What?"

Dalton shifted form once more, this time taking Cesar's appearance.

"Who the hell are you?" Cesar shoved his chair back. "What are you doing?"

"Stay seated," Dalton said. "Why did you destroy Bright Gate?"

"I didn't," Cesar said. "The place was booby-trapped."

That made sense to Dalton as he remembered Hammond relaying that Kirtley had warned her he had a contingency plan in case he was killed. It didn't matter— Cesar's attack had initiated that event.

"Do you know who you work for?" Dalton asked.

"I work for me."

Dalton shook his head. "You're being manipulated." He sat down across from Cesar, a mirror image. "Where is Professor Souris?"

"Company," Barnes yelled.

A woman entered the courtyard, pistol at the ready. She took in Barnes and Jackson, their right arms ending in tubes, then blinked at the two Cesars seated at the table.

"Valika!" Cesar cried with Dalton barely a second behind, saying the same thing.

"Kill him," Dalton pointed across the table.

"No!" Cesar cried out. He jabbed his finger back at Dalton. "Shoot him. He's one of those things."

The pistol in Valika's hand shifted back and forth between the two of them. Barnes and Jackson were still, waiting to see how Dalton was going to play this out.

A pair of guards burst through a doorway and began firing at Jackson, who jumped, re-formed, and fired, hitting one of them. Barnes took out the other one. Valika took advantage of the distraction to grab one of the "beer cans" off her belt and pull the pin. She tossed it right at the table. Dalton saw it land and was surprised that she would risk killing her own boss.

Then it exploded.

"I've got major power disruption!" Hammond yelled as the screen that showed the status of the three Psychic Warriors went crazy and then blacked out. Her fingers slammed into keys as she tried to regain contact. "I've lost them."

The effect on the real plane was negligible. A simple pop, no larger than that of a firecracker. On the virtual plane it was another story.

The electromagnetic burst hit Dalton's avatar like a searing hot wind, blowing away the form in bits and chunks of energy. He felt no pain, just shock, his psyche blown back with the avatar.

Then there was only grayness, no form, no substance. He reached for the connection with Sybyl, but there was nothing.

Chapter Twenty-two

The three main engines on the shuttle ignited, spewing
flame, drawing their fuel from the external tank. Inside
Eagle Six experienced the familiar feeling as the entire
craft shook with restrained power, the entire system still
bolted to the launch platform by eight hold-down bolts at
the bottom of the two solid rocket boosters. The roar in
creased as the SRBs ignited. A split second later small ex
plosives cut the bolts and the shuttle began lifting off the
launch platform.

Eagle Six was slammed back in his couch as the shut
tle accelerated. Sixty seconds after liftoff the pressure
reached its maximum, then began to recede. One hundred
and twenty seconds into the flight, the two SRBs had used
all their fuel and detached, falling back toward the ocean
for recovery.

For six more minutes the shuttle's engines continued
to fire, pushing them up, before finally shutting down. The
external tank was jettisoned and the orbiter was finally in
its basic configuration. There was another burst from the
maneuvering thrusters to thrust them into the designated
orbit.

Eagle Six unbuckled from his chair and stood. He
keyed the intercom. "Begin preparation for EVA in"—he
checked his computer screen that held the mission pro
file—"three hours and forty minutes."

Vhat happened to them?" Cesar had finished screaming
his security detail. Even though he knew there was
othing they could have done to stop the intruders, it
ade him feel better. There was no sign of the three in-
iders—they'd simply vanished when the strange grenade
ılika had thrown had popped. Cesar had felt nothing, al-
ough he'd had a moment of doubt when he saw it land
ıder the table.

"The grenade exploded on the plane they travel on,"
ılika said. "I don't know if it killed them, because that
asn't really them."

That didn't make sense to Cesar, but he was thankful
onetheless. "Who do you think they were? I thought
ight Gate was destroyed."

Valika had been thinking about exactly that question
hile Cesar ranted at his guards. "Somebody might have
caped from Bright Gate."

"But don't they need equipment? Like Souris does?"

"I don't know," she said. She remembered the helicop-
rs they had spotted departing the Bright Gate site and
ld Cesar about them.

"We leave here now," Cesar ordered. "We'll meet the
ip on its way here."

ven in his cell in the Hanoi Hilton on the darkest and
·eariest of days, after being tortured, Dalton had never
iown such despair and isolation as he felt now. He didn't
·en have the pain from his body to let him know he was
ive. He had consciousness, barely, but for all he knew, he
ight indeed be dead. This might be what happened
hen a person died, disconnected from their body.

He saw nothing but featureless gray all around. He felt
othing, heard nothing. There was no link to Sybyl, no in-
cation of Barnes or Jackson.

He had no mouth to speak with. He had no idea if he

was still in the virtual plane near Saba, or if the explosio
had sent him elsewhere.

A part of him simply wanted to let go. He was sur
that if he gave up the tight grip he had on his thoughts, h
would simply fade away into nothingness. He remem
bered the pilot who had been brought to the cell next t
his, beaten half to death by villagers, stunned by the sud
den change from living on board an aircraft carrier to th
hell of the POW prison. Dalton remembered how he ha
held the pilot's hand all night long, to let him know h
wasn't alone.

And the pilot had died the next day, more of despa
than of his wounds.

Dalton held on to the core of his being ever tighter. H
had made a promise to himself then and he wasn't abou
to give up now. He had promised that day that he woul
never let go of life like that.

He wasn't certain he *was* alive, he realized. But he ha
feelings and that was enough.

"Are they alive?" Mentor asked, staring at the three bodie
suspended in their isolation tubes. The machines contir
ued to function, slowly sending breathing fluid to them.

"The bodies are," Dr. Hammond said. "But we've los
contact with the psyches."

"What happened?"

"I don't know. Sybyl recorded a surge on the virtua
plane. What caused it is anyone's guess."

"Can you bring them back?"

"Not without a connection," Hammond said. "They'r
like the other bodies, the ones we rescued. Still alive bu
no one home."

Mentor slapped his hand on the top of the compute
"Goddamn it!"

"I'll keep trying," Hammond said.

inda McFairn had never liked enclosed spaces. The mas-
ve opening on the side of Cheyenne Mountain that led
own to Space Command wouldn't be considered small,
it it was enclosed, especially as the car taking her passed
y the huge steel door that would be closed if the site were
ver attacked. She clutched her briefcase tighter as the car
escended further into the mountain.

Ostensibly she was here on an unannounced inspec-
on. Given that Space Command was one of the nerve
enters for national defense, the Deputy Director of the
SA doing such a thing was not unprecedented.

A one-star general was waiting for her just outside the
ner door where the car came to a halt. He opened the
oor before she had a chance to reach for it.

"Welcome to Space Command, Deputy Director
IcFairn. I'm General Mitchell."

McFairn shook the offered hand. "General."

He indicated they head through the large inner door.
Vhat can I do for you?"

McFairn hesitated for just a second; whether her hesi-
tion was from going into the complex or the task she
ad to perform, she wasn't sure, and she quickly hustled
ter the general.

"Given all the flap over the loss of secrets from Los
lamos," she said, "I'm making these inspections to check
ternal security of computer systems. I need access to one
'the terminals that connects to your mainframe."

"Certainly."

ouris was peering out the side of the helicopter that
esar had arranged to pick her up at the Colorado Springs
rport, where the Lear had landed. They had flown
ound Cheyenne Mountain and were now hovering over
e west side of the mountain. She was seated in the front

right seat, the pilot in the front left. The aura transmitte
took up the entire back of the helicopter along with th
batteries to give it power.

She closed her eyes briefly, remembering the imag
she had been sent, then opened them. "There." Sh
pointed at a narrow gap between two rock spurs. "Closer,
she ordered the pilot.

As he edged in toward the mountain, she reached be
hind her and drew out the leads and began placing then
on her head, the movements habit. The pilot glanced a
her quizzically but said nothing. He had flown numerou
flights initiated by a thick envelope of cash and knew bet
ter than to open his mouth.

"Hold here," Souris finally said when they were abou
fifty meters from the opening.

She closed her eyes, then flipped on the transmitter.

Immediately she could sense the psychic shield insid
the mountain guarding Space Command. But that wasn
her objective. She passed out of her body, her mind float
ing down on the psychic plane.

McFairn flipped open her metal briefcase. She was i
General Mitchell's own office, the door locked shut. Sh
always appreciated the military mindset where rank wa
all that mattered. As a GS-16 she technically outranke
the general and he was quite aware of that.

It was impossible to hack into the computers i
Cheyenne Mountain from the outside, but doing it fror
the inside was another matter. She connected leads fror
the computer inside the briefcase to the general's termina
Even with access to the mainframe, she didn't have th
code to enter the part of the master computer that store
National Command Authority codes. But because th
NSA had devised the "lock" it also had a way to inver
a key.

She knew the unlock code, like all other NCA codes, ᴄhanged constantly on a rotating basis that was also part ᴏf the code. Thus, to break in, she would have to find both ᴛhe base code and change code, and then combine them.

McFairn's computer had a sniffer program and found ᴛhe "door" and then began running through thousands of ᴄode combinations per second, looking for the right one. ᴀll she could do was sit back and wait.

ᴓouris found Sybyl without much trouble, the computer ᴦiving off a strong signal on the virtual plane as Dr. ᴴammond searched to contact the lost team members. ᴓince the Ranch wasn't shielded, Souris was able to slide ᴉnto it on the virtual plane and into Sybyl unnoticed. Since ᴓybyl had been hooked to the power line from Cheyenne ᴍountain, it was the one weak point in the virtual shield ᴛhat surrounded the base.

Souris followed the power line into the complex and ᴛhen into Space Command's mainframe. The "door" ᴃlocking the way into the code section was easy to find, ᴀnd she began to weave her way through the electronic ᴌogjam.

Then she noticed the program running through comᴃinations also trying to get through.

ᴉt took six combinations to get through the door, and the ᴄomputer had five. McFairn edged forward on the seat, ᴡaiting for the last one to be decoded.

ᴓouris was in. It didn't take her long to figure out the unᴌock code.

A second later the sniffer program broke through and ᴀnd it also.

Souris had no idea who was running the program, but ᴓhe reacted anyway. On the way out of Space Command's

computer, she triggered the emergency alert, putting th
base on DefCon Four footing.

McFairn has just pulled out the disk with the unlock coc
when an alarm stridently sounded. For a second sh
thought she'd been caught, and then she realized wh:
was happening. DefCon Four had been triggered. She r:
to the door and down the corridor.

The massive blast door was swinging shut, locking h
inside.

Souris had found manipulating the mainframe from insic
exhilarating. As soon as the base was secure, she disable
the program to allow it to stand down from the ale
footing. Then she disabled the secure communicatio
trunk line on her way out, completely cutting off Spa
Command from the rest of the world.

The cool breeze on his cheek. Dalton focused on remen
bering that feeling from the moment he had scattere
Marie's ashes.

He felt it again. The gray gave way slightly with
tinge of red. Then it was gone.

Dalton concentrated. There was something, someo
close by. He felt the breeze once more. He reached o
to it.

"I've got something," Hammond announced.

"What?" Mentor was hovering over her shoulder.

"I'm boosting power," Hammond said.

Dalton felt the connection, grabbed on to it like a drow
ing man to a lifeline. As he raced back toward the Ranc
there was a presence next to him, doing the same thin

e couldn't spare the energy to reach out to it, to find out
ho or what it was.

Then he was inside his frozen body, his mind still with
ccess to the virtual plane. He felt the power come back
to him from Sybyl.

"Dalton and Jackson are back," Hammond said. "I'm
ringing them out."

"What about Barnes?" Mentor asked.

"Nothing."

n her way out, Souris paused inside of Sybyl, contem-
lating the changes that had been made since she left
right Gate. She saw what Jenkins had done, the modifi-
ations to the computer and the programming.

s the connections with Sybyl grew stronger, Dalton
ould sense Jackson. He was on the virtual plane inside of
e Ranch, watching as Hammond began the process of
ringing his body back. He knew he'd have to go back into
is brain shortly, but he wanted one last chance to figure
ut what had happened.

"Are you all right?" he asked as he searched the virtual
lane for the third member of their team.

"I think so."

"Where's Barnes?"

"I don't know—" There was a pause, then her voice
ame back. *"Someone else is here. In Sybyl."*

He immediately picked up the presence she was refer-
ng to. *"Hold!"* he sent to Hammond, but the link through
ybyl wasn't strong enough. He could feel the virtual
orld slipping away from him. With a desperate effort he
unged" toward the foreign body. His virtual essence ca-
ened into the other and he was overwhelmed with a

flurry of images and emotions; shining through it all like
beacon was the fact that whoever or whatever the pre
ence was, it had just come from out of Space Command
mainframe and had the unlock code for the MILSTAR r
transmitter.

As that startling piece of information resounded
Dalton's consciousness, the virtual world faded away ar
he was back in his own mind, inside his body.

Chapter Twenty-three

The helicopter carrying Valika and Cesar landed on the rear deck of the *Yuri Gagarin*. They quickly off-loaded and were met by Tanya Zenata. Cesar wasted no time on pleasantries.

"Have the modifications been completed?" he demanded.

"Yes, sir," Zenata responded.

"The computer?" he asked.

"We're putting it on-line as per Professor Souris's instructions. She left it programmed. All that is needed is for someone to initiate the program."

Cesar smacked his hands together. "Excellent."

He headed forward, leaving Valika and Zenata.

"What is going on?" Zenata asked. "What does he have planned?"

Valika had a weapons case in each hand. "It is best for you not to know."

Souris was back in her body, inside the helicopter, but she was still connected to Aura. A quick systems check told her power was very low and she would have to shut it down soon, but she was still relishing the contact she had made with the Psychic Warrior in the other computer. She had felt the man's essence, an experience unlike anything she had ever encountered before. Reluctantly, she returned to the real plane and shut down Aura.

"To the airport," she ordered the pilot.

"What happened?" McFairn demanded.

General Mitchell was at the back of the main control room for Space Command, trying to make sense of the various reports his people were giving him.

"Something got into the computer," Mitchell said. "We're off-line and sealed in."

" 'Something'? Like what?"

A young officer ran up and gave the general several computer printouts. McFairn waited impatiently as the general read.

"We don't know," Mitchell finally said, sparing her a moment before going back to the paperwork.

McFairn felt a trickle of sweat go down the center of her back. "What did it access other than the DefCon Four alert and knocking your mainframe off-line?"

"Damn," Mitchell swore as he flipped a page. "It got into the DefCon Four codes."

For a moment McFairn thought she had been found out, but she realized it was worse than that as Mitchell continued.

"Which codes?"

"Whoever did this got the unlock code for something in MILSTAR." Mitchell frowned. "Why would someone want that?"

McFairn knew exactly why someone would want that and the pieces fell into place–the Ring experimenting using a satellite as a retransmitter and now stealing the unlock code. They were going to appropriate the system and use it with Aura.

"How long will it take to get the computer back online and get communication with the outside world?" McFairn demanded.

General Mitchell shook his head. "We don't know. We hope in a couple of hours, but this is unprecedented."

McFairn checked her watch. A couple of hours. By
then CS-MILSTAR would be deployed and on-line.

"What about the shuttle?" she asked. "If we're off-line,
who's ground base control?"

"Houston would automatically have taken over,"
Mitchell said.

"I need an outside line," McFairn said. "ASAP."

"We're doing the best we can," Mitchell said.

"Do better."

"If the code has been compromised, we can't take any
chances," Dalton said. "We stop both. HAARP and the
Ring/Mithrans."

"How?" Jackson asked as she tossed aside the towel
she had been using to wipe embryonic fluid off her face.
"The Ring's got some sort of weapon they can use against
us as Psychic Warriors."

"And HAARP is shielded on the virtual plane," Mentor
noted. "We have no influence with Washington. We're
helpless."

Dalton had been considering the problems as he was
warmed up and brought out of the isolation tank. "How
long until the CS-MILSTAR satellite is on-line?" he asked
Mentor.

"Two hours, five minutes."

"They were leaving Saba," Dalton said. "And the psyche I ran into ..." He paused as he mentally searched
through the various images he had picked up. "Naldo said
something about a ship. I saw a ship in the psyche I ran
into. A large one. With big satellite dishes taking up most
of the deck space."

Mentor was already at a computer, typing. "For-
tunately we're not locked up like Space Command. We tap
into the commo trunk going both ways, but we're outside
the complex, not under control of their mainframe, so we

still have an outside link." He continued typing, the paused. "Here it is. The *Yuri Gagarin*. It's Russia According to the CIA, it's currently located about tw hundred miles from Saba."

Dalton nodded as he peered over Mentor's shoulder the image on the screen. "That's it. That's what I saw."

Hammond was also looking. "They could use that as mobile HAARP-type platform. Those dishes would perfect."

"We know where the Ring is now," Dalton said, "ar we know where HAARP is."

"In opposite directions from here," Jackson noted.

"And what about Barnes?" Hammond threw in. T body of the third member of their PW team floated in isolation tank. "He's out there somewhere, but I ca reach him."

"Keep trying," Dalton said.

"I will."

"I'll take care of the ship." Dalton turned to Jacks "You've got HAARP."

"How?" Jackson asked.

"We don't have time to get there any other way th via virtual jumps," Dalton said.

"But—" Jackson began.

Dalton halted her by holding up his hand and turni to Mentor. "You said we're tapped into Space Command commo. Can we order the shuttle to abort the mission?"

"No. We don't have the proper authorization codes."

"What do we have codes for?" Dalton asked.

Mentor frowned. "What do you mean?"

"This thing was founded as an alternate commar post for the President, for God's sake," Dalton said, sla ping the side of the computer. "We've got to have at le access to all National Command Authority functions, ev if we don't have the authorizations, right?"

Mentor shook his head. "We don't have any control. The President would bring his own authorizations here."

Dalton had figured that would be the case. "Then we have to get some help that doesn't require authorization, right?"

"What kind of help?" Mentor asked.

"We have access to both normal MILSTAR communications channels and GPS, right?" Dalton pressed.

Mentor was thoughtful. "Yes."

Dalton grabbed a chair and indicated for Jackson to pull one close. "I have a plan if we can find the right pieces to play."

Souris transferred from the helicopter to Cesar's Lear at Colorado Springs. As the plane accelerated down the runway, she contacted the *Gagarin* via SATPhone.

"Yes?" Cesar answered on the first ring.

"I have the code."

"Give it to me."

Souris rattled off the letters and numbers.

"I've got it," Cesar acknowledged.

"I will be there in six hours," Souris said.

"It will be over by then," Cesar said.

"I know." A smile crossed Souris's face. "I know." She had her laptop on her knees and was typing in what she had learned about the Psychic Warrior program. Aura no longer interested her, nor did Cesar. She cut the connection.

McFairn stood in front of the large stainless steel vault door. Her pulse was racing and she forced herself to slow her breathing before she fainted from hyperventilation. A part of her was almost grateful that she couldn't send the code to Boreas. But that part was overwhelmed by the knowledge that the code had been stolen; regardless of how much she agreed with Boreas, she knew that she would rather be on his side than whoever his enemy was.

Dalton felt the embryonic fluid around his feet, then legs as he climbed into his isolation tube. The process was as brutal as all the previous ones, but his focus was on the up-coming mission. They had found the right piece for Jackson to use in Alaska, but hadn't been able to find him anything near the *Gagarin*. He was going in on his own and hoping he could come up with something once he was on the ship. At least it wasn't virtually shielded.

"Focus on the white dot," Hammond's voice echoed inside his head.

Chapter Twenty-four

The cargo bay doors of the shuttle swung open to space. Sitting in the lower level of the flight deck, facing the cargo hold, Eagle Six had his hands on the controls for the Remote Manipulator System (RMS), a fifty-foot-long articulating arm. The tip of the RMS was attached to CS-MILSTAR. Earlier, while the doors were still closed, he had gone in and removed the locking bolts on the satellite, freeing it.

Boreas checked the computer program for the tenth time in the past hour. It was all set. Millennia of battling would be over in a minute. If he had the unlock code for CS-MILSTAR. He pressed Redial on his SATPhone once more.

He cursed as the phone rang and rang without an answer.

The dishes on the *Yuri Gagarin* shifted in orientation, aiming toward the nearest MILSTAR satellite. In the communications center, Cesar was with Valika, the crew under strict orders to leave them alone.

"We will destroy HAARP first," Cesar said. "Then, I think, maybe the Pentagon."

Valika frowned. "Señor Cesar, I do not see why–"

Cesar smiled. "Valika. Call me Hector."

"Why are you doing this, Hector?"

"Because it is—" A confused look came across Cesar's face. "Because." The confusion disappeared and anger replaced it. "Goddamn it, can't anyone do what I tell them to, just because I tell them?"

"I'm sorry, sir," Valika said.

"We have the power!" Cesar said. "Don't you see that?"

"But it makes no sense for you to do this."

"You are like Naldo," Cesar said. "A coward."

Valika stiffened. After all she had done for Cesar, he was treating her like the Soviet Union had done to its faithful soldiers, turning its back on them. She got up and left the communications center, slamming the hatch behind her, leaving Cesar staring at the program on the computer screen that Souris had set up.

In the small cabin she had been allocated, Valika looked around. Her weapons cases were laid out on the bed, along with the small bag containing her few personal items. She tried to calm down, but her chest hurt and she felt as if she might be ill.

She realized this was the sum of her life. The original of the photo that Souris had used in the simulation, of her parents, was in her bag. Valika sat down next to the case holding her sniper rifle and took the picture in her hands.

Jackson saw the field of antennas. And she could feel the psychic wall like a dog would feel an electronic fence. She hung in the virtual plane, waiting, close by. While she was there, she cast about, searching for others, but there was nothing, just the cold wind over the icy mountains.

"Mentor?" she relayed through Sybyl. *"Are you there?"*

"I'm here."

"Have you pinpointed my help?"

"Yes," Mentor replied. As he relayed the information she needed, Jackson was already moving.

———

The two B-2 bombers were "hot," meaning they had live ordnance on board. They'd been in the air for eleven hours, having taken off from their home base at Whiteman Air Force Base in Missouri and flying a complex route, designed to test the crews' abilities en route to their "target."

Each plane was loaded with a conventional Block 30 weapons package: forty MK-82 five-hundred-pound bombs and thirty-six CBU-87 combined-effects munitions, each weighing a thousand pounds. Almost forty thousand pounds of ordnance was packed inside each aircraft, more than ten B-17 Flying Fortresses could carry. The bombs were loaded inside the fuselage on cylindrical racks, which allowed them to be dropped at a high rate of speed.

The two bombers were flying north at high altitude, having gone "feet dry" over the southern coast of Alaska. Their designated target was an Air Force bombing range in the middle of the state.

They were using GATS/GAM to conduct their mission: Global Positioning System Aided Targeting System/GPS Aided Munitions. In normal speak, that meant the two-man crews were basically surrendering control of targeting and even flight path to the computer, which had the location of the objective programmed in and which was updating the flight path every one thousandth of a second using Ground Positioning Satellites that fixed the aircraft's position within two meters. The computer would not only get them to the target, it would release the bombs in a predetermined order to cause maximum destructive effect.

It was cutting-edge technology and something the crews of the planes didn't particularly care for, as they were little more than observers.

Jackson found the two B-2s by following the GPS downlink. She flew above them on the virtual plane, admiring their sleek lines. While only 69 feet long, each aircraft was over twice that wide, at 172 feet. The smooth black surfaces were designed to make the aircraft virtually invisible to radar, and also served to make them almost invisible as they flew through the dark night sky.

Jackson slid into the first bomber. She found the master computer and entered it, flowing along the electronic paths inside.

Eagle Six's hand barely twitched on the controls, but the RMS magnified the effort and the CS-MILSTAR satellite lifted off the floor of the cargo bay.

"The mainframe is still booting," General Mitchell told McFairn. "But we have found access to an outside line. It's an old one. Landline. As far as we can tell, it's a regular phone line that someone forgot about."

"Where?"

Mitchell led her out of the building they were in, into another that held stacks of crates. In the rear an old rotary dial phone hung on the wall. "One of my men checked it. It has a dial tone."

McFairn grabbed it. There was a dial tone. She began dialing.

Dalton saw the ship below him, the large dishes facing the sky. He jumped once more, to the unoccupied flight deck at the rear of the ship behind the smokestack. He slipped from the virtual plane to the real. He assumed the form of Cesar and began moving forward along the port side.

He wished he had as clear a plan as Jackson did. He was winging it at best, but he figured thirty-five years of Special Operations experience would come up with something.

———

Mentor checked his watch. Five minutes until CS-MILSTAR was supposed to be on-line.

Hammond was at the computer console. "Barnes is out there, but he's not responding to my attempts to contact him through Sybyl." She scrolled down. "His pattern isn't right."

"What do you mean?" Mentor asked.

Hammond shook her head. "I don't know. It's just not right."

Boreas glanced out the windows of the control center. Even on this moonless night he could make out the white peaks of the Wrangell Range. He glanced at the red digital countdown at the front of the control room as it clicked through four minutes.

His desk phone rang. He ignored it and hit Redial on the SATPhone. The desk phone continued to ring. He stalked over to the desk and grabbed the receiver.

"What?" he yelled.

"It's McFairn. I have the code."

Jackson left the first B-2 and went into the second. She knew what she was doing now and this time it went quicker.

Eagle Six had the arm at full extension. He locked the controls for a second and removed his hands. His palms were wet and he wiped them on his flight suit before regaining the controls.

"Status?" he called out.

"Green," the payload master replied.

"Position?"

"Right on."

"Attitude, velocity?"

"Within parameters."

Eagle Six pulled a trigger and the end of the arm released the satellite. He spun ninety degrees to the right, to a communications panel, and accessed his private, secure link.

"Boreas, this is Eagle Six. Over."

"This is Boreas. Over."

"CS-MILSTAR is deployed. Operational in two minutes. Over."

"Roger. Out here."

"What the hell?" the pilot on the lead B-2 exclaimed as the plane banked to the right. He checked his navigation computer, then turned to the mission commander in the right seat. "We're off course."

The commander had already noted that and was furiously typing into his keyboard. "I can't access control."

"Shut it down then!"

"I can't." The commander slammed a fist down on the keyboard. "Where are we headed?"

"I have no idea."

A red bulb lit up in front of them. The mission commander swallowed hard. "We're weapons hot."

Dalton cut through a cross corridor on his way toward the bridge and paused.

Jimmy.

He was perfectly still as he faded slightly from the real plane, accessing the virtual. He knew he was vulnerable, floating on the cusp between the two planes, but he felt Marie. He waited.

Two doors down. Left.

Dalton waited, knowing as he did so that he was running out of time to act, never mind come up with a plan. But there was nothing more from Marie.

He returned solidly to the real plane. He walked down

he corridor and pivoted left in front of a door. He grabbed
he knob and threw it open.

A woman was sitting on a bed, several plastic weapons
:ases next to her, a frame in her hand—the woman who
ıad thrown the strange grenade at the villa in Saba. She
umped to her feet.

"Cesar! You've reconsidered?"

Dalton had to trust Marie. She wouldn't have sent him
ιn here without knowing more than he did. He shifted
ιvatars, assuming his own form.

The woman was as fast as his change, her hand snaking
:o the shoulder holster and having a gun pointed at him be-
ore he had finished transitioning. "Who are you?"

That was an interesting question, Dalton realized, one
ιe wasn't sure how to answer.

"You're American?" the woman asked.

Dalton nodded.

"A Psychic Warrior?"

"Yes. Sergeant Major Dalton."

"I'm Valika." The gun was still pointed at him. "Why
ιre you here?"

"To stop the transmission."

"It is bad, isn't it?" Valika asked, the muzzle of the
veapon lowering slightly.

"Yes."

"Cesar is not himself."

"He's being manipulated."

"By who?"

"A group. They—" Dalton searched for words. "Live on
he other side. In the virtual plane."

Valika nodded. "Souris has also been corrupted by
hem. And they have changed her. I knew it. I knew some-
hing was wrong all along."

"They mean to kill everyone on the planet."

Valika shook her head, but not very convincingly.

"Cesar says the satellites will target specific places on the planet."

"The MILSTAR satellites blanket the world," Dalton said. "And he's not in control like he thinks. Is Souris here?"

"No."

"Why do you think she's not here?" Dalton didn't wait for an answer. "She's going to a shielded location. Everyone on this ship will be killed when you transmit."

"The bitch," Valika muttered. "I never trusted her."

"There isn't much time," Dalton said.

"What can we do?"

He noted a long case on her bed and he had the spark of an idea. "What's that?"

"Barrett fifty caliber."

Dalton smiled and he knew Marie had pointed him in the right direction. "Strategic target interdiction."

"What?"

"Something I trained on in Special Forces." Dalton was opening the case. "Grab a couple of extra magazines."

Boreas's eyes were locked on the red numbers counting down.

:58

:57

:56

Cesar was also watching the same numbers on the screen of the computer that Souris had programmed. He briefly wondered where she was. She had not called in for a while.

It did not matter. His gaze went back to the screen and the distant stare returned.

Jackson released out of the trail B-2's computer into the virtual plane, flying along with the two bombers. She watched as they both smoothly completed the turn, led by heir guidance and targeting systems, and their bomb bay doors opened.

The first cylinder of the lead plane dropped down into he opening and cycled through, spitting out bombs.

Boreas leaned forward to hit the red transmit button just as the first MK-82 landed on the leading edge of the field of antennas. The second impacted a half a second later.

Mixed among the five-hundred-pound high-explosive bombs were the cluster bombs. Two hundred meters above the ground, the casing of each thousand-pound cylinder split open, dispensing 202 bomblets. The "footprint," as the Air Force called it, for each CBU was two hundred meters by four hundred meters. As the heavier MK-82s dug out ten-foot-deep craters, the CBUs cut huge swaths through the antenna field, slicing metal like cheese.

Boreas was stunned as the thud of the first explosions reverberated through the control center. He ran to the window and looked out, seeing flash after flash in the darkness as bombs exploded.

Jackson was satisfied the HAARP field had been wiped off the face of the Earth by the first B-2. She was right behind the second one as its first cylinder unloaded.

She'd manipulated the GATS/GAM on that one to target the HAARP control facility. She knew forty thousand pounds of ordnance was overkill for one two-story building, but the bombs were available.

Boreas never saw the B-2, five thousand feet above in the night sky. He also didn't see the first MK-82 as it hit the roof and tore through to the first floor.

He did have a brief glimpse of the fireball that consumed him before he died.

The screen cleared and a smiley face appeared. Cesar frowned. What was going on?

"Cesar."

He recognized the voice. Souris.

"It is too late for anyone to stop this. We will rule the world."

"Who? Who are you talking about?" Cesar jumped to his feet and slammed the monitor to the ground, glass shattering. The smiley face was still on other screens, grinning at him.

The face disappeared, replaced by a single blinking word.

TRANSMITTING

Dalton settled down with the butt of the Barrett tight into his shoulder. Valika was kneeling next to him, a set of binoculars oriented on the closest satellite dish. They were on the walkway that ran around the rear smokestack of the *Yuri Gagarin*, over a hundred feet above the main deck and on level with the top of all the dishes.

He pulled the trigger and the rifle rocked back against his shoulder. The half-inch-diameter bullet hit the exact center of the dish, blowing the core into a thousand parts.

"Adjust, up one twenty meters," Valika said.

Dalton reacted, shifting the gun.

"Fire," Valika ordered.

He pulled the trigger and the second large dish was out of commission.

"Adjust, plus one ten up ten."

He had the rhythm, the feel of the Barrett, a weapon he had fired in training, and it took less than a second to find the new target. The third bullet took out the next transmitter. This was a mission he had been trained for a

Fort Bragg, using the Barrett to hit critical components of various systems to disable them.

Red lights were flashing in the bridge of the *Gagarin*.

"What is it?" Lonsky demanded.

Zenata was staring at her displays. "The two main and first alternate dish are down. Transmission is rerouting to the final dish."

"What the hell is going on? Who's doing this?"

Dalton pulled the trigger.

"Miss," Valika told him.

Dalton felt the snap of bullets whizzing by before the sound reached him. "What is it?" he asked as he resighted on the last remaining dish.

When there was no reply, he pulled his eye back from the scope and glanced to his left. Valika was against the smokestack, a large splotch of red on the upper left quadrant of her chest, a thin trickle of blood flowing from her mouth. Her lips twisted slightly in what might have been a grin, then her eyes glazed over and the body slumped back.

"Damn." Dalton spared a look down and he could see Cesar running forward, a submachine gun tight against his shoulder. A string of bullets tore into the walkway just to the right of Dalton. He ignored them, knowing he had run out of time, and aimed at the center of the fourth dish.

"Reroute complete," Zenata announced. Lonsky was on the left wing of the bridge, looking back, trying to find the source of the firing.

"Transmit in two seconds," she yelled to him.

Dalton pulled the trigger and the bullet hit the center of the dish, silencing it. Even while the bullet was in flight he was fading, disappearing from the real plane into the virtual as Cesar fired another burst that tore through where he had been. The Barrett fell to the deck with a loud clang.

Dalton jumped and was on the deck just behind Cesar. He re-formed in the real plane, his left arm shifting into a firing tube. He didn't hesitate or feel any compunction about shooting the other man in the back. He fired and the ball of energy hit Cesar in the middle of his back, blasting him forward.

Cesar was dead before he hit the deck plate.

Dalton shifted back into the virtual and jumped, heading back toward the Ranch.

Chapter Twenty-five

The computers on the two B-2 bombers had been released from the reprogramming that Jackson had done. The planes were on their way to the nearest Air Force base outside Anchorage. The crews were certain their careers were over. Dropping eighty thousand pounds off-range was an offense they were sure they would never recover from. They could only hope they had hit wilderness and not killed anybody.

Behind them, there was little to indicate that 540 steel towers had once occupied the torn and savaged ground. On the hillside where the control center had been, there were just a few chunks of smoldering concrete.

Captain Lonsky looked at the body of the man who had fought the ship for a few moments, then issued an order.

"Throw it overboard."

Once that was accomplished, Zenata waited for the next order.

"Let us head back to Russia," Lonsky said. "The less said about all this, the better."

Dalton raced along the power connection with Sybyl, back to his body at the Ranch.

Souris diverted the Lear to Dallas. She "knew" that Cesar had been unsuccessful, but she also knew that the Psychic

Warriors had been responsible for destroying HAARP, s
the two canceled out.

She had failed in the mission she had been assigned
but gaining the Psychic Warrior update was a coup. The
would appreciate that. It would give them a way to ente
the real world and fight the Priory.

Dalton climbed out of the isolation tube, his body shiver
ing uncontrollably. Jackson was already back, a towe
draped over her shoulders, and she handed one to him a
he reached the floor. He immediately noted Barnes's bod
still in its tube. "Do you have contact with him?" he aske
Hammond.

"No," Hammond said. "I've been trying, but he hasn
responded."

"His signs?"

"Strange."

"Strange how?" Dalton demanded.

"Not like the others. He's out there being supporte
with power somehow, just not from Sybyl."

Dalton turned back toward his tank. "We need to g
look for him." He halted as Mentor entered, coming fror
the operations center.

"You did it," Mentor said, slapping him on the back.

"MILSTAR is still up there," Dalton said, "with the re
transmit capability."

"I can work on correcting that, now that I have som
time," Mentor said.

"And the Priory and Mithrans are still out there, wher
ever they are," Dalton added. "We've only stopped ther
for the moment."

To that, Mentor had no reply.

Jackson put a hand on Dalton's shoulder as he pre
pared to climb back into his isolation tube. "You need

break. Wherever Barnes is, he can wait for a little while. You need rest."

Dalton was about to argue with her when he realized she was right. He sat down wearily on a crate, Jackson doing likewise across from him.

"We have to reconstitute Nexus here in the United States," Mentor said. He pointed at the other three people in the room: Dalton, Jackson, and Hammond. "The four of us."

"Five of us," Dalton said, indicating Barnes. "We need to do better than reconstitute Nexus," he continued. "This war between the Priory and Mithrans has been going on for a long time. With the advances in technology we're seeing, this conflict almost just destroyed us. I say for the next round, we go on the offensive."

He put his hand out, palm up. "Are we agreed?"

Jackson immediately reached out and put her right hand on top of his. Hammond followed. The three of them looked at Mentor.

The old man slowly nodded. "It is time." He placed both his hands over theirs.

Dalton could feel the power, the aura of strength, coming off the other three. It wasn't much to fight the Priory and the Mithrans with, but it was a start.

Robert Doherty is a pen name for a best-selling writer of suspense novels. He is the author of *Psychic Warrior, Area 51: The Grail; The Rock; Area 51; Area 51: The Reply; Area 51: The Mission;* and *Area 51: The Sphinx*. Doherty is a West Point graduate, a former Infantry officer, and a Special Forces A-Team commander. He currently lives in Boulder, Colorado.

For more information you can visit his Web site at www.nettrends.com/mayer.